Pop. 199

A novel

by Ann Magaha

I

This book may be purchased through
　　　　Amazon.com and Amazon Kindle,
　　　　Taylor and Seale Publishing.com,
　　　　Barnes and Noble.com,
　　　　Books a Million
　　　Phone: 386-481-0502
　　　　　396-760-8987
　　　　www.taylorandseale.com

TAYLOR AND SEALE
PUBLISHING, LLC

Dedication

In loving memory of my mother, Virginia Singer, the wonderful artist and the dearest and best of mothers.

Acknowledgments

My thanks to the early readers of the manuscript— Karen Rose, Gwen Carson, Mary Kaye Schilling—whose enthusiasm and praise were invaluable; to Mary VanBuren for her expert editing; to the late Steve Glassman who insisted I write the book to begin with and who read and applauded me along the way; to authors R.M. Kinder and Randy Attwood, who urged me to seek publication; and especially to Steve Jones for his wit, his wealth of knowledge, and his unfailing affection.

Epigraphs

"What we, or at any rate I, refer to confidently as memory—
meaning a moment, a scene, a fact, that has been subjected to a
fixative and thereby rescued from oblivion—is really a form of
storytelling that goes on continually in the mind and often
changes with the telling."

   William Maxwell, *So Long, See You Tomorrow*

"I think it (memory) is all a matter of love: the more you love a
memory, the stronger and stranger it is."

    Vladimir Nabokov
   (from BBC television interview July 1962)

Advance Praise

The dam posed a threat to all of Aldrich and the surrounding countryside. The dam would mean the wrecking of all the downtown buildings. It would destroy homes, churches, schools, and bridges, and then it would flood the whole area, swallowing roads and creeks and all of the low-lying farms up and down the Little Sac River, even swallowing the river itself. There were no dissenting voices. (p.131)

Janet Stephens remembers her parents' divorce and being sent off to her grandmother and uncle, both of whom were mere strangers. Her recounting of the memories of the wrenching years she remembers resemble a dream sequence. They have interesting overtones of Fellinesque neo-realism with mythical proportions. At times it seems as if Janet is outside of herself looking at her young self when she is unaware of the importance of what is happening and unaware of the nuances of importance in what others are saying to each other and how they are treating each other. But she does feel that something big is always imminent.

Although a small town, Aldrich can be compared to a modern-day Olympus doomed to extinction. Janet, the main character, becomes aware of the threat notices, somewhat like the mythical Cassandra, but she discounts the opinions of others though she later records them …"The flood was imminent … driven by an indifferent, all-powerful and ruinous force."

The small town was an imperiled Eden whose importance as a microcosm of the essence of peace and serenity and beauty of the lost American Dream was scarcely appreciated until it was lost and its unique characters gone or scattered. This story draws upon Longfellow's epic poem *Evangeline,* which takes place in the doomed town of Acadia.

The novel is evocative of the play *Our Town* by Thornton Wilder. Small happenings assume importance on a grander scale when remembered with nostalgia.

This is a very worthwhile literary work which transports the reader through a film-like sequence of slices of real lives and may evoke personal memories long forgotten. It is a work worthy of being a classic for its engaging human interest and historic value. .

Dr. Mary C. Custureri
Author, Humanities Professor,
Reading and Curriculum Specialist

PART I

Chapter 1

When my mother was seventeen, she impulsively married a soldier, my father, who had just come back from WW2. It was the uniform not the man. For years she blamed her bad marriage on my grandmother.

"Why did Mama let me get married? I was seventeen years old for Lord's sake," as if my grandmother or anyone for that matter could have intervened.

"Wild horses couldn't have stopped Marge Stephens when a man was involved," one of my mother's high school friends told me much later. "Your mother was stubborn as a mule and had an awful thing about men." That made me feel bad even if it was the truth.

"How come," I asked, "was she so… stubborn?"

"Who knows. Marge was Marge. She came along at the end…after your grandfather had flown the coop and the family had fallen apart, a menopause baby…"

That didn't make me feel any better, either about my mother's stubbornness or about her "thing" for men, of which I knew all too well. After I was born, my mother ran off with three or four men that I know of and married one of them at one of those chapels in Vegas. Even so, she harked back to her first marriage as her defining downfall, and as much as she loved my grandmother, undoubtedly more than anyone else in her life, she faulted her. After every breakup, she posed the question to family and friends.

1

"Why, why did Mama let me marry George Stephens?" And then, bemused and aggrieved, she would repeat my grandmother's "lame" reply: "'Well, Marge, I thought you could have done worse.'"

The second man my mother ran off with, the one she left my father and me for in 1949, didn't last long, just a few weeks. At that time Daddy was stationed in South Carolina. I was in the fifth grade. One morning I found an envelope and a package from her. "For Janet" was printed in large letters on the outside of the envelope. Inside she had drawn a birthday cake with eleven candles and written a message.

> *Dear Janet,*
> *I'm going out West for a while. Here is an early birthday*
> *present. I'll be in touch.*
> *Love,*
> *Mom*

I didn't know HOW she'd be in touch. Every day for three weeks when I got off the school bus, I checked the mailbox, but there was never anything from her. Then one Monday I got off the bus, checked the mailbox, which was empty, came through the back door, and there was Mom in the kitchen crying and frying chicken. I dropped my book on the floor and ran to her. She wiped her eyes with a dish towel and stooped to hug me.

"How are ya, kiddo?" I don't know why, but I began to tremble. I couldn't stop. She kept on hugging me until my shaking finally ended.

"What's the matter? Why were you shaking?" she asked.

"I didn't know if you'd come back."

"Oh brother. Of course, I was coming back." She wiped her eyes again.

"Why are you crying, Mom?"

She looked at me for a long time, tears trickling from her swollen eyes.

2

"I missed you," she said, finally. We hugged again. That was maybe the happiest moment I ever had with my mother— knowing how much she had missed me.

Before dinner that night, before Daddy got home, she put on her mascara. I loved to watch her wet the little brush, move it back and forth across the Maybelline mascara tray, and lean toward the mirror, squinting, eyebrows raised, to apply the black to her eyelashes.

"Thank the Lord for mascara," she would say through partially pursed lips. "You and your grandmother don't know what it is for us plain girls. After two kids, your grandmother gave out of the pretty genes. The last one of us? Just plain as dirt."

"I think you're pretty, Mom."

"That's because I know how to fix myself up." She pulled the top off a tube of lipstick and rolled up a bright orange shade. "Now, you got lucky, ya little skunk. You're a throwback to Rose." Rose was my grandmother's first name. "Milk-white complexion, azure eyes. Whew! You're gonna have to fight the men off!" We giggled.

"Did you like the outfit I got you?" She was talking about the package she'd left me with her goodbye note.

"Uh huh. Wanna see it on?" I had tried on the matching skirt and top several times and danced around the house. It was pink with white stripes. The skirt was gathered around the hips but the top of it was flat so that the blouse fitted over it. It was a snug sailor blouse with a flap collar and a white sailor tie. I loved it. When I came back in the room with it on, Mom started singing:

"A pretty girl is like a melody…" Mom had a good voice. She'd sung that song to me ever since I could remember. "Nobody's ever sung that song to ME," she said. "Of course, your father can't sing a note. His people are hardworking and good, but not fun or talented like we are." She turned and winked at me and then, reverting to the mirror, studied her image. "Thank the Lord we all got good skin in our family," she said.

3

Good skin mattered more than anything to Mom. "I'll tell ya one thing. I don't ever want to be so poor I can't afford a good moisturizer." As she aged, Mom continued to thank the Lord for modern day cosmetics and beauty products. "Gray hair is a dead giveaway. Thank the Lord for hair dye."

Before Daddy got home that night, she brushed my hair hard, which hurt, and with a comb worked out the rats that had built up over the last two weeks. Then she brushed it again until every blond strand "shone."

"Look at those golden tresses, down to your shoulders" she said, "A blond-haired Dysart! Who woulda thought it!" Dysart was Mom's maiden name and she attributed all of my assets to her side of the family. "Luck of the draw, kiddo. Luck of the draw." She pulled back a handful of hair from my forehead and looped a rubber band around it twice.

"Ouch!"

"Stand still. You wanna look good for your father, dontcha?"

"It hurts."

"You have to suffer to be beautiful," she said, tying a pink bow over the band. "Even if you did get lucky, nature's never enough. Remember that. Now. How's that."

I looked at myself in the mirror. "It looks good."

"Well, your mother has the knack."

Mom would have made a good hairdresser. She had the right philosophy about nature and she had the "knack," but being a "beautician" was something "cheap" girls did, girls who didn't go to college.

When we heard Daddy's car late that afternoon, we met him together at the door.

"Mom's back," I said, with a big smile, decked out in my sailor dress and matching hair ribbon.

Daddy didn't even glance at me. He stood in the doorway gaping at Mom, then walked right by both of us, took off his cap and his uniform jacket, and hung them on the hall tree.

4

Daddy was always quiet and undemonstrative, but even a child could see something was wrong. While I was staring at him, Mom disappeared into the kitchen. After a while I could hear her humming a popular tune with words of the song interspersed. "I'll be loving you, always. Hmm hmm hmm hmm hmm always." I wondered if she was singing to herself as usual or if she was sending a message to my father. When she called out, "Okay. Time to eat, you two," he came to the table, sulled up like an old possum. That's how Mom described someone who was mad and hurt and wouldn't speak. Poor Daddy.

To break the tension, Mom chattered about her "trip out west" as she passed the fried chicken, mashed potatoes, and wilted lettuce, the best meal we had had in weeks. (Wherever else my mother failed, it was not in the kitchen). She told us all about Yosemite, which, as a joke, she pronounced YOSE MIGHT. She acted as if she'd just gone there as a student of nature.

"Over eons, rivers and glaciers somehow carved 3,000 feet into solid granite to create YOSE MIGHT."

When Daddy didn't respond to the geology, she went on to animal life. She said there were bobcats, mule deer, and big horn sheep. Daddy just kept looking down and eating the limp lettuce, his favorite dish, a throwback to his midwestern roots.

"Mom, you could be a ranger at YOSE MIGHT," I said, to show my appreciation since Daddy wouldn't say a word.

"I could've been any number of things with the proper education. Remember that, kiddo." Mom had a thing not only about men but about never having been to college. Then, adopting her jokey tone, she said, "Ya know how close I got to an American black bear?"

"How close?"

"I could just barely see it. Barely. Get it?"

I laughed and asked, "Did you really see a bear?"

"I'll tell ya, if you'll just BEAR with me." I laughed harder.

"Tell the truth!" I demanded.

5

"I am," she insisted. "Those are the BARE facts."

As soon as I stopped laughing, I said, "Knock Knock."

"Who's there?" Mom said, happy that I was playing along.

"YOSE MIGHT."

"YOSE MIGHT who."

"Yose might as well admit you didn't see a bear."

Mom laughed to beat the band.

"She's pretty AND she's smart, isn't she, Daddy?"

She addressed him directly for the first time. He didn't answer, but I could see he was beginning to crack. We kept up the banter throughout dinner until finally, after Mom brought out the strawberry shortcake, Daddy broke down and spoke.

"How'd school go today, pal?"

I told him the music teacher had chosen me to sing "Away in a Manger" in the Christmas program and that I had asked if I could tap dance AND sing the song, and she said the two didn't go together. Daddy said she was probably right, but I told him that the waltz clog went perfectly with "Away in a Manger," and I could prove it.

"Okay, prove it," he said.

I put on my tap shoes and showed them, and Mom said it was the best "rendition" of "Away in a Manger" she'd ever seen and that if Jesus had learned to tap dance when he was a boy, his whole life might have been different.

"But my singing isn't too good," I said. "I don't know all of the words. I have to sing all three verses."

And then Daddy said as if in passing, "Your mother can help you with that."

His reference to Mom, quietly creeping into the conversation, made me flush and I and Mom, who rose from the table with a secret smile, knew the three of us were mended.

As Mom washed the dishes, we could hear her in the kitchen: "Hm hm hm hm hm hm... She'll leave you and then, come back again. A pretty girl is just like a pretty tune."

6

***

Even at the age of eleven, I sensed the importance of the part I had played in restoring my parents' marriage that night. For a brief time, I entertained the dizzy idea that I held some special power in that regard. But before long, as Christmas of that year neared, my inflated hope was countered by a dream. In it, my mother is in the kitchen singing. Daddy and I can hear her from another room. We know that we will be happy and that all will be well for as long as the song goes on. When the singing stops, we run to the kitchen to see if Mom is all right. Mom is wiping her eyes with a dishtowel.

Sobbing, she says, "I'm not a pretty girl."

"But you're smart and funny, and a very good cook," I say.

"I know," she says, "but that isn't enough."

Then Daddy says to her, "I love you."

And I say to her, "I love you, too."

She says, "I know, but that's not enough."

"Why isn't that enough?" I ask.

"I don't know."

Angry now, I say, "You could have done so much worse."

"I guess you're right about that, kiddo," she says, sniffling.

And I say, "Go ahead then and leave. Get out. Daddy and I like it better without you. We hate you. You're stubborn and wild and plain as dirt."

Mother picks up her big Samsonite suitcase and leaves by the kitchen door. I am in agony when I wake up still wanting to persecute my mother.

My mother's high school friend used an old rime to describe how fast and whimsically my mother had "torn out of town" right after she married Daddy:

7

"Down the road they went a whizzin'
His hand on hers and her hand on his'n."

About a year and a half after the Christmas program, during which I sang "Away in a Manger," just as my mother had taught me, Mom tore off down the road with another man, "his hand on hers, and her hand on his'n."

Chapter 2

This time there was no note to me, no package. It was my father who told me Mom had left. When I came in the door after school the day of her departure, the house was still, the shades pulled. It felt like the kind of afternoon hush when your mother is having a nap and you have to keep quiet and let her get a rest. I was surprised and happy to hear a stir in the kitchen.

"Mom," I called out, bounding to the kitchen. But oddly, the noise turned out to be Daddy, who should have been at work. He was getting a beer out of the fridge.

"Hot hands, cold beer," I said, repeating one of my mother's expressions that got her a laugh when Daddy brought around his fishing buddies.

But Daddy didn't laugh. He seemed worn out and slow, the way I had felt during those three weeks when I woke up and realized that Mom was gone and that I had to get dressed, and eat by myself, and catch the bus, and then come home on the bus and be in the house alone. He set the beer bottle on the table and faced me.

"Looks like your mother has gone out West again," he said with a sad, numb look that went to my core.

"Oh," I said, as if he'd told me Mom had stepped out to the commissary to pick up a few groceries.

He kept looking at me with his heartbroken eyes.

"I'm sorry, pal," he managed to say. I looked away from him and stared at the beer bottle as if it could save me.

I read the label aloud: "San Miguel."

Daddy smiled pathetically, "That's right."

9

"Is it good?" I asked, though I knew it was my father's favorite.

"Very good... It's made in the Philippines where..."

"When is she coming back?" I interrupted.

"I don't know" Daddy said, "if she'll be coming back..."

The tears were welling up in his round, blue eyes. I didn't think I could stand it, looking at him or hearing what more he might have to say, and I ran out of the kitchen and down the hall to my room. He called after me, but I pretended not to hear, closed the door to my room, and curled up on my bed with my panda, Bear-de-Rowe.

Now when I replay that scene, I wish I had stayed with Daddy instead of running off. I can still see him standing by the fridge in his starched, khaki shirt on the verge of tears. It was bad enough that my mother had left him again, but she had left with Dingbat, who was in Daddy's outfit and who was a known womanizer.

Of course, I didn't know that until later. I just thought she'd gone "out west" again. Or maybe I did know—that she'd gone off with another man, but I would never have thought of Dingbat. I had thought when I grew up, I would marry Dingbat myself. Only in retrospect did the pieces come together—how much Mom enjoyed frying the fish Daddy and his buddies, Dingbat among them, brought home from their trips, for example, or how when Dingbat told me corny fishing jokes, she laughed too hard.

"Why didn't Noah do much fishing on the ark?" Dingbat had asked me once. I couldn't think of an answer. "He only had two worms," he said.

Mom laughed like it was going to kill her. I'll admit he could be funny. He paid attention to me, and he was by far my favorite of my parents' friends, but the joke wasn't THAT funny.

"Two worms? I don't CATCH on" I said, "CATCH, get it?" But my comeback Mom barely noticed.

10

When Dingbat complimented her cooking, she said coyly, "Just brag on me a little and I'll knock myself out." If Dingbat was fishing, Mom was definitely on his hook. He had the two qualities she admired in a person: Dingbat was "fun," and he had "personality." He also had dark hair and a thin moustache, and he was a gambler like my mother.

I didn't put all that together back then. But I wonder now how much my father had put together. I still don't know exactly what he knew at the time. Did she tell him she was leaving him or just leave?

I like to think that they quarreled and made a decision, but Mom wasn't one to undergo any pain she could avoid. She hated the feeling of being held back once she had given over to an idea. The problem with Mom was her fear of being trapped. She was happiest when she was acting on the spur. It wasn't only the joy of escape but the sense that an automatic good derived from breaking away, acting on one's own.

"Bid 'em high and sleep in the alley!" she would exclaim, slapping down a card that would make or break the hand. That was one of her favorite sayings. Mom believed a gamble was not only fun but, in and of itself, worthy. It was how life was supposed to be lived.

"There's nothing worse than getting stuck in a one-horse town for the rest of your life. You don't want to be one of those who never got away. If you don't take a chance, don't expect to win."

When Mom took her chances with Dingbat at the expense of me and Daddy, she just might have told herself it was the right thing to do—that the possible good that would come from the venture outweighed the harm. Maybe she thought after they got settled, she'd come back and get me and I would go live with them, although she never proposed such a thing to me, not at the time that she was with Dingbat.

In any event, my mother left us, just as her father had left her and maybe, I have often wondered, BECAUSE her father

11

had left her, time and again. If he'd just stayed away that would've been one thing, but Grandpa Clay came and went, unpredictably, and the painful, repeated disappearances she ingrained. Grandpa Clay had skipped town, flown the coop, hit the rails, and that made it all right for her to do the same. He did it, and by God she could, too. I could hear her saying it, even though she never did say it to me. I could hear her thinking it over and again, each time she wanted to go off on a lark. "He did it, and I can, too, God damn it. You have to takes your chances." But who can say what she told herself and how much of it she actually believed?

"Doesn't matter," most would say. "It was pure selfishness." And maybe they would be right, but I honestly believe that my mother's motives were not entirely self-serving. And even if they were, that would be better than the thought that, after it occurred to me, I could never set aside—the idea that she was bent on self-defeat; because that might mean that a child who had been deserted might have no control over the impulse to desert responsibility, and that I, too, might unwittingly make self-obliterating choices. "She turned out to be exactly like her mother," I could hear them say of me. "Two peas from the same pod."

After I fled the kitchen the night Daddy told me Mom had left and wasn't coming back, I stayed in my room clutching Bear-de-Rowe for what seemed like forever. I think I knew that once I came out of my room, things would be very different and that there would be no way I could hold on to what I had known and believed about the world.

When I finally came out, Daddy was sitting in the kitchen nook bent over a legal pad.

"You all right, pal?" he said, looking up.

I nodded, my eyes lowered on Bear De Rowe. He took a drink of San Miguel.

"What about a sandwich?"

"Okay."

When he got up to fix the sandwich, I went over to him, head ducked, and put my arms around him, and he leaned over with his arms around me, and we had a brief bawl together. That night was the first and last time I ever saw my father cry, and I am thankful that I at least allowed him that.

After we let go of each other, he stooped down and looked at me squarely as if he had an important confession or instruction, and then he said, "Do you want mayo on it?"

"Yes. Thank you," I said.

I sat Bear-de-Rowe up on the window ledge by the table and waited while Daddy fixed me a lettuce sandwich. I wanted to tell him something—that I loved him, or that I was sorry, or something, anything that would make him feel better, but the moment had passed, and we were already girding ourselves for the future.

I knew that Daddy would leave for the Philippines in a few months. He and his buddies ate fish and drank beer and talked about their orders. I'd overheard who was being transferred and where. Dingbat was going to Vegas; Daddy was going to Manila. Everybody knew that. And everybody knew there were travel restrictions and that families couldn't go to some places overseas, like Manila, where there were Huks who lived in the hills and raided the villages and even the cities. But I still couldn't bring myself to frame the obvious question: Now that Mom was gone, what was I going to do when Daddy left?

Mom had said while Daddy was in Manilla, we might go out west or we might visit her family in Missouri, but whatever we did we were gonna have a big time and then in six months or so, when the travel restrictions were lifted, we might even join Daddy and explore the Pacific en route, and go to Hawaii and learn to do the hula, and I would get a grass skirt. Now none of that would happen. Who would take care of me?

Before, during those three weeks when Mom was "out West," I was alone for two hours in the afternoon until Daddy got home. I had one townie friend, the girl I sat next to at school,

13

whose mother picked us up and took us to dance class one day a week; but the other days I had ridden the bus home with the other base kids, checked the mail, unlocked the kitchen door, and stayed in the house.

"What will you do in the afternoons until I get home?" Daddy had asked me.

"I'll play with my bears and tap dance."

"Okay," he had said.

And that's what I had done. But that was then. Soon Daddy would be half way around the world. When he vacated our quarters, I would have to go somewhere.

A few days after he broke the news about Mom, Daddy broached the problem. "We'll have to figure out a battle plan for when I'm gone."

But I couldn't think that far ahead. We had two months to figure out what I was to do, and I was bent on the hope that one afternoon when I got home from school Mom would turn up in the kitchen, so I evaded the battle plan and addressed the present.

"Maybe," I suggested, "we can get Kay to come over afternoons for the next few months."

Kay was the teenage girl who rode my bus and babysat me when Mom and Daddy went to the club. She told me all about *Jane Eyre* and *Anne of Greene Gables* and how they were orphaned and mistreated and had to go live with other people but how it worked out for them in the end. Kay hated the ninth grade and had an idea that she might go live with other people, too.

"I like Kay," I said, but Daddy just swigged his San Miguel.

"Tomorrow, after work, let's go to the Chicken Hut," he said.

That was my favorite place. They had chicken in a basket. It was off base a few miles from the gate. We went there only on special occasions. The last time had been a year ago on Mom and Dad's anniversary. He and his friends and their wives, and I— none of my parents' friends had children—all went.

14

"Okay," I said. "Is anyone else going? Is Dingbat coming?"

Daddy looked at me with the awful, worn look he'd had earlier.

"No, it'll just be the two of us, pal. We need to talk over how we're going to handle things when I leave..." He looked at the yellow pad on the table. On it was a list, things, I supposed, that he needed to remember to do. "We'll have to make arrangements..."

When the phone rang and Daddy jumped up to answer it, I twisted around to look at the pad without touching it. The narrow spaces were divided by thin green lines, most of them blank. On the first lines were Daddy's large printed letters, unadorned and decided, easy to read. At the top of the list was "MOM," followed by a phone number. I had the happy thought that Daddy had Mom's phone number, that maybe she was on the phone with him now returning his call, and that maybe I could talk to her and ask her if I could go "out West" with her while Daddy was away.

I heard him from the hallway practically yelling into the receiver. "That's okay. I understand. You're probably right. She'd be better off in Missouri. Tell Dad I said 'hello.'"

When he came back, he said, "That was an awful connection. They could hardly hear me."

He looked so sad I began to choke up. I kept hearing the words, "She'd be better off in Missouri."

"Was that Mom?" I asked. "Why didn't you let me talk to her?"

"It wasn't your mom, pal. It was your grandmother in Oklahoma. I was just letting her know I'm being deployed."

"Oh," I said, wondering if deployed meant the same thing as divorced.

"It's bed-time, pal. Tomorrow we'll figure everything out. I'm looking forward to the Chicken Hut, aren't you? You probably won't want your French fries, but I'll take care of them for you..."

15

As he rattled on drinking another San Miguel and trying to make me and himself feel better, I read the rest of the items on his list. In his bald, unassuming hand, followed by phone numbers, were three names: "ROSE," "PAT," and "GREYHOUND." They practically pulsated on the page, especially the last.

"Daddy?" He stopped talking. "Who," I asked him, "would be better off in Missouri?"

"What?"

"You said on the phone someone would be better off in Missouri. Who did you mean?"

Chapter 3

The next evening at the Chicken Hut, Daddy tried to answer my question.

"Anybody," he said. "Missouri is a great state. You know that's where President Truman is from..." Daddy kept building up Missouri, "and you can't beat the fishing... Remember what a good time we had there? She's a real nice lady, your Grandmother Rose. You remember her, don't you?"

I had been to Missouri with my parents four years before when Daddy had leave. I remembered a tall, dark-haired woman who had a funny little "whee" at the end of her laugh. Hahahaha, whee! When she picked me up, I could see tiny red lines on her cheeks that made them rosy. "She has that Welsh skin" Mom had said. "By the time I came along she'd run out of the pretty genes, or I might've had that high color, too."

I pretended not to remember a thing about my grandmother, because now that we were at the Chicken Hut, I knew what Daddy was leading up to. Off and on all day, I had told myself that it might be Mom who would've been "better off in Missouri," better off there than "out West." That is something my father's mother might have said to him, but the way Daddy was placating me, I knew now that I was the one who would be "better off in Missouri" and that Daddy had asked my Oklahoma grandmother to take me and that she had said no.

As I was assimilating this, Daddy sang the praises of Missouri and of my Missouri relatives.

"Your Uncle Pat is a fine man. You remember him, don't you, pal?"

"No," I said, lying to my father. I wasn't going to make it easy for him to send me away.

"Your Uncle Pat was in World War I."

I wasn't impressed. Daddy tried another tack.

"He went all the way to Springfield to see *Oklahoma*. Remember how he liked to sing?" I shook my head. "Well, he has a good voice like you."

I did remember Uncle Pat, not him so much as a song he sang to me: "I've got a wonderful feeling. Janet is coming my way. Oh what a beautiful day."

I remembered the song and the fact that Uncle Pat had gone to see *Oklahoma* and had taken Mom with him and not me. I had heard her joke about how they sat on the front row and how all the men in the chorus were probably fairies and how they ought to call it OklaHOMO. I didn't catch on to the joke, but everyone, including Dingbat, laughed when she sang, "OHHHHH KLA HOMO where the queers come rushing out on stage."

But Daddy didn't know how much I knew, how a young girl absorbs all of those adult indiscretions. The truth is I was closer to Mom. She knew me much better than Daddy did. Daddy was away a lot, and his hours were long.

But that night at the Chicken Hut, because I thought he was getting rid of me, and because his parents had rejected me, and because my mother had deserted me, I said cruel things to my innocent father: "Uncle Pat lives in a little town and so does Grandmother Rose. People who live in little towns in Missouri are ignorant and boring."

My father was dismayed.

"Well, I don't think you can say that. I don't know where you got that from. Small town people are the salt of the earth."

"That's why they're so boring," I shot back, though I had never heard the expression. "They don't ever have fun, and they don't have a smidgen of personality. They just go around... salting the earth."

18

Daddy put down his chicken thigh. I was going after Daddy, making him feel bad in the same way my mother had when she took off on "country ignoramuses."

"I think you'd better change your tune, young lady," Daddy said.

But I couldn't stop. "They don't have any talent and don't care about improving themselves," I said like a spoiled, imperious child in a fairy tale. "That's why they live in Missouri, and Oklahoma is even worse. There's nothing as hokey as an Okie."

Daddy was stunned into silence. The things I had said wounded him in a way that was worse than if my mother had said them, which in so many words, she surely had, but coming from me—the denigration of his family and of him—reiterated by his own daughter, was especially cruel. I put my napkin on the table and pushed my basket of chicken away. I had eaten just a few bites of a drumstick and a couple of fries. After a few minutes, the waitress came over and asked if there was anything wrong. Daddy had stopped eating, too.

"We'd like to take these home... if that's all right," Daddy said.

"Why, of course." The waitress answered sympathetically, hoping to be of help to a man and his little girl who were obviously too upset to eat.

When she returned with the wrapped up chicken, Daddy got up without a word, walked to the register and paid the bill, then turned and said to me from across the room, "Are you coming or not?" That was so harsh for my father, I thought for a minute I had misunderstood.

After we got in the car, I began to sob.

"That'll be enough of that." It was a direct order. I gulped back my tears. "Here," Daddy said, handing me a napkin from the bag of chicken. "Lock your door," he said for the millionth time in my life but for the first time leaving off "pal," which came as another blow.

19

At least he didn't want me to fall out of the car, which I had done twice with Mom. But back when that had happened, I had been in the back seat of an old Pontiac huddled by a door that was hard to close, and I was only four. "It was snowing outside and the car heater drowned out everything," Mom had later explained. Evidently, I had leaned on the door, tumbled out of the car in my snowsuit, and fallen on the road without a yelp or a thump. On two different occasions, like a mime set to the drone of the heater, I had rolled from the car and landed in the snow. Twice Mom had no idea until she saw me in the road in the rearview mirror. "She's really getting good at it. She'll be able to join the circus," Mom had said, laughing it off. But Daddy thereafter automatically told me to lock the door, even though I was seven years older, even though I could now close the heaviest car door, even though I wasn't riding in the back seat of a car driven by a careless, impetuous mother.

As I rode home with Daddy, stifling my sobs, I thought about a bedtime story my mother had made up about a trip the two of us would one day make back to Missouri. We would go fishing in the Little Sac River, and maybe build a fire on the bank, and boil corn on the cob, and sing "In the Evening by the Moonlight."

Now that Mom was gone I often thought of the story as I went to sleep. I would fantasize about swinging out on a rope tied to a tree on the bank of the river and dropping into the cool water. Then I would catch the fish my mother would fry and, in the evening by the moonlight, like magical beings, we would fall asleep on a soft bed of leaves.

But now, instead of making me happy, my fantasy made me convulse again. I tried not to make a noise. It's hard to weep quietly to just let the tears pool and spill over without uttering a sob. If I'd had Bear-de-Rowe, it would have been easier. I could have held him to my face, caught the tears, and muffled the sound. Thankfully, my father turned on the radio, and someone was singing "Dark Town Strutters Ball," which drowned out my sniffling. It was one of my tap numbers, so I was able to concentrate on the steps. "I'm gonna dance off both my shoes when they play those jelly roll blues." I moved my feet to the words, reflexively, thinking the steps, the way you do after you learn a dance. In that way, the bare movement of my shoes on the car floor in a mute, imperceptible dance, I got all the way home without breaking down.

Ever since, I have considered tap dancing a life skill.

Chapter 4

That night I dreamed I was tap dancing on the stage in the auditorium of my school, but no one could hear the taps. When the kids in the audience began laughing, I stopped and looked at the bottom of one shoe and then the other, but there were no taps, either on the toes or the heels just the little holes where they had been nailed to the sole. When I looked back up, I was in the school lunch room. My classmates, seated at long tables, were eating chicken and fries out of baskets. I tried to explain to them that I had been doing a soft shoe, no taps necessary, but they kept biting and chewing, unable or unwilling to hear me.

When I woke up in the morning, I was immediately relieved but then like the throb of a fresh wound, I remembered Daddy—how I'd hurt him on purpose at the Chicken Hut and how he had cut me off. Daddy had already left for work. I was alone with what I had done.

If I hadn't had Bear de Rowe, I don't know if I could have gotten out of bed, put on my jumper and blouse from the night before, and made my way through the emptiness of the house. On the kitchen nook table was a page ripped from Daddy's yellow pad and weighted down by my blue Shirley Temple bowl. On the page was a note in large, glowering print: "BE HOME AT FIVE."

Daddy had filled the bowl with Rice Krispies. I poured milk over them and waited for them to go "snack, popple, and crap," as Mom would have said, which had always made me laugh. Bear de Rowe looked on as I ate and then I returned him to my room and put him on the pillow on my unmade bed.

As I traipsed to the bus stop, my grief was over-ridden by dread. Since I was in the sixth grade, I had to ride the bus into town with the junior high schoolers. As always, I would have to face Sam Heigel, the older boy who teased me. When I climbed on the bus, sure enough, Sam yelled out from the back. "Yessir, that's my baby," he said, and everyone laughed, because he was a teenager and I was just a kid.

Thankfully, Kay was sitting near the front.

"I saved you a seat," she said, moving her books. "How's it going? You look sleepy or just funny, like your eyes are all puffed up."

"Puffed up?"

"Yeah. It's not bad. So when am I coming to babysit? she asked. "I could use the money."

"I'm not sure."

"Is it true that your mom has...made a sudden departure?"

"How did you know?"

"I'm psychic. That means I can divine what's happened." She smiled sympathetically. "I guess that's why you look.... forlorn?"

"I guess so."

I wasn't sure what forlorn meant, but I liked the sound of the word. It made me feel like I was a character in a fairy tale or a book about a girl whose circumstances would change for the better.

"Tell your dad I could come over afternoons if he would like to avail himself of my services. You want to know what I'm doing with my savings as soon as I have accumulated enough?"

"What?"

"You can't tell a soul."

"I won't tell."

"Especially not your dad. Then it would get right back to MY dad."

"My dad and I aren't talking."

"Good."

"Well, I'm taking all the money I get and leaving this place... I'd take you with me, if I could, Janet, I really would, but that wouldn't be possible."

"Where are you going?"

"An undisclosed destination."

"What does that mean?"

"It means I can't say. But in case I don't see you again soon, I want to leave you with some words of wisdom."

"Okay."

"Don't let them send you to an orphanage."

"An orphanage..."

"An orphanage is even worse than seventh grade, which is the worst thing most people ever go through. In an orphanage you aren't locked up all day and mentally tortured by your classmates the way you are in seventh grade, but you're locked up and mentally tortured by adults, and that's worse. I wish I'd had someone to advise me when I was your age. Anne of Greene Gables had a good life if she could have skipped the orphanage part and moved straight to the country."

"Country people are... the salt of the earth," I said.

"That's right."

From somewhere in the back of the bus, Sam Heigel had made his way to the seat behind me and Kay. Sticking his head between us, he began singing to me.

"Let me call you sweetheart, I'm in love with you..."

"Stop it," I said, bursting into tears like a sissy, some mother's darling or daddy's girl, which I was not.

"Leave her alone, Sam," said Kay. "Don't you know she's been abandoned?"

"Abandoned. Did you hear that? She's been abandoned," Sam announced to the whole bus, overemphasizing the ban in abandoned.

"I guess it's up to me to unaBANdon her." The kids behind us roared. He started singing again, "Let me hear you whisper that you love me, too."

"That's not funny, Sam Heigel." Kay lit into him like the heroine of a novel. "Go away or I'll tell them all how I beat you at your own game," she whispered fiercely.

24

Sam Heigel became tongue-tied, which cured my whimpering.

"You cheated," he finally spluttered, his nostrils and upper lip uncontrollably twitching.

"Goodbye," Kay said, blithely, and Sam retreated.

"Wow," I said, wiping my nose on my sleeve.

"That's how you handle a spoiled General's son," she said, once he was out of earshot.

"How did you beat him... at his own game?"

"With a paddle."

It took me a minute to catch on.

"With a PING PONG paddle?"

"That's right," she said with a smug, slight smile.

Kay had told me how she had won the ninth grade girls' ping pong championship, how it had been announced over the intercom, and how it was "the only good thing that had ever happened in three years at the institution of torture" she was forced to attend.

"When? When did you beat him at his own game?"

"It was at Teen Town. Everyone else was dancing in the other room, so he deigned to play with me. When I beat him, he was so mad I thought he would hit me. Mr. Ping Pong champion."

"That was a... a great..."

"Triumph."

"Uh HUH."

"Yes, it was," Kay replied. "I advise you to take up the game."

"And you never told anyone about it?"

"Shhh," she said. "It's between you and me. I wouldn't deign to tell the others. That way we have something over him."

I was dying to know what "deign" meant, but as the bus pulled up to the school, Sam resurfaced and stood in the aisle beside our seat, blocking us from getting out. He stood there ushering everyone off the bus and then got off himself and walked behind the others up to the edge of the parking lot where the walkways to the elementary school and the junior high met. After the others were out of sight, Kay and I could see him skulking ahead of us. He was bent over, getting something out of his book bag on the ground. When he stood up, I could see it was a paddle, which he began to swing as if he were serving the ball. He stood there, serving the imaginary ball, over and over, waiting for us, daring us. I slowed down hoping he would move on.

"Just keep walking," Kay said, stepping in front of me and leading the way.

I trailed her looking straight ahead glued to the back of her blue sweater.

"Watch it with that paddle, Heigel," she said to him as we passed. But when I turned my head to see how he took her warning, he lunged toward me, serving the ball, but this time the ball was my back side. The paddle sent a sharp pain up my back and threw me off balance. I yelped and stumbled but caught myself and began running on the walkway toward the elementary school. I thought he might be chasing me, and I ran almost to the steps at the entrance, before I looked back.

When I finally did, he wasn't behind me. I stood there below the steps panting, searching for Kay, for the blue of her sweater. I thought she had taken off for the junior high, but I didn't see her anywhere on the walkway. Then I looked back to see where Sam was, and he was still at the edge of the parking lot and below him lying on the white gravel was Kay. She was curled up on her side with her head turned to the side. Sam was standing over her with the paddle in his hand. I watched him as he raised it like a spear over his right shoulder and swiped it down toward her hunched body as if he were killing the ball. It was a mock stroke, mainly to scare her, but I found out later, he had already taken intentional aim, brutally striking her in the gut, which was how she had fallen.

I ran back down the walkway toward them. He swung the paddle again. It just missed her arm. And now he took an open shot toward her face that you could hear cutting the air. She kept

26

scooting in the gravel away from him as he advanced with another swing. Then he raised the paddle again, over his left shoulder and swung a ferocious back hand this time grazing the hand that was shielding her face.

"What are you doing?" I shrieked. Kay was groaning. "Leave her alone," I yelled.

Sam stopped swinging, his back to me, but he wouldn't move away from her. I was afraid to get too near for fear he would turn and swing at me. Looking up the walkway toward the school, I yelled as loud as I could, "Help!"

And then Sam did turn on me. "Shut up," he said, so vicious and red-faced I tripped where the gravel met the concrete as I backed away.

But someone had heard my scream. From behind Sam, a figure was coming up through the parking lot.

He called out, "What's going on here?" It was the Private who drove our bus.

Ignoring him, Sam pointed the paddle at me, shook it, and said, "She's a liar. You'd better not ever repeat what she said."

"I… I wouldn't deign to," I said, backing further away.

"I asked you a question," said the Private, briskly coming up behind Sam. "What's going on here?" He was young, probably not a lot older than Sam but taller and commanding in his uniform.

"My father is General Heigel," Sam snarled over his shoulder to the Private. Then, smarting and tremulous, he snatched his bag from the gravel, tried to put away the paddle, which refused to fit, resorted to placing it with his quavering hand under his upper arm, and walked away with long strides and then faster practically running toward the school.

I knelt down by Kay. "Are you all right?"

"He hit me in the stomach," she whispered.

"What?" I asked, leaning nearer to her.

"I've lost my breath."

"She's lost her breath," I whimpered to the Private.

27

"She'll be okay," he said, consoling me. "Let me help you up, Miss." The Private bent over behind Kay, gently reached under her arms, and pulled her up.

"What do you want me to do?" he asked. "I can go get the school nurse."

"No. I'm not going in that building," Kay said in a weak, wobbly whisper.

Strands of her long hair had come out of the rubber band and fell on the sides of her face. "Could you take me home on the bus?"

"Well," he hesitated, "that would be highly irregular." But after a second he said, "General's son or not, that Heigel is a worthless piece of shit."

We didn't know what to say. We had never heard such vile language and had no idea how gratifying it could be. When Kay found her voice she murmured, "Thank you."

"Thank you," I echoed.

"Will you be all right, Miss?" the Private asked me.

"Yes, thank you."

"What about on the bus coming home from school today?"

"I take the early bus... for the little kids... He, the worthless... piece of shit, doesn't ride that bus."

He smiled. "Okay. That's good. After I report him today, you girls won't have to worry."

Kay was looking at the Private, the open collar of his shirt, his soldiers cap at an angle. She was in love.

"You take care, Miss," he said, looking me in the eye.

I was in love, too.

28

Chapter 5

I almost asked the Private if he would take me home, too, but he and Kay turned and started walking back to the bus, and I headed back to school and got to my room just as the last bell rang.

It was the day that the art teacher came to our class. I was grateful. Art engrossed me like a good daydream. It took my mind off Sam Heigel and the talking-to from Daddy that was coming up at five o'clock.

The art teacher brought paper, starch, and paints. I made a papier-mache Bear-de-Rowe with black ears and a white face, pasted him on a piece of cardboard, and painted below: "Have a Beary Christmas." The teacher pointed out to me that Christmas had passed. I told her I was thinking ahead to the next Christmas.

And I was. Even if Daddy said Mom wasn't coming back, I didn't believe she would spend a Christmas without me. We had too much fun making up Christmas jokes and singing all the songs. We Sang "Away in a Manger" in harmony, and I didn't get off on her part. We sang, "Here Comes Santa Claus," and I would do the time step, which is perfect for that song. We made up gestures to go along with every line of "Rudolph the Red Nose Reindeer."

"We know how to have fun, don't we, kiddo?" Mom would say. Daddy didn't join in unless he had had a beer or two. "Don't ever get to the point that you can't have fun without alcohol," Mom would advise me.

Drinking was not one of my mother's problems. And I never once ever saw her smoke a cigarette. People don't think of her virtues when they think of my mother, but when I miss her, which I do to this day, I think of them. My mother, if she'd been at home instead of out West, would have loved my ''Beary Christmas'' papier-mache. She would have hung it up on the wall

29

in our quarters, and we would have sung "Have Yourself a Beary little Christmas."

I carried the poster home with me on the afternoon bus that day. There were only three other kids. It was quiet. The bus jiggled me to sleep and I didn't wake up until it came to my stop. I walked home with my poster in a haze. All day I had wanted to call Kay to see how she was. Also, I had wanted to know how she knew my mother had "abandoned" me and tell her that just because someone abandons you doesn't mean they don't think you're fun. But when I got home, I propped the poster against the foot of the bed, lay down on the rumpled sheets with Bear-de-Rowe, and didn't wake up until Daddy came looking for me at 5pm.

Our meeting was more of a briefing than a talk. Daddy told me that I was going to Missouri just as soon as school was out, which was only two weeks away, and that he would be moving into the BOQ and then flying to the Philippines, where families were not allowed.

"Could I live with you in the BOQ, just until you leave?" I wondered.

"No. Only military personnel are allowed in the BOQ. I'll need time to clear out our quarters and to get ready to leave… There are legal matters to get in order."

"Are you and Mom getting a divorce?" I asked for the first time.

"Yes."

His "yes" was final, not angry or clipped, but fixed and indisputable. It triggered a host of unutterable questions: Was divorce forever? Would my parents never see each other again? Is a divorced soldier allowed to have a child on a base? Would I always live with other people? But they seemed impossible to pose —the answers too frightening—so I asked a question of lesser consequence, an old one that had gnawed at me but that I had been too afraid to ask.

"Where out West is Mom?"

"I'm not sure," he said. "Maybe in Las Vegas."

"Where Dingbat went!" I exclaimed, as if that were a mitigating factor.

The name made Daddy flinch. What a dumbbell I was. I still didn't catch on that Mom and Dingbat were more than just friends.

"Can I talk to her?" I asked.

"I don't have a phone number."

"But how will she know where I am? What if she can't get hold of me?"

"Oh, she'll know. She'll figure it out... I'll let her know somehow. Don't worry about that, pal." The "pal" was a huge boon. "As soon as I can, in six months or so, I'll be back to visit you up in Missouri...Okay?"

Six months was unfathomable, but I understood that my father's demands were incontrovertible.

"Okay," I said.

"You should start thinking about what you want to take with you. You can't take too much, but if there are things you want to put in storage for a while, we can do that. Everything has to go in one suitcase. Okay?"

"Okay."

"Is there anything else we need to talk about?"

I didn't tell Daddy about Sam Heigel. I guess I somehow felt in the wrong, as children will, though I knew Daddy thought there was nothing worse than a kid who pulled rank. But also, as I look back, I didn't really know my father. I knew him mainly through my mother. I loved him, of course. I treasured my reinstatement as "pal," but I also needed him. He was the lifeline to my mother. I couldn't risk alienating him by telling him what had happened that morning at school.

Instead I asked, "Can Kay come over in the afternoons after school, until I leave?"

"I don't see why not."

"She needs the money."

31

"Well, you can tell her I'm good for fifty cents an hour."

Daddy got up from the table. "I could use some chow. What about you?"

"I could use some." Since we had left the Chicken Hut, I had eaten exactly one lettuce sandwich—in the school lunch room.

"Well, let's see here," he said, opening the fridge.

"Daddy, I have another question."

"What's that, pal?"

"Do I have to put everything in a suitcase? My dolls and my bears like to see the countryside. They'd rather ride in the back seat."

Daddy sat back down.

"Well, you're not going in a car, pal. I'm gonna have to put you on a bus."

"A bus?"

"You're a big girl. And I have it all arranged at the other end for someone to pick you up… I wish I could drive you out, but it just isn't possible for me to do that, attend to things here, and get to Manila to report in, too."

"I don't like to ride busses," I said.

"Well, the Greyhound bus is a lot bigger and more comfortable than a school bus."

GREYHOUND. The large, printed word on Daddy's list, now sprang to mind, unleashed and growling.

"Look at this," Daddy said. He picked up a road map and began unfolding it. "It's a map of the United States."

The map scared me, too. The whole of the United States was too vast. I could not place myself in its enormous context. A trip by myself on a bus, on a wild, mad animal, racing through the United States made me feel faint. But Daddy kept unfolding, one section after another, the map getting bigger and bigger.

"I don't want to look at it. Do I have to look at it?" I must have looked scared because Daddy backed off.

"No. Not now. I think we ought to get some grub now."

Daddy got the wrapped-up food out of the fridge, and we chowed down on the cold chicken and fries we had taken home with us from the Chicken Hut.

***

Daddy didn't know it, but in the days that followed, Kay came more than afternoons. She came after he left in the morning and stayed all day. For a week the two of us, holed up in our quarters, skipped school. She said it was "a necessary survival tactic and not cowardice," but in truth, we were afraid to get on the bus.

"I'm never going back," Kay said.

"You're quitting ninth grade?"

"Yes."

"You're just aBANdoning it?" I asked.

"Yes."

But at the end of the week, she said, "He won't bother us as long as we have the same bus driver."

"I don't want to go to school," I said.

"We'd better go back, Janet. Our parents will find out. Besides, there's just one week left. We have to go back to pass. You don't want to have to repeat sixth grade, do you?"

I still didn't want to go, but she talked me into it, explaining that the Private had reported the incident and that by now we had nothing to fear as long as he was the driver.

"But what if he isn't our driver." We had different drivers all of the time.

"Well, then we won't get on the bus."

"Oh."

So we started going to school again. The first morning, instead of getting on at her stop, Kay came to my house, and we walked to the stop together. When the bus pulled up, Kay nudged me and smiled. Our private was driving. When I climbed on, he winked at me. Kay and I sat together as near him as we could. I

33

half expected Sam to sing something out at me or make a catcall, but he didn't.

"Is he on the bus?" I asked Kay.

"I don't know. I didn't look back there."

"I didn't either."

"The Private winked at me," I said.

"Me, too. I thought I'd faint on the spot," Kay said.

We tee hee'd, which made us feel better and rode in silence all the way to school.

Sam Heigel never sang to me or came near us again. After the first few bus rides, I knew he never would. Kay said he should have been punished, that he was guilty of assault, that the law had failed us. But like me, she was thankful for the fact that he was leaving us alone.

During that last week before I left for Missouri, as soon as she got home from school, Kay came over and stayed with me. She said her mother had told her to be nice to me, that I would need a friend.

Her mother was right. Kay helped me decide what I should leave and what I should take on my "sojourn to the Midwest." She folded my clothes and packed my suitcase, bought me a bottle of deodorant and a tiny tube of pale lipstick, neither of which I had ever had before. Together we tackled the road map. She drew circles around the main cities I would go through to get to Missouri. We talked about how long it would take to get from point to point and where I would change buses. She showed me how to fold the map back and forth like a fan so I could keep it in my red velvet pocketbook, which I was to carry with me on the bus.

Best of all, she told me the truth—what every adult on the base knew—that my mother had left Las Vegas with another man, and that the man was Dingbat. The "upside," she said, quoting her mother, was that it was "just another fling" for the likes of Dingbat and that she "wouldn't give it six months."

Kay told me that Mom would probably join me eventually in Missouri and that even if she didn't, I was going to have an "unforgettable adventure." Kay comforted me as well as any adult might have, far better than Daddy knew how. Without her, I would have been very much alone. She helped me reconcile myself to my mother's desertion, to my father's move half way across the world, and to my own displacement to Missouri, by myself, on a Greyhound bus.

After I left South Carolina, she wrote me and I wrote her back, but when her father was transferred, we lost contact as army brats will. She never told me the name of the "undisclosed destination" where she wanted to go, but I made it up that the twenty-five dollars Daddy had paid her to take care of me were enough to get her there. I also made it up that our Private visited her there, that they became engaged to be married, and that they asked me to be the maid of honor.

***

Once I had a dream that mangled my wedding fantasy of Kay and the Private. Kay is in a white dress with a train a mile long. I adjust her veil and walk down the aisle in a pink tutu carrying Bear-de-Rowe. When I arrive at the altar, the groom turns out to be Dingbat and his groomsman is Sam Heigel. Dingbat has grown a villain's moustache. He twists it and raises one eyebrow, and I start to laugh. When the wedding march begins, everyone turns and looks down the aisle. It is Daddy who is giving away the bride. The minister says, "Who gives this woman to this man?" and Daddy says, "I do." "Then you may raise the veil," the minister says to me. And I raise the veil. But instead of Kay behind the veil, surprise: It is Mom. She is luminous—fully mascaraed, lipsticked, and powdered. She walks to Dingbat and says, "Kiss me, you fool." He bends her back in a dip, kisses her, and drops her on the altar floor. She stumbles on the dress but gets back up and says to the minister, "He didn't mean to drop me. It was an

35

accident." The minister proceeds, asking if there are any objections.

I say, "She isn't the right bride. He isn't the right husband. Don't let them be united. Daddy and I object to the union."

But Mom laughs and says, "It's over, kiddo. We're already united."

"But you never said you were going to get married."

"You were supposed to be able to tell that, ya dumbbell. We were meant for each other. How did you miss that? Now do your tap dance and your song."

I refuse to dance. Sam Heigel begins singing, "Let me call you sweetheart." I run down the altar steps. Halfway down the aisle, I see Kay, lying on the floor in her wedding dress. She is tangled in the train and can't get up. When I wake up, I am yelling, "Help! Help! The bride needs help."

I only had the dream once, but it played over in my mind so many times it seemed like a recurring dream. For the year after Mom left for Vegas, it was a lurking torment. However hard I tried to keep it submerged, at night when I went to bed, my mother in a wedding veil, flanked by Dingbat and Sam Heigel, flashed up and then the horror was on. At the beginning with Kay and the Private, a beautiful church wedding forebodes a perfect union, but when Mom and Dingbat take over, the marriage made in heaven morphs into a hopeless, fly-by-night coupling made in some tawdry chapel in Vegas.

It is the story of my mother's life—the happy, hopeful beginnings with men and the awful, ugly separations that follow. My mother's flights with men became more nightmarish with each repetition. Eventually, I realized that the trap Mom needed to escape was the always-needing-to-escape itself. But that was something I didn't understand until much later and that Mom probably never understood though, as she herself would have said of another, it was plain as the nose on her face.

***

The day before Daddy put me on the Greyhound bus in Beaufort, South Carolina, I received a letter from Mom.

> *Hi Kiddo,*
>
> *How are you? I hope you were able to finish the sixth grade with a bang. I expect you got all A's as usual. I guess you know by now that your father and I decided to get a divorce. That's been coming for quite a long time. Maybe you guessed that, being the smart one in the family. Anyway, now I need to make a living for myself and the chances of finding employment are better out here than back east so that's why I had to travel so far away.*
>
> *Don't be mad at me. In time you will thank your lucky stars that it all worked out this way. You could do a lot worse than go back to good ole Missouri!*
>
> *I'll be in touch soon and maybe up to visit you as soon as I get a job and they let me have time off.*
>
> *Do you know what the horse said when he first met a zebra? "What's with the silly pajamas?"*

In the margin she'd drawn a picture of striped pajamas.

> *Get it? Regards to Bear-de-Rowe.*
> *Love,*
> *Mom*
>
> *PS Guess who I bumped into out here. Your old pal Dingbat! Can you believe it? Dysart luck! We get along like a house afire. He is going to help me find a job.*
> *PSS Give my love to your grandmother and to Uncle Pat.*
> *PSSS When I get some moola, I'll send you something cute to put on your back.*

PSSSS The Little Sac River is a great place to swim. See if one of those Miller kids will take you. The third oldest is about your age. But it's better to go with one of the older boys, who knows the ropes. Get it?

She'd drawn a picture of me holding a rope that was attached to a tree. In the background were wavy lines for the river. I was wearing my bathing suit that had the stars on it, which she had bought me in fourth grade and which I loved but which I would never be able to squeeze into.

PSSSSS I'm proud of you, kiddo. I'll call ya in the near future.

There was no phone number where I could call her, but the final words of the letter, an afterthought, tossed last-minute into the final PS, bore the hope that would keep me going. She would call me. She would call me. I folded the letter, the way she had, the short way first, then three folds so that it just fit into the envelope, stamped Las Vegas, Nevada, and put it beside the map in my red velvet pocketbook, which I would hold close when I boarded the racing dog that would whisk me away from home and carry me into the strange, lonely middle of the country.

PART II

Chapter 6

In 1950, without a car, the best way to get from South Carolina to the town where my grandmother lived in Missouri was on the Greyhound Bus. It didn't go through her town, but it went through a somewhat larger town just eight miles away. It stopped on a county road at one of those little one-room filling stations that had a roof that extended out over the two pumps in front. Daddy had described it to me. It was painted red and white. I kept looking out the bus window for the station, afraid the driver would pass it, but at 8pm the rural countryside rolled by in utter darkness. If the driver overshot the station, I had decided to get out of my seat and go tell him, but how would I know if I didn't see it? I knew we couldn't be far away because the previous stop was Bolivar, which according to the map, was just down the road from Fair Play, which was where the filling station was. So I sat on the edge of my seat, clutching my red velvet pocketbook all the way from Bolivar to Fair Play, prepared to spring up and into the aisle. When the bus slowed down and the driver announced "Fair Play," I was so relieved I said, "That's my stop!" right out loud, and the woman across the aisle sat up from a sound sleep and asked, "Are we in Humansville yet?"

The bus door whooshed open, and the driver helped me pull down the large Samsonite suitcase my mother had used travelling all over the country with my father from one army base to the next. It had all of my clothes, carefully packed by Kay, two books— *Ben Hur* and a *Nancy Drew*—my tap shoes, and Bear de Rowe, which Kay said I was too old to carry openly.

39

The driver set the suitcase by a bench at the gas station and left. The bus had rumbled down the road and disappeared into the night by the time I realized that I had left the roadmap on the seat beside me, folded back to show three towns which I had circled: Bolivar, in small dark print, Fair Play in smaller, lighter print, and Aldrich in print so tiny and light you had to squint to see it. I didn't really need the map now that I had arrived, but Daddy had given it to me, and he and Kay had gone over it with me. It had become my guide to the future, and it was also the guide to where I was from and maybe where I could someday go back. Of course, I didn't think of all that at the time and maybe I am exaggerating, but why else did losing the roadmap, make me feel so lost? It was the last thing Daddy had given me. It was like losing the way home, a final untethering from my father.

The gas station was closed, but there was a bare light bulb on inside. It was the only light anywhere, just that poor, solitary beam, which faded into the murk a few feet past the bench where I was sitting. I looked up and down the road into the darkness. My great Uncle Pat, who lived in Fair Play, was supposed to pick me up, take me to his house for the night, and drive me to my grandmother's little town the next morning. I only knew Uncle Pat from the last time my mother and I had visited my grandmother, but I knew him better than I knew his brother, my grandfather, which was not at all.

My grandfather, according to Mom, tickled my toes and made funny faces until I held out my arms to him, then picked me up and threw me in the air to make me gurgle and laugh, and after that went his merry way. Mom said he was like a fisherman with too many fish.

"He lured you in and threw you back. Oh, he could be fun, all right, best quail shot in the county. And you couldn't beat him at marbles, your Grandfather, but he certainly fell by the wayside. Turning up in town with some new scheme, then disappearing without so much as a kiss my foot... But your Uncle Pat? He can be counted on. He's the one who stepped in and

40

helped Mama. He might not have the looks or the personality of his brother, but he is the Rock of Gibraltar."

You'd think my mother could have applied her knowledge of men to make better choices in her own life. Her preference for men with "personality" over those who "could be counted on" should have been obvious to her. But, of course, it doesn't work that way. I know that now. Back then, I was just glad it was Uncle Pat and not my grandfather who had agreed to pick me up.

However, after a few minutes of waiting on the bench, I began to wonder if Uncle Pat had forgotten me. I also wondered about reliability. A Rock of Gibraltar is always there, but does it always remember? Or get things right? The most reliable person in the world could make a mistake on day or time. What if no one came after me? How would I get to my grandmother's? I remembered Mom's story of a woman who had walked barefoot through the night all the way from the Fair Play bus stop to Aldrich.

"She was dang near defeated," Mom had said. "De-feeted, get it?"

At the time I had slapped my knee the way Mom did, but now it wasn't funny. I felt sorry for the "hillbilly" whose shoes didn't fit and who had to walk miles alone in the dark on a "washboard road."

At least I had good shoes, I was thinking when I heard the motor of a car in the distance. I jumped up hoping to be better seen, but without ever seeing the car lights, the whir of the engine began to fade, quieter and quieter, into obscurity leaving nothing but the drone of tree frogs. I sat back down, picked my pocketbook back up, and held onto it as Daddy said I should, and tried to think.

I had been to Uncle Pat's house once when I was little. Mom and I had driven from my grandmother's town to Fair Play to the beauty shop. The owner was a pretty, fat lady who smiled and laughed and gave me a bag of curlers to play with while she dyed Mom's eyebrows. Her shop was in a row of red brick buildings on

41

the main drag. When we left her shop, we had walked to Uncle Pat's house, which was just up the street, right there on the main drag of town. It was just a small house. From the beauty shop, I could find it. But where was the main drag? I wondered if I should start walking toward the town. But the darkness enveloped everything. Once I strayed beyond the station, there was no way to see—no moon, no stars, just pitch darkness. If I struck out on my own, I wouldn't be able to find the red brick buildings, much less find Uncle Pat's little house. And the suitcase was too heavy.

So I sat on the bench afraid to leave the station. Maybe, if I got Bear-de-Rowe out of the suitcase, I could curl up on the bench and wait until dawn. I was too tired to think. I just kept looking at the lone light hanging on its long electrical cord from the ceiling inside the station. On the wall behind the light was a telephone. I wanted to call my father. Looking at the phone made me begin to cry. I bent over my pocketbook and unzipped the lining to find the handkerchief Kay had given me.

When I looked back up from dabbing my eyes, I saw, through the murk, a muted light from the direction of town, a hazy glow which became brighter, divided and turned into headlights, moving toward me slowly, the hum of a motor increasing as the lights approached, slowed down, and turned into the station. From the open window of the car, I could hear a man singing: "It's a grand night for singing…"

I couldn't hear the words, just the waltzy, carefree, melody, but later I learned the lyric, including the line, "Somewhere a bird that is bound to be heard is throwing its heart at the sky." It's a song of pure, unadulterated hope. I was in a place and time when a man might drive down the road singing out the window into the summer night. The car stopped, the door opened, and out came the singer. He came around the car and into view—a wiry, gray-haired man in shirt sleeves who walked with a spring. I wiped my cheeks and blew my nose. It was Uncle Pat.

"Well, that looks a little bit like Janet, only a lot bigger," he said, tilting his head to get a better look at me. "By gonnies, it IS Janet! Is this your suitcase?"

Uncle Pat picked up the suitcase, walked to the car, and opened the door for me. While he put my suitcase in the trunk, I reached up and touched the soft, gray fabric stretched across the roof of the interior, the same as in Daddy's Packard. The night, which had frightened me just minutes ago, now balmy and beautiful, floated into the car through the open windows.

After the clunk of the trunk lid, I heard Uncle Pat say, "Best looking one of Rose's clan, by a longshot." He pretended to be muttering to himself, but I later realized he did that, with every intention of being heard.

Chapter 7

Uncle Pat was the only person in my family who ever lived in Fair Play, and that was only because he married Aunt Pansy, who lived there and couldn't leave. Fair Play wasn't considered desirable. The nicer people lived in Aldrich. Fair Play was common. The people weren't as smart or well-educated. Examples of these deficiencies were unclear, but one mark of education, I later learned, was one's knowledge of Latin, and I can remember wondering if the people of Fair Play didn't "know their Latin."

I'm not sure if the prejudices of my family reflected those of the general population of Aldrich, but they were fraught with contradictions. For example, Aunt Pansy, born and raised in Fair Play, was the unquestioned "salt of the earth," and her niece, the pretty fat lady who ran the beauty shop, though a beautician, a vocation no "nice" girl aspired to, was just as "nice as pie." Nonetheless, the very words "Fair Play" called up inferiority, not only social but moral. Part of that had to have been because Fair Play was where women went who were "in trouble." When they whispered, "She couldn't keep her skirts clean and had to go over to FAIR PLAY," everyone over sixteen knew what she went for, and it wasn't to get her eyebrows dyed at the beauty shop.

But Uncle Pat, of good Aldrich stock, moved to Fair Play just the same. And he would have done it twenty years sooner if his mother hadn't lingered on. In those days some men, the kind you could count on, cared for their ailing old mothers until they died. That duty fell to Uncle Pat. That is why he couldn't move away from Aldrich. Pansy, like Uncle Pat, also had an old mother to look after. She, therefore, couldn't move from Fair Play. So Uncle Pat and Pansy dated all those years until his mother, my great grandmother, finally died, and he married Pansy at the age of fifty, and moved in with her and her old mother, and became a FairPlayan.

But I never thought of him as such. His heart was always in Aldrich, at least that's what I imagined as a child. It was Aldrich where he spent most of his time. He drove there every morning to the store that he ran with my grandmother. He spent all day working there with her and associating with the people of Aldrich who happened into the store. Sometimes he would even sleep overnight on the cot in his office at the back of the store. On the other hand, he returned most nights to Fair Play, so maybe I was wrong about where his heart really was. Maybe it was with Pansy in their little house on the north end of the main drag of Fair Play, a house that was no more than a gunshot rectangle made of native stone, surrounded by a scalloped wire fence.

When Uncle Pat and I arrived there late that spring night after he picked me up from the gas station, Aunt Pansy and her old mother never appeared. I pictured them sleeping in the small rooms off the dark hallway that ran through the middle of the house. With a flashlight Uncle Pat led me past the closed doors to a back porch, which had a narrow bed for me and a large bowl with a pitcher of water where I could "wash up." Uncle Pat showed me how to turn the flashlight off and on in case I needed to go out the back door to the outhouse, which I did. Then he patted me on the head and "turned in."

The outdoor toilet was new to me, and I was afraid, but I had to go. With the flashlight I could see boards on the ground that formed a long narrow walkway from the back door all the way to the outhouse. The boards were even, smooth, and straight. If it hadn't been nighttime and everything hadn't been so new to me, I might have thought they were fun to walk on, or run on, or maybe skate on, but after Uncle Pat left me, my fears of the night returned. The boards were a trial I had to cross alone. Desperate to use the toilet, I screwed my courage, stepping back out into the blackness and walking as fast as I could down the narrow planks. The boards seemed to go on forever. They were probably no more

45

than fifty feet from the house, but I might have been walking all the way to downtown Fair Play or to Aldrich or even Bolivar.

Forbidding and strange as those towns were, a mere triangle of pinpoints on a map, they were the places that mattered. Uncle Pat's and Aunt Pansy's lives revolved around "the big three," as Uncle Pat jokingly called them, and once I arrived, so did mine. Our portion of Polk County, he once told me, *est divisa in partes tres.* It was rare that he or I or anyone I came to know in Missouri ever travelled outside that ten-mile radius. But Uncle Pat, I was soon to learn, rose above the limited boundaries of his physical existence. He was by no means a worldly man, but he was educated. He knew his Latin.

By the time I got up the morning after the first night I spent with him in Fair Play, I could hear voices. I had slept in my underwear. As soon as I got back into my sailor outfit, I ventured down the long hallway and followed the voices into the kitchen. Pansy's old mother and Uncle Pat were drinking coffee in the kitchen.

"So you're Marge's girl," the old lady said to me in a creaky voice.

"Yes, ma'am," I said, as I had learned to reply in the South. I had never seen anyone so old and tanned by age. Her brown skin had a sheen like glazed papier-mache. Uncle Pat clinked down his cup and picked up and jangled his car keys.

"We have to be on our way," he said.

"I hope you'll come back so that we can visit." The old lady's parched lips curved into a little smile. "How old are you, Janet?"

"Twelve years old."

"I remember when I was just your age," she said in a dry, reedy whisper.

Uncle Pat had made me some toast that he said I could eat in the car on our way to Aldrich. I put on my shoes and socks.

"Come back and see me," the old lady beckoned as we left the house. I was glad I didn't have to stay and look at her, so

46

old and hunched over, her coffee cup shaking in her bony hand.

"Pansy works in the big city of Bolivar," Uncle Pat explained to me, as we were driving along.

"Bolivar..." I said the word for the first time the way he did—to rime with Oliver."

"That's right. She goes to Bolivar. I go to Aldrich. And in the evening we go back to Fair Play." What he said made me think of the map I had left on the bus, and I felt bad again about having lost it. "How was the toast?" I had eaten both pieces by the time we had gotten to the other end of the main drag.

"Good."

"I'm a pretty good toaster."

We drove by the filling station, which was now open and busy. The owner was pumping gas. Two men in straw farmers hats were sitting on my bench. The place looked different in daylight.

"How long does it take to get to Aldrich?" I asked.

"Oh, about thirty minutes. If we don't have a flat." He turned off the paved highway onto a washboard road.

"I hope we don't have a flat."

"Me, too. Nothin' keeps you from taking in the morning like a flat."

"How often do you have one?"

"No more than one or two a week."

"Oh," I said, not knowing if he was teasing or not.

As we bumped along, the scent of roadside honeysuckle wafting through the open windows, Uncle Pat began singing "Oh What a Beautiful Morning." He had a clear baritone voice that was pleasant. When he got to "Everything's going my way," right after "I've got a wonderful feeling," he slowed down and stretched out the final, "Oh, what a beautiful day."

"Oh, what a beautiful day," I sang softly to myself, mimicking him. I was thinking I could do the waltz clog to the song.

"Best voice of the whole bunch," he muttered to himself.

'Huh?" I said.

"There's a whole bunch of fish in this branch we're about to drive through." The road began a steep descent down through a dense woods.

"We drive THROUGH the water?"

"It isn't far. We'll probably make it without stalling out."

When we got to the bottom of the hill, I could see the road disappear under the water.

I gripped the armrest and peered out the window. I could see the rocky bottom of the branch through the clear ripples. Uncle Pat slowed way down and crossed, bumping over the pebbles, the water lapping the tires.

"Whew," he said as we climbed up the other side of the hill. "Made it, by jacks."

"If you don't make it, what happens?"

"You mean if you get stuck in the water?"

"Yes. What would you do?"

"Well, first YOU'D get behind the wheel and I'd get out and push, and if that didn't work we'd both get out of the car and hope someone would come along with a tractor or a couple of mules and pull us out."

"What if no one came along?" I asked.

"Well, that's when we'd start praying." I didn't know if that was a joke, but I started laughing and Uncle Pat, who wasn't a big laugher, just smiled.

"I can remember when your mother used to sing on the stage, he said after a few minutes."

"Really? She never told me. What stage?"

"The Aldrich High School stage."

"Oh," I said, deflated. Uncle Pat smiled as if he'd pulled off a good one. I was beginning to catch on to his sense of humor.

"They used to put on some pretty good shindigs… nothin' to snort at."

48

"Mom and I sing a lot together. I can harmonize.

"What's your favorite song?"

"Away in a Manger."

"Uh huh."

"Do you know that one?"

"Away in a manger, no crib for a bed," Uncle Pat broke out, and we sang the first verse, enjoying the scented morning breeze coming through the windows. After our duet, Uncle Pat and I bumped along in silence, "taking in the morning."

We passed a country church on a little hill, a farmhouse off in the distance on the other side of the railroad tracks that ran alongside the road, and nothing else but sparse woods until we came out into a clearing at a crossroads where we had to turn one way or the other. Uncle Pat stopped and asked which way I thought we ought to go. In one direction, the road led by a big white house and vanished into trees. In the other, it led to an iron bridge and up a steep hill.

"Is that the way to the river?" I asked, pointing to the bridge. And then I remembered Mom's stories: "That's where the swimming hole is!

"That's right" said Uncle Pat. "So which way?"

"So that's the road into town," I said, pointing in the opposite direction.

"You're a pretty good navigator," he said, turning toward town.

The road into town cut through a woods of silver maple trees, a thicket of pointed leaves forming a wall of rustling green on either side, only broken by houses with dirt paths and flowerbeds. I had never been in the midst of a barely tamed countryside. It was too absorbing to think or worry. I could only look at the wonder of it.

After we passed the big white house at the edge of the woods, I saw on the other side of the road a funny little weathered house that looked like a boxcar. A boy was playing with his dog in the front yard. Uncle Pat raised his index finger and the boy waved.

"One of the Parsons brood. You know that rime about the old woman who lived in a shoe?"

"Uh huh," I said, waiting to hear what he had to say next.

"The old woman could be Mrs. Parsons." I guessed that Uncle Pat meant that the boy had a lot of brothers and sisters or maybe that their boxcar house looked like a shoe.

After a while I asked, "Was that a collie... that the Parsons boy was playing with?"

"I wouldn't go that far."

"I've always wanted to see a collie."

"Well, you never know. That dog might have a little collie in him."

A truck came toward us and passed and then a green Packard like Daddy's. The drivers of each raised their index finger and Uncle Pat raised his. I didn't know how such a small gesture could be seen from one steering wheel to the next, but it could be, and with my hand on the seat, I practiced raising my finger in the same way.

Finally, we came to the main intersection of town. On the road to the right, beside the railroad tracks, I recognized a tall metal building with a square room at the very top that had a window.

"That's the way to my grandmother's house!"

"How do you know that?"

"Because you go by that funny building over there."

"That's a feed mill."

"A feed mill..."

"So which way is town?" he quizzed me.

"That way," I said enthusiastically, pointing to the left.

"Pretty smart kid," he said under his breath.

Uncle Pat crossed over the tracks, turned toward town and drove by a long row of red brick stores, none of which looked familiar. Then he turned onto a street with another row of redbrick stores and pulled up in front of the first and biggest one of them. It had three large display windows, a canopy that extended out over a wide concrete walkway, and long benches on both sides of a wide, two-door entrance. A metal sign over the doorway said Dysart Brothers. I don't know if I remembered the storefront from experience or if it was from a photo I had of my parents standing in front of it, but I felt like I had been there, maybe in a dream.

Uncle Pat and I stepped up onto the high concrete walkway and entered Dysart Brothers.

"There's no one here," I said, entering the huge, dim interior. There were shelves on either side that went all the way to the high ceiling and tall racks on both sides of a long middle aisle.

"It's still early."

"But I thought..." A tall woman wearing a long white apron appeared from the darkness of the back of the store. She put down something she was holding on a counter, and walked toward us, each step distinct on the concrete floor. She didn't look like anyone I had seen before, but as she moved toward us into the morning light coming from the display window behind me and Uncle Pat, she removed her glasses, and at that moment her features began to take shape—her large deep-set eyes, her pale complexion, her dark pinned-up hair, and I knew it had to be my grandmother. I knew it because my mother had described her to me many times, and because I had that remote memory of the time she'd picked me up and laughed and spun around with me, and of course, because Uncle Pat WAS, after all, taking me to meet her as planned. But despite all that, I was unprepared for the sight of the woman emerging from the shadows and materializing before me. The images of her that I had conjured were nothing beside the reality. In fact, it wasn't until the moment that morning at the store, when I looked up at my grandmother standing there in her white apron and she looked down at me that she came into being.

"Here she is, safe and sound. All the way from Fair Play to Aldrich and not a single flat tire!" said Uncle Pat. I kept looking, wide-eyed and mute, at my grandmother, who was smiling at me.

"I'll swan. Look how you've grown," she said. But I was at a loss to reply.

Finally, I uttered two syllables, which came from nowhere: "GranRose," I said and then went dumb again. I don't know what happened to the "mother" part of her name. She had always been alluded to as "grandmother Rose." But my grandmother laughed the laugh with the little whee after it, and my shortened version became my name for her thereafter.

Chapter 8

GranRose's house was on the outskirts of Aldrich, just beyond the end of the town sidewalk where a dirt path took over and the road turned and led out into the country. It was a modest bungalow, set back behind silver maples with a porch that crossed the front and wrapped around one side and had a railing wide enough to walk on between the pillars.

The house had a living room with a piano, a dining room with a coal stove, a kitchen with a Coldspot, a bathroom flanked by two bedrooms, and a big attic with three abandoned iron post beds. GranRose gave me the front, downstairs bedroom. The room had doors to the bathroom, the living room, the porch, and a closet. For a time it had been my mother's room. I could picture her sitting on the small bench in front of the big round mirror of the vanity powdering her nose or lying on top of the faded pink chenille spread, the cotton tufts worn down to nubs, several pillows behind her head, reading a book. The room wreaked of Mom—the old robe left behind in the closet, the forgotten trinkets in the vanity drawers.

The house heated up during the summer afternoons, and I slept in my new room with the door to the porch open to let in the night air. In the mornings by the time I got up, GranRose had fed the chickens and left for the store. Sometimes she had boiled an egg for me and mashed it up with some oleo. I would find it on the kitchen table covered with a feedsack dish towel. Otherwise, she expected me to "fend" for myself. GranRose had no rules, and she assigned me no duties. It wasn't in her nature to regulate others. She expected others to regulate themselves.

"What's Marge's girl up to?" I once overheard a store customer in a sunbonnet inquire of GranRose. I was unseen on the floor of the store playing jacks.

53

"Oh. She's just fiddling around," GranRose said, as she wiped down the counter.

The customer had decided to sit for a spell. "Hmm... fiddlin'"

GranRose was not being critical. It was okay for a kid to fiddle around. She was thankful that I was spared the deprivations that her own children had suffered during the Depression or the many chores that had fallen to her growing up on a farm. GranRose, like others of her generation, hadn't really thought much about child rearing. She had trusted that her own children would do their best, as she had. And with the exception of my mother, they had. My aunt, despite the Depression, had gone to college, unlike my mother, become a teacher, and married well. My uncle was a decorated military officer. He had bought the house that GranRose now lived in. He had made it possible for her to move out of the tarpapered rental she'd been reduced to after Grandpa Clay absconded, people couldn't pay their bills, and the store nearly went under.

"Those kids certainly did right by you, Rose. They have that to their credit," the woman in her sunbonnet said, unaware of my presence. She shifted from one subject to the next, a constant, unbroken ramble. "Of course, they had the money to do it. Not wealthy, mind you. But they did well enough. Made it their business to provide for their old mother. Yes, your kids did well, Rose," she paused and then added, "with the one exception..."

When I heard "the one exception," I dropped a jack and the ball went rolling. Only my mother, the menopause baby, had taken after her father and fallen by the wayside.

"Will Marge's girl be stayin' on with you then, Rose?" the woman asked from her rocker by the stove.

"I expect. For a while."

"The burdens of old age... So her mother is off gallivantin', through Texas is it?"

"Nevada."

54

"Well, the girl doesn't seem a bit like her. Pretty and polite… She didn't get that from her mother! Marge was a wild hare!" The woman leaned back in the rocker cackling. "The time she and Oneita got into it! By the time Lila Bauer got out to the schoolyard to split them up, Oneita was covered in mud and Marge was a bleedin' from the nose." She babbled on unaware of my presence.

GranRose tried to divert her. "Pat, these cans go over here on the shelf by the Vienna sausage, is that right?" But the woman kept on.

"Scripture says if yer an example to your children, they will follow in the ways of the lord. But a muleheaded girl like Marge? Why no example in the world could've swayed her…"

Now GranRose interrupted her. "Janet?" She called to me over in the pharmacy part of the store where the concrete floor was smooth and not porous, good for both jacks and tap dancing. "Are you ready for a sandwich?"

The sunbonnet began to bob, the woman having realized her mistake. "She sure could sing, though. Marge could sing like a lark," she said in a loud croak to make sure I heard. "Lila Bauer said she never did see a kid learn to read so fast, faster than a steel trap."

I stood up and came into view.

"Well hello there," she said, throwing her hands up as if surprised. Her face was sickly white, covered with large tan splotches. "We were just reflecting upon your mother's many virtues. My, my," the sunbonnet moved back and forth in disbelief, "you don't look a bit like your mother. Of course, she had that Buster Brown haircut…Your grandmother used to sit her up on the counter…wasn't easy to cut those bangs straight. There's a trick to it." The woman forgot about me and drifted off, "I don't know how you kept her still long enough to cut it," she said to GranRose, "Always chompin' at the bit, Marge was, always rearin' to go someplace…couldn't be tamed…" She cackled again, then remembered me, "unless she had a book, of course… She was

55

quite a reader, Marge. Faster than a jackrabbit. Do you like books?" she asked me.

***

Miss Sunbonnet was right about my mother's being a reader. Mom had told me more than once how she had felt when she had finished reading all of the books in the Aldrich school library, how bereft she was and how she longed to leave Aldrich. But she wasn't what I would call a book lover, though I have to say she was rarely without a book. There was usually one face down, marking her place, on the bedstand or beside the easy chair. But a bibliophile? If she'd had to choose between a good book or a mediocre man, probably even a bad one, she would've shelved the book without thinking.

For me, during those first troubled months in Aldrich, books were critical. They gave me a respite from the nagging thoughts of my missing parents, especially Mom. Despite the openness of Uncle Pat and GranRose, I suffered from a profound emptiness. I know now that I was grieving, almost as if my parents had died. The feeling, a penetrating pain, recurred throughout the day. It hurt most when I first awoke and had to remember, afresh, that my mother had left me by choice and that my father had put me on a bus and shunted me off. By the time I got out of bed, GranRose was long gone. I was alone in the house until noon. Books became my morning refuge.

Each day, I took my breakfast to the swing on the porch outside my bedroom door and read all morning. After I finished *Ben Hur* and *Nancy Drew*, I began reading whatever I found in the house—a gold bound *Grimm's Fairy Tales* that I found on top of the piano in the living room; an illustrated *Call of the Wild,* which someone had left on the floor by one of the beds in the attic; all of the stories in the stack of old *Redbook* magazines on the back porch; even a beat-up paperback copy of *Beau Geste,* which was in the outhouse and from which a few pages had been torn.

56

The books not only provided a reprieve from my woe, they triggered my fantasy play. After I read the Grimm brothers, I picked the flowers from the trumpet vine that grew over the porch rail and put them on my fingers and pretended to be a fairy queen who had long orange fingers. In the vanity in my bedroom, I found a little, orange box that I believed to have been my mother's. On it were drawings of little white poofs with black handles, which I finally figured out were powder puffs. Inside the box was fine, loose powder. I powdered my face rachel, put on the lipstick that Kay had given me, and pretended to be the beautiful Jewess Esther from *Ben Hur*. That's how I fiddled away the mornings. That's how I survived, by fiddling.

At noon, each day, I said goodbye to Bear-de-Rowe, who occupied one end of the porch swing, and left for the store. GranRose and Uncle Pat welcomed me. Mom had been right about my life at the store.

"After you 'learn the ropes' around the store, you'll have 'free rein.' Get it?"

It wasn't long before I sliced the bologna for my own sandwich, helped myself to a Grapette out of the big metal cooler, and thought nothing of reaching into the glass cabinet to the candy bin for a handful of red hots. After lunch, I played jacks in the pharmacy or fiddled around in Hardware. One afternoon, my mother, for the second time since I had arrived, called the store. When I came out of Hardware, I could hear GranRose on the store phone.

"We haven't had any rain all month.... Yes. Well, it's hot as the dickens... No, she doesn't.... I gave Betty Miller some feedsacks to make her some, but she'll need more than that if she's here for school... When do you think you'll come?... Well don't tell her you are if you're not... Because she's got her hopes pinned on you... George sent me a check... Well what's she supposed to do? He's on his way to the Philippines, and you've gone off hoop-te-la... She's all right. She's had the wind knocked out her sails... but I expect she'll be okay." She took the receiver from her ear.

57

"Janet," she called out in the direction of Hardware, "your mother is on the phone.

"I'm here," I said, startling her from behind.

"Here, hold this." She handed me the receiver. "Just a minute," she said, getting the stool she used to reach the high shelves. "You can stand on this."

I stood on the stool and spoke into the mouthpiece. "Mom? It's me."

My mother was apologetic about not having called sooner. She asked me about the bus trip and told me she had some good news.

"Guess what!"

"What?"

"Your mother landed a job working in a doctor's office."

"Will I be able to…"

"Dysart luck!" she said. "Just when I was down to my last dime!"

She went on to say she was sending money to GranRose to take me to Bolivar to get some clothes for school. When she said that, I began to cry, noiselessly, the way I'd taught myself. Up until then, without quite knowing it, I had been hoping she would come for me and take me to wherever she was, and I would go to school there. Now I knew I was going to be away from her indefinitely. What had happened to me—the change in my life that had already taken place—became more real, the effects more permanent. What I had known was irretrievable. I was going to have a different family and lead a different life altogether. Before she hung up, she said she would call again and let me know when she'd be coming for a visit.

Her visit became paramount in my life. Every time I experienced the empty, deserted pang, I would counter it with the thoughts of her arrival in Aldrich. As long as she was coming for a visit, I still had a mother. She might not be like other mothers, but I still had one who cared enough to come see me, and on one of those visits she might decide to take me back. Each morning after

58

that call, I read in the swing with Bear-de-Rowe and at noon, each day, I walked to the store, thinking about her visit.

It was a fifteen-minute walk. GranRose had no qualms about my walking to the store on my own or going anywhere else on my own for that matter. But I had never had so much freedom before, and the first day I ventured forth, even though there was only one way to go, I wasn't sure I would find the store on my own. The first few minutes of the walk were on the road. The gravel was hot at noonday and burnt my bare feet. I was glad to cross over a ditch to the dirt path on the one side of the road. I could see someone on the railroad tracks that ran down the opposite side of the road. When I came to where the path met the sidewalk into town, I could tell that the figure was a boy. His back was to me. He was walking on one of the rails with his arms out for balance. Ahead of him was a dog. I walked fast along the sidewalk to get up to where he would see me.

"Hi," I called out. He looked up and stepped off the rail.

"Hi," he called back. I was sure he was the Parsons boy I had seen in the yard of his boxcar house.

"Is that your dog?"

"Yeah."

"What's his name?"

"Eudorrie. She's a girl." I walked on the grass over to the edge of the road. The dog was black and white, about half as big as the boy.

"What kind is she?"

The boy shrugged. "Don't know." He bent down and stroked her head and back. "She came from over in Eudorrie." I later learned that Eudora was the name of a neighboring town. "She's a retriever. Watch this." He picked up a stick and threw it in my direction. The dog raced out into the road between us.

"Here, Eudorrie," I said, to see if she would come to me, but she got the stick and raced back to the boy.

"Do you want to play with her?" the boy asked.

"Okay." A car passed, the driver raised his finger at me, and I raised mine back at him, a tiny gesture that gave me a rush of satisfaction.

"Come over here," the boy called out. "You can throw the stick in the field so she don't go in the road." I tripped across the hot gravel. The dog stayed beside the boy, watching him as he handed me the stick. I threw it in the direction of the mill. The dog looked at me and then at the boy. "Go get it, Eudorrie," he said, but the dog wouldn't move. The boy began running into the field and the dog raced ahead of him, stopped where the stick had landed, and waited for the boy. When the boy leaned down, Eudorrie went for the stick and wouldn't give it up. The boy finally wrested it from her, threw it overhand a long way in the opposite direction into a field of weeds, and walked back to me. "It'll take her a while to take to ya." The dog disappeared into the weeds.

"Where'd she go?"

"She'll be back."

"Do you live out toward the river?"

"Just this side of the bridge. Eudorrie and I go fishin' down there."

"There's a swimming hole." I said, feeling how hot it was in the sun.

"Uh huh. It's pretty low. There hasn't been any rain."

"What grade are you in?" I asked him.

"Seventh. I will be... when I go back..."

"Me, too!" I said.

"I don't see Eudorrie," the boy said looking off in the distance. She might've found something. Wanna walk over there?"

We began walking in the direction the dog had gone. Beyond us through some trees, I could see the back of a large white structure.

"What building is that over there?" I asked.

"That's the Christian Church. I don't go there." The air was dead still and yet the leaves of the trees in the church yard were flickering.

"Where do you go?" I asked as if it were my business, but he didn't mind.

"I go to the Methodist, sometimes."

We found a path. The weeds on either side were coated in dust. I could hear the dog sniffing in the weeds ahead of us. She had found something.

"What has she got?"

"A lizard or a mouse or somethin."

The dog had her nose in a pile of old boards. She was pawing and sniffing.

"See that?" the boy asked, pointing to a circle of stones.

"Those rocks?"

"That's a well in there." We walked up to the stones. "Where's the stick, Eudorrie? Maybe it went in the well." He smiled at me, got down on his knees, and looked over the side of the circle of rocks. "Can't see it. Don't see a stick down there." I didn't know if he was kidding or not. I looked into the well and couldn't see the bottom.

"Does it have water?"

"Oh yeah. Not as much now. We're havin' a drouth."

"I can't see any," I said, bent over, narrowing my eyes. The boy found a stone.

"Listen to this," he said, dropping the stone into the well. I heard it splash.

"Did you hear it?" I nodded. "It's a pretty deep well."

The dog stopped digging and sniffing and began barking.

"Eudorrie," I said, patting her side. "What's the matter?" She stopped barking, looked at the boy, cocked her head, and then started barking again.

"She's thirsty," the boy said, "That's why she likes it over here by the well." I was thirsty, too.

"I'd better get going," I said.

"Me, too." I didn't believe him. He looked down and pushed one of the old boards aside with his foot for lack of anything better to do.

"See you later." I started back across the field. I lifted the side of my skirt and wiped the dripping sweat from my face. As I got to the railroad tracks, the boy called out to me.

"What's your name?" I turned back. He and the dog were almost to the trees beside the Christian Church.

"Janet," I called back, shielding my eyes from the sun.

"What?" he shouted.

I cupped my mouth. "Janet."

"I'm Ray," he yelled out. "Ray Parsons." I raised my forefinger at him in a kind of diminished half wave, and he raised his back at me.

Chapter 9

The next few days on my walk to the store, I wondered if I would see Ray and Eudorrie. Sometimes I stopped in the shade of a tree by Doc Lawson's house and looked across the street into the field between the mill and the Christian Church, but the boy was never there. Finally, I stopped looking. The bees were always buzzing in the honeysuckle that cloaked the wire fence around Doc's yard. It wasn't a good place to dawdle.

One day weeks later when I got to town, I could see a man sitting on the bench outside the store, petting a dog. When I got closer, I recognized the dog.

"Eudorrie!" She came up to me wagging her tail. I wondered if she remembered me or if she was just friendly.

"Is she your dog?" the man asked.

"She's Ray Parsons' dog."

I sat on the other end of the bench and asked the dog how she was doing, if she was thirsty, and where Ray was. There was a cocklebur in the long hair around her neck, but she wouldn't let me get it.

"You don't want an old bur in your hair, do you? Com'ere, Eudorrie," but she wouldn't come back.

"She'd probably make a pretty good bird dog, come October," the man said.

"Just a minute," I said to him. "I'll show you something."

On one side of the store, between it and the post office was a large grassy area that had been freshly mowed. In the grass clippings up against the outside wall of the store was a stick. When I came back around the corner to the front of the store, I saw GranRose standing inside watching me through the display window. I waved the stick and she waved back with the feather duster in her hand.

"Watch this," I yelled out to her and to the man on the bench. I threw the stick all the way up the walkway to the café. The dog took off, skidded into the stick, picked it up, and brought it back to me. It was the first time a dog had ever retrieved anything for me. The man clapped his knee and nodded at me.

"Good dog," I said, jubilantly, but when I looked up at the window for GranRose's approval, she had gone. As I raised the stick to throw it again, a woman and a girl, both dressed in blue, came out of the café.

"Better throw it around the corner on the croquet yard," the man said.

"Wanna see how far I can throw it?" I didn't understand what he had said, the something "yard," but I knew I shouldn't throw the stick on the walkway again where there were people. "I'll throw it on the grass," I said.

The man followed me around to the mowed lawn, and I threw it as far as I could. As the dog bolted across the green, Ray came from behind the post office on the path that cut through from the back of the store to the other strip of stores. When the dog saw him, he dropped the stick and bounded over to him.

"Hi, Janet," Ray said, stroking Eudorrie's head.

"He won't play fetch with me if you're here," I said walking up to him.

"They'll be playin' croquet as soon as it gets cooler," Ray said.

"Who will?"

"Anyone who wants. He's the best one," Ray pointed to the man I'd been talking to, who was now down the road, loitering in the shade, his head tilted drinking from a small bottle.

"What is crogay?"

"Cro-KAY," he said. "You hit a ball with a mallet. I can do it. I could show you, but we don't have a set. They'll set it up out here, on the grass. You have to have an even mowed yard." A car approached in a plume of dust. "I'll see ya," he said to me looking at the car. "Hey," he hollered at the driver. He started

64

running toward the car. The car stopped and the driver leaned across the seat and said something to Ray, who stepped up on the running board. I watched as the car drove off. Ray turned back and smiled at me and waved. Eudorrie ran beside the car as it moved down the road stirring up the dirt. It was hot. The sweat was trickling down my forehead.

When I went back to the store, I could feel a current of air coming from the far side of the store. The woman and the girl in blue were in front of the main counter. The skirt of the woman's dress fluttered when the fan turned her way. I idled in the background beside the stove ogling the girl. She was wearing shorts and a matching top that tied in a knot in the front and was made out of the same print as the woman's dress.

"Janet, sashay on over here and bring me those feedsacks on the chair," GranRose said when she noticed me. "How would you like some shorts and a top like Betty Sue's?" I handed her the red and yellow feedsacks. Betty Sue had short, dark, curly hair. She was the prettiest girl I'd ever seen, and she was just my height.

"It'll have red rickrack on the part that ties in front," said the woman, who was Betty Sue's mother.

"I would like it." I did not add "more than anything in the world."

"We'll have enough for a dress for you, too, Rose."

"Well, I could use something."

Uncle Pat came down the aisle from where he had been stocking shelves.

"Hear that?" he said to me, jangling the coins in his pocket. "Want a nick?"He pulled out a handful of change, picked out a nickel and gave it to me. "What about Betty Sue?"

She grinned at him, which made her eyes almost close.

That afternoon Betty Sue's mother, whose name was Betty, left Betty Sue at the store and together, with our nickels, we went up the walkway to Posy's café and sat up on the stools at the fountain and bought a cherry Coke that fizzed white around the rim of the glass. On the wall was a calendar with a picture of Betty

Grable in a bathing suit and high heels looking over her shoulder. Her hair was swept up with curls all over the top the way my mother had worn hers when she really wanted to look good and had all morning to work on her hair and makeup.

"Her name is Betty like yours," I said to Betty Sue, pointing to the calendar, "and her hair is curly, too."

"She has pin curls. Mine are permanent. They won't go away, not for a long time," she said fluffing the dark curls up with the bottom of her hand.

"At my school in South Carolina I knew a girl with naturally curly hair."

"Mine's not natural. It's a Toni! I just had it yesterday. Before that it was straight as a board, just like yours. Your grandmother orders them, the Tonies. You can do it yourself. Oneita Hicks gave me mine. She used to work in a beauty shop in Fair Play. She'd give you one, too."

Betty Sue and I had a lot to talk about. We moved outside the café and sat on the shady edge of the walkway with our legs dangling down above the road. I told her I wanted to go swimming, and she told me about the best Aldrich spots. Rocky Ford she said was, "better than the sliding board at the Bolivar swimming pool," which I later learned was true. At Rocky Ford the water rushed across a long, slab of slate and you could slide with the current across the smooth rock and under a low bridge into a shallow pool. "We could go there! Or, we could go to Coffman Branch," she slowed down building the suspense, "…where there's a deep spot that swirls around, silver on top and real dark below like a mirror. And you can wade out, deeper and deeper up to your waist, and then," she paused dramatically, "swim right over to the deep part, and go under or float on your back and when you come back out of the water, you're like… reborn!" Her culminating word, "reborn," appropriated from a Bible verse or a sermon, was new to me. I was entranced by the mystery and romance. Betty Sue and I had an immediate affinity. "Rocky Ford is out in the country past your grandmother's house, but Coffman Branch is just down over the other side of that hill," she pointed to the steep hill that rose up just beyond where we were sitting.

"We drove through it, Uncle Pat and I. On the road from Fair Play," I said.

"Uh huh. It's a long branch that winds all around. The part on our farm is the deepest. Deep enough to swim. When you get out you're all cooled off for the rest of the day."

"You're reborn."

Betty Sue smiled, her eyes became twinkling slits, "Yeah."

"I don't have a bathing suit…"

"I wear my old shorts and an old top. Or an old dress."

"Okay. I can go tomorrow."

"Not tomorrow!" she exclaimed, then, explaining herself, like a kind missionary to a heathen, added, "Tomorrow is Sunday."

As we talked, cars and trucks were pulling up along the high curb and parking diagonally all the way from the store up to where we were sitting. I could see a bunch of kids clamoring out of the back of one mud-splashed truck parked in front of Dysart Brothers. The town was filling up with people. An old man with a stick that he tapped on the pavement walked toward us. He was wearing suspenders and a straw fedora.

"Everyone seems to be convening at the *polis*," he said as he approached us. We didn't know what he meant, but that didn't bother Betty Sue.

"Hello, Mr. Sharp," she smiled.

"Betty Miller's girl, isn't it?"

"Yes."

"And who is your friend?"

Betty Sue knew everyone who passed by and what they did, and they knew her. She introduced me.

"I believe I taught your mother," Mr. Sharp said to me. "Her Caesar wasn't bad, but as I recall, Cicero was a challenge. Gifted, mind you, but didn't live up to her potential." The mere reference to Mom gave me a pang. "Will you be attending Aldrich School?"

"I don't think so. My mother is... in Las Vegas, Nevada." What I said didn't make sense. I didn't know how to explain my situation, and I couldn't think of a way to answer for my mother's Latin.

"Well, it's nice to meet you, Janet." He turned to Betty Sue, "I'll see you soon at the *schola*." He tapped his stick two times and proceeded down the walk.

"Have a nice day, Mr. Sharp. See you at the... *schola*," Betty Sue said.

Betty Sue had the manners of someone twice her age. Her small talk was imitative but unaffected. I've often thought that growing up the darling of a small community gave her a special grounding. She was nurtured by many but not pampered. She respected others, old and young, educated and ignorant, and recognized her limitations to exactly the right degree. She was neither shy nor bold. She was modest, unspoiled, and confident. And she was twelve years old.

Posie spoke to us through the screen door of the café. "Are you girls still here?" She was holding a fly-swatter.

Betty Sue's new curls jiggled when she turned her head. "We're still here, Posy." I could tell how good the bounce of her curls felt to her. Posy swatted a fly on the screen.

"It's getting pretty late."

Betty Sue stood up. "We got to talking."

"Your mothers will be looking for you." Posy disappeared into the café. Her words gave me another pang. Of course, she couldn't have known that my mother wouldn't be looking for me.

"We'd better go," Betty Sue said. "My house is at the top of the hill, the first one on the right." And then remembering something she'd heard, perhaps in Sunday School, she said, "You're always welcome in our home." It came out a bit stilted. It might have been the first time she had said it. But she didn't let it

68

bother her. She just reverted to her twelve-year-old voice and invited me to come to her Sunday School class and told me to memorize a verse from the Bible because tomorrow was recitation day. I stayed there in front of Posy's and watched as Betty Sue began her climb. There was another more travelled road, a much more gradual incline, but it was farther away, and Betty Sue struck out, up the rocky, steep hill, on her way home. About half way up she stopped on a flat rock, a huge stone outcropping, I guess to catch her breath, and then began climbing again.

When I got back to the store, it was getting cooler. There were several men with mallets gathered around the front, some sitting on the bench, one fanning himself and batting away flies with his hat. Others were setting up wickets and posts in the yard around the corner. I watched as one man walked off the distance between wickets and another bent over placing them just so. The one who was measuring the course had on glasses that had a missing arm that he'd replaced with a piece of string that hung down over his ear. When he took them off, I recognized him as the man who had watched me play fetch earlier in the afternoon.

"Hi," I called out.

He waved at me with a white handkerchief and then mopped his forehead with it.

There was coming and going in and out of the store. I had never seen the entrance so crowded. I made my way through the laughing and talking outside into the store. Uncle Pat was behind the counter ringing up an order. There were people milling all about, people from the country I had never seen before.

"Is GranRose here?" I asked Uncle Pat coming behind the counter. He was surprised to see me.

"Your grandmother went home early. Where have you been?" The telephone rang, two longs and two shorts. "Can you get that for me?" I went to the back wall. The stool was beneath the phone so that I could step up when it rang.

"Dysart Brothers," I answered, as I had been instructed.

"Get Rose for me. I have some news," said Nola, the Aldrich operator who listened in on most conversations and knew what would be of interest to GranRose.

"She's gone home," I said.

"Is this Marge's girl?"

"Uh huh."

"Well, you tell your grandmother I heard someone was in town."

"Who is it?" I asked.

"She'll know," Nola said, who operated the switch board out of her two-room house at the end of the row of businesses, just beyond the café.

When I off got off the phone, Uncle Pat had gone to the back of the store where he had a desk and a cot and his personal things. Other men had sat down around the stove in the middle of the store. One had a harmonica and another a washboard and a stick. They were laughing and bragging.

"Got my shotgun and hid behind the door and when the rat comes out runnin' along the rail," the man held up the stick and took aim, "Bam! Got 'em, by jacks."

More people were coming into the store, farmers in overalls and women and kids. They were all talking at once, the kids asking for candy and pop. A woman was popping off the bottle caps in the opener of the cooler. After she'd passed the bottles to her kids, she snapped open a little black coin purse and placed several coins, one at a time, on the counter. All the chairs around the stove were taken. There were people standing up and down the main aisle. One teenage boy had a banjo. He had brown hair, a lock of which fell down over his forehead. I lurked behind the counter for a while and then sat on the stool under the phone, where I could still see the boy. He laughed at something, which made me smile, too.

Uncle Pat appeared from the back with a violin and bow and walked to the men who had gathered around the stove. He spent a few minutes tuning up then put the bow to the strings and produced a sweet high-pitched tone, a long, stretched out sound that was new to me, followed by two short pecks. A hush fell over the store. Then he began a lively tune, some song I didn't know. After the first strains, the other musicians gradually joined in and when the tempo picked up, people began to nod and clap in time. Some shuffled their feet and the little ones began to hop and skip. After the music reached a climax, Uncle Pat slowed the pace, and when it grew soft and the others quit playing along, he plucked the strings of the violin, and the song ended. It was a perfect conclusion. I jumped up clapping. When we were applauding, Uncle Pat noticed me for the first time. People went back to talking as he walked over to me.

"Who was it on the phone before?"

"It was Nola with a message for GranRose."

"Your grandmother will be looking for you. You'd better get on home. It'll be dark before long."

I wanted to stay for at least a little while longer. This was the first carefree day I had had in Aldrich—playing fetch, meeting Betty Sue, witnessing a Saturday night hootenanny. Why had GranRose gone home? Why wasn't she here having "a big time" like everyone else? But I couldn't argue with Uncle Pat, so I walked down a side aisle, looking back through the racks at the boy with the banjo and then leaving by the back door, and taking the path over to the post office.

Outside the sun had almost gone down and the last croquet match was finishing up in the remaining light. Only two players were still in the yard. The others stood on the side watching. I heard one of them say, "He was poison before I got halfway through." He was talking about the player who was bent over holding the mallet with both hands planning his shot. I recognized him—the man who was Poison—as the man on the bench I'd spoken to earlier. He had on his glasses with the piece of string as he took aim. His opponent was standing over his ball at the far end of the yard, about fifty feet away.

71

"Let's see yer stuff," he goaded in a loud voice for the benefit of all.

Poison raised the mallet and swung. There was something poised and easy about him. He wasn't blunt. I sensed this without knowing him or being capable of articulating either then or now the quality I observed. His ball jumped and rolled slower and slower toward the other ball. When it tapped the side of it, a hoot went up from the crowd that had gathered in the dusk. The man who had come close to winning threw down his mallet.

"Dang you," he said. "You're a lucky son of a gun, Clay Dysart."

Oddly, that was the first time I had ever heard anyone say that name. I had heard "Clay," "Daddy," "Grandpa Clay," and "your grandfather," but I had never heard "Clay Dysart." The factuality of the words themselves—who he was to others, and the accord they paid him, redefined him. It was as if he had gained the status of a person, a member of the community of Aldrich. In that moment I wanted to claim him as my grandfather and be claimed by him.

"You old rascal," the loser said, picking up his ball and his mallet.

"Dysart luck! You can't beat it," my grandfather, Clay Dysart, called back with a slight, modest smile. He looked over in my direction. I thought he might be acknowledging me, but to this day, I'm not positive that he was looking at me or knew who I was. Sometimes I wish I had gone up to him, but the truth is, I was too afraid of his reaction. So when the hangers-on gathered around to congratulate him, I walked behind the post office out onto the cement walkway toward home.

By the time the house was in view, the sun had gone down, and a sliver of moon shone above the dark maples in the front yard. There was a light on in the back of the house. Just as I came to the end of the dirt path, I heard a vehicle behind me. It was a truck with a load of kids singing in the back. As I waited for them to pass, I could hear the words: "Oh Mr. Moon, Moon, bright and shiny Moon, won't you please shine down on me..." After they turned the corner, one of the kids saw me and called out, "Hi, girl," and they all waved. I waved back absently, still trying to figure out what had just happened at the croquet game. In the back of my mind, I was afraid that my grandfather DID know who I was and had ignored me.

In the house I could hear the clank of a bucket in the kitchen. GranRose was heating water which she'd pumped for her bath.

"There's a potato and some salmon croquettes," she said, lifting the heavy bucket. I followed her into the bathroom and watched her pour the hot water into the tub.

"How was the hootenanny?"

"Uncle Pat was good."

"He's as good a fiddler as you'll see around here."

"There was a croquet game, too," I said tentatively, but GranRose just pointed at my knees.

"You can use my water after I'm done. Those need some scrubbing."

"GranRose?" I hesitated. There was a lot I needed to say.

"What is it?"

"Nola phoned the store and said someone was in town, but she wouldn't say who."

"Well, now, I wouldn't worry about that." I didn't know why she thought I would worry about it, but she was right. I had worried about what Nola meant. I had become wary of vague, cryptic language designed to spare me.

"Anything else worrying you?" GranRose sensed something was bothering me, or maybe she was projecting her own worries, about Clay, the "someone" she had known was in town ever since he had parked himself on the bench in front of the store early that afternoon, the "someone" she had doubtlessly avoided by leaving for home early and skipping the hootenanny that very night. As I stood there in the bathroom, I wanted to tell her about

73

the croquet match and about seeing my grandfather, but something kept me from it.

"Do you have a Bible?" I asked instead.

"It's some place on the buffet."

"I have to find a verse for Sunday School."

I found the Bible underneath the dictionary. On the cover was "Rose Dysart" in gold. I had never even heard of the old practice of opening the Bible randomly in order to discover a God-given passage, but the page I turned to has since struck me as uncanny, and I am not a particularly religious person. By that, I don't mean I'm not semi-religious. I am. I just mean I'm not religious the way Betty Sue and her family were. Oh, I learned the books of the Bible by heart, and I memorized the well-known psalms and proverbs, of course. We all did that in Sunday School. But I never began to savor the Bible the way Betty Sue did over the years. My Bible, like GranRose's, might be found underneath another book or books, some novel like *My Antonia*, which I first read in tenth grade and which I have read over and again for sustenance and renewal at different times in my life; but for all my skepticism, I have to admit that the verse which I alighted on in GranRose's Bible that night was heaven sent.

"Behold, children are a gift of the Lord, the fruit of the womb."

Later that night as I washed in the tub, I practiced saying it aloud, emphasizing, "gift of the Lord." I said it as I slid the soap over my dirty arms and legs, changing the language to make it apply specifically to me: "Behold! I am a gift of the Lord." My eyes squeezed closed, I put the soap on my hair, slid down in the tub, and held my head back. "Behold! I, Janet Stephens, am a gift of the Lord." I swished my hair repeating the phrase. The words made me feel that I counted or, as Betty Sue would have said, that I was a "child of God," and that my grandfather's discounting of me, if that's what had in fact occurred, did not determine who I was.

Chapter 10

The next day when I woke up, GranRose was already dressed for church. She had washed and ironed my traveling outfit, which was too tight and too short. After I got it on, she said my knees were still dirty.

"It's just shadows," I protested, but she got a bucket of water and a bar of soap and I sat up on the edge of the tub with my legs inside the basin while she washed the shadows away and made the golden hairs glisten. I put on socks and shoes for one of the few times since I had arrived, and we walked to church because she couldn't get the Pontiac started.

"Did you find a Bible verse?"

"Uh huh." I said, concentrating on the sidewalk.

"What are you looking at?" GranRose asked me.

"If you step on a crack..." I didn't finish the line.

"Ohhh," she said, dragging out the sound, the way she did to mean "nonsense." "Whoever thought of that rime ought to be shot. You couldn't break your mother's back whether you wanted to or not. It's not within your power."

I've always been glad GranRose and I happened to walk together to church that morning. The cracks were a torturous symbol of the fracture between me and Mom. What bothered me wasn't so much the idea that I could accidentally injure my mother, which is terrible enough, but that somehow I might WISH to, which is so much worse. GranRose, by pointing up my powerlessness, banished in a few words a fear that had beleaguered me since I had come to Aldrich where the sidewalks figured in my daily life.

I call our unlikely walk together that day, "Dysart luck." Betty Sue would call it God's will, in support of which she would note that we were on our way to church. Betty Sue would consider family luck to be a poor substitute for belief. And, of course, she

75

would be right. Had I been truly lucky or better yet brave, I might have resolved another more substantial matter on my walk to church with GranRose that morning. Had I apprised her of my encounter with my grandfather the night before, she might have put to rest another, more grounded apprehension, one that still rises up in me today. But I could not. I was too afraid that she might confirm what I feared most: that my grandfather simply had no interest in me. And so, after GranRose's comment on the cracks, we hurried along to church in silence.

The Aldrich Methodist Church and grounds took up the better part of the downtown square. Every Sunday, I went with GranRose to the 10:00AM service, but until our walk to the church that morning when the Pontiac wouldn't start, I had resisted Sunday School, mainly because it was new to me. We could hear the bell tolling as we hurried along. In my red velvet pocketbook was the piece of paper with my verse written on it. We were a little late, but GranRose headed down the aisle to the front to her special pew. We stood and sang songs, sat and prayed, and then the long sermon began.

On the wall beside the pulpit was a portrait of Jesus. The print was under a piece of glass in a thin gold frame close enough to be studied and dreamed about. Jesus was kneeling by a large rock, hands folded, praying in the garden. He had long brown hair and a flowing robe. His face shone against the dark greens and blues of Gethsemane. Looking at it, I forgot about my mother, my father, and my grandfather. It calmed me. I don't know what to call the time I spent gazing at the portrait—a reverie? some form of prayer? Others, I suppose, would call it daydreaming, a kind of drifting romance. Whatever it was, the image consumed me and assuaged my childish worries.

Many years after I had forgotten the portrait, I saw it in a used bookstore and junk shop in the Ozarks. It was in a back room on a wall with other dusty, unsellable prints in rickety wood frames. I don't know why I even bothered to enter the room. The sign above the door read "Christian Art." I might not have noticed the print at all, hidden as it was behind display cases of chubby ceramic angels and plastic saints. I might have walked right by the wall, crowded with embroidered verses from the Bible and depictions of the bleeding heart of Mary, but the moment I spotted the image, the gentle rendering of Jesus, emerging from all the surrounding kitsch, I had to steel myself against the onslaught of my tenderest childhood feelings.

I don't know why I didn't buy it. All it needed was a delicate gold frame. But for some reason I resisted. I have often wished I were less hesitant. A man once told me I would never get married because my mother's impulsive behavior had made me non-committal and overcautious. But the truth is I just didn't want to marry HIM. Another man, who understood me better, told me I was irresolute in reaction to my mother's stolid determination. He was probably right. In any case, I didn't buy the print. Perhaps, I feared that the image would become commonplace and that I would lose the memory of what it once meant to me, or maybe I just didn't know where I would put it. I simply didn't have the proper place to enshrine it… best to remember it as the object of my childhood reverie.

Always the minister broke in on my communion with the image of Jesus, inviting those who wanted to take Him as their savior to come forward. That part of the service was the best by far. The congregation sang the slow, whispered songs of longing and repentance. "Just as am without one plea, but that thy blood was shed for me."

I was captivated by the intimacy of giving oneself over and the shedding of blood. I sang along with the others the murmured hymn of consecration to see who would "walk forward" to kneel at the rail and be saved. Then "Praise the Lord!" the preacher concluded the dreamy rite. The pianist struck up a lively song of renewal. The congregation, made whole, was released, free to converse and depart or stay for Sunday School. After the benediction on the Sunday I had agreed to attend, I was on the verge of backing out and returning home when Betty Sue appeared beside the pew.

"Good morning!" she said, decked out in a yellow-and -white feedsack dress.

"Do you know your verse by heart?"

"I think so."

I could see there was no getting out of going. Betty Sue led me to a small room which opened off one side of the church. We sat in small chairs around a long, low table. The new Sunday School teacher, who didn't look at all like a teacher but more like a dime store clerk, told us she had "studied the scripture" in a course at Bolivar College. She stood at one end of the table beside an easel with a poster board that had on it "Matthew19:14." Her name, Charlene, went perfectly, I thought, with her dark hair and long eyelashes. To begin the recitations, she said she would go first. It was fun just to look at her as she delivered her verse from Matthew.

"Suffer little children and forbid them not to come unto me: for of such is the the kingdom of heaven."

She wagged her finger when she said "forbid" and held up open palms and looked at the ceiling on the "kingdom of heaven." Then she broke her pose and asked, "Does anyone know who said that?"

"Did Jesus say it?" asked a little boy.

"Yes! Jesus said it!" Charlene said, her eyes shining below the lashes. She explained that Jesus wasn't saying that children should suffer but that they should be allowed to come unto him and that one of the ways of doing that was to memorize the words of God. She spoke in a dramatic, elementary way that not only held your attention but left nothing up for question that you might later worry over.

"Now it's YOUR turn to come unto Jesus!"

I got the wrinkled paper out of my pocketbook and holding it in my lap out of sight, re-read it, hoping she wouldn't call on me first. Thankfully, she called on Betty Sue, who recited

John 3:16 perfectly, getting things off to a strong start. After that, a girl recited The Golden Rule and a shy boy with averted eyes said, "Jesus wept," the fall-back verse chosen by the unprepared. Finally, a confident, eager boy named Percy delivered his verse, relishing all of the words that ended in "eth."

"If a woman PUTTETH away her husband and MARRIETH another, she COMMITTETH adultery," he said, spitting out the words like a threat.

I didn't know what adultery was, but I was sure it was a bad thing and that my mother had committed it. Even Charlene was thrown off guard. I could tell by the batting of her eyelashes. Before she could call on the next student, Percy, grim and accusing as a minister, hastened to explain his verse.

"What it means is that a married woman who goes off with another man is nothing but a," he paused and sneered, "floozy."

None of us knew what a floozy was, but the word was funny, and we all broke out laughing at the sound of it. Percy, grudgingly, joined in. The laughing relaxed me and when it was my turn, the words tripped off without a hitch, or so I thought:

"Behold, children are a gift of the Lord, the fruit of the loom. How blessed is the man whose quiver is full of them."

If Charlene hadn't corrected "loom" with "womb," I wouldn't have realized my mistake and neither would any of the other kids. But she did, and the word stirred Percy.

"What's a womb?" he asked, with suspiciously narrowed eyes.

"It's the part of a woman that gives birth," Charlene said, with forced equanimity. That she was able to come up with that answer I have since thought admirable. "Children are the fruit of the WOMB," she said, with an even voice but batting lashes.

Percy said with assurance, "I feel blessed that MY quiver is full of them.'"

This time, when the class laughed, Percy didn't join in. He was mad. We had mocked his quiver. He shot me a dark look as if I were responsible.

"All right, class," Charlene said, still blinking. "It's time for Bible study. This Sunday's lesson is about the punishment of evil and the reward of righteousness."

She removed the letters and numbers from the flannel graph board, which came away like magic, and began pulling from a box the cut-out characters and objects of her story. First there was Noah, a paper doll with a gray beard and a white robe. She stuck him up on the board with a bare press of her hand.

"Noah was a righteous man!" she said, asserting herself, regaining control.

At each turning point she produced a new cut-out—two giraffes, a dove, a rectangle of blue for the rising seas, and a square of brown for an ark. We hung upon Charlene's rising and falling voice, her delicate gestures, the way the cutouts silently adhered to the board.

Despite the embarrassment of my suspiciously Freudian slip-up—the replacement of "fruit of the womb," (my mother?) with "fruit of the loom," (my father?)—I never again wanted to miss Sunday School, and with one exception, when I was sick and contagious, I never did.

***

In fact the church, along with the store and everything in between, became a part of my turf. Together, Betty Sue and I explored it all. First the storefronts and formal walkways and then the network behind the stores—the narrow stream in the ditch that ran the length of the row of buildings and the wooden planks that crossed it, and all of the paths—the one to the public outhouse, the one past the back entrances to the other stores, and the barely trodden way that led through weeds, down a small gully, then up to higher ground and through the tall, unmown grass to the smooth

80

green lawn of the Methodist Church. If we were tuckered out, we rested under a shady sycamore beside the serene white church with its pointed arch windows and its tall, white bell tower. Or we went inside and sat in one of the long, wooden pews and caught our breath. On some days we played at the store back in Hardware, which had its own unused display window with a stage that looked out over the loafers' bench. We sold tickets and put on shows in the window. Our first production was a hit. The loafers outside pulled out their bench and turned around to watch us sing and dance in our matching feedsack shorts and tops. They clapped and egged us on.

"Why those girls 're ever bit as good as they got at Branson."

Betty Sue sang "How Much Is That Doggie in the Window," and I danced off both my shoes to the jelly roll blues.

As the summer bore on, I read less and sang more. Betty Sue and I began singing duets. We rehearsed in the church where the floor was raked, the pulpit was on a platform, and there was a piano—a perfect theatre at our disposal. Betty Sue sang soprano, and I sang alto as Mom had taught me. We harmonized on all of the old hymns. *Sweet hour of prayer, sweet hour of prayer that calls me from a world of care...*

GranRose sent us around town to sing to the sick. We practiced our songs on the elderly and bedridden in homes up the hill from the store and on the streets that jutted off from the road to the river. On Sunday afternoons, Betty Sue's mother took us out to the country churches to singings where we performed for people who congregated from Eudora, Walnut Grove, and farms all around.

In seasons of distress and grief my soul hath often found relief. And oft escaped the tempter's snare, by thy return sweet hour of prayer...

Betty Sue and I sang all over Polk County that summer.

"Can I go with Betty Sue to sing at Dunedin Park?" I asked GranRose. The park, on the north end of Bolivar, had the large, shady grounds where the singing would be held. People would come from all over the county.

"You can sing to your heart's content," she said, "but how will you get there?"

"Betty Sue says we can ride over on the mail hack, with Noble." That was the name of the driver.

"Who'll bring you home?"

"Her mother says we can ride home with Solomon Sharp." Solomon was the old man with the walking stick who still taught Latin at the school.

"If Betty has looked into it…"

"She has."

So Betty Sue and I sang "Have You Talked to the Man Upstairs" on a big wooden stage that had been erected in the middle of the park. On the way home, Solomon Sharp said we had done Aldrich proud and that we out-sang the two Bolivar girls who followed us. "*Agas bene*," he congratulated us. Solomon taught Latin in and out of school.

***

If I were a religious person, I would probably say that God had intervened in my life. That is what Betty Sue would say if she were alive today. But what I say is that it was the singing that intervened; for those songs—the melodies and harmonies, the rhythms and the lyrics—broke up the unremitting thoughts of my mother. They wrenched me apart from her as surely as other songs had once bound me to her. They gave me a barrier which she could not penetrate, and perhaps that barrier constitutes a God, a savior of sorts. All I know is that those songs allowed me to endure. My musical tastes have changed over the years. I almost never listen to the music of my childhood, but let me happen upon a rendition of "Peace in The Valley," Betty Sue's favorite solo, and I am assailed by memories, overcome with gratitude—for her, for Uncle Pat, and for GranRose, who let me sing to my heart's content.

Chapter 11

By the time school was to begin, my mother still hadn't come for the promised visit, but Daddy wrote me regularly. It took a month before I got the first letter stamped from Manila, but after that I got one every week. Uncle Pat began sending me over to the post office to pick up the mail.

"There's a letter for you today in there," the postmaster would say from behind his window as he handed me a batch of mail. "All the way from Manila."

Mom's letters were bulky and uninhibited, full of jokes and drawings and observations in free-flowing cursive. Page after page was folded together and crammed in an envelope that had to be scotch-taped. Daddy's were the opposite.

I loved the smoothness of the sheer blue envelope edged with little blue and red bars. Inside there would be just one thin folded sheet. Daddy was a man of few words. His letters were brief, but precious. I sat in the rocker by the stove and poured over every word.

> *There are trees here that have white flowers on them. The women and children sit under the trees and make flower necklaces. You would be good at that! We eat Filipino food here in the BOQ. My favorite is called lumpia. It is vegetables and meat rolled up in some dough and fried. I miss good old fried chicken and mashed potatoes and your grandmother's angel food cake. Does she make it for you? Say hello to her and give her the enclosed check and hello to Uncle Pat, too. I sure miss you, pal.*
> *Love, Daddy*

"What does your father have to say?" Uncle Pat would ask me. "Has he seen any Huks?" Uncle Pat gave me paper and a pencil, and I wrote to my father at the desk in his alcove in the back of the store.

Dear Daddy,

I made a friend. It is Betty Sue Miller. She lives on top of a hill. It is steep and rocky, but I can walk up it to her house. I am always welcome in her home. I walk to her house and we go swimming in the branch on her father's farm. It is hard to get to. You have to go through a barbed-wire fence and walk down through a cow pasture. There is one mean cow named Juanita to watch out for. Also, you can get a leech when you are swimming. I found one on the back of my leg and GranRose ripped it off, which left a bloody spot. We are in a drouth here. Betty Sue and I pray for rain. I made up a rain dance, and we did it in her yard under a hose that we put up in a tree, but it still has not rained. Well, I have to go. Betty Sue and I are walking to the river. I will be careful there. NO SWIMMING is allowed unless an adult takes us. Uncle Pat puts us in an innertube and we float with the current to the big tree, but he cannot go, so we will just wade. Hope you have a good day and don't have to fight a Huk. I do not want to go to seventh grade, especially in Aldrich. Mom is coming to get me so I won't have to go!! If the Huks go away, maybe I can visit you one day. I want to sit under the tree and make the flower necklaces. The main flower in Aldrich is the hollyhock. Everybody has them in their yards. You can not make necklaces out of them.

LOVE,

Janet

***

The August afternoon Betty Sue and I planned to walk to the bridge, the gravel on the road was so hot we had to wear shoes. Before we headed off, we went to the post office to mail my letter to Daddy.

"Looks like you girls are puttin' on a show today," the postmaster said. Betty Sue and I were dressed in our matching feedsack tops and shorts.

"We're going wading at the river," Betty Sue said.

"Uh huh. That'll cool you off."

As I was licking the stamps, the mail hack pulled up outside, which was Dysart luck. Betty Sue raced outside to see if we could hitch a ride with Noble to the river. Even with the windows down, the hack was stifling. As we neared the bridge, we passed a green truck parked on the side of the road in a parched cornfield.

"Looks like you may have company," Noble said. "We'd better warn them." He honked the horn. "Give those boys a chance to get their britches on," he said.

He dropped us off just before the bridge where a well-worn path sloped through tall weeds down to the river and led to the swimming hole. We descended into the shade of poplars with peeling bark and thick-leaved maples that bordered the bank. A musty scent rose up from the dark, barely rippling water. We could hear voices coming from the swimming hole. We made our way stepping on the hard dirt between the tree roots. As we got closer, I saw a boy beside the huge trunk of an old tree on the edge of the bank.

"He has on his britches," I said to Betty Sue.

Balanced on the roots that twisted like a pretzel out over the water, the boy was holding a rope and talking to another boy who was treading water.

"Hey," he called out when he saw us, "Watch this!" He swung out and let go.

The one who was already in the water yelled out, "Hey, Betty Sue Miller," and the other one, when he came up, shook his hair out of his face, looked up at us grinning, and said, "Come on in."

"Want to?" Betty Sue surprised me.

"We're supposed to wade."

"We'll be okay. I know them. They're older."

"You can swim, can't you girls?" asked the treader, whose name was Bill. He was the older of the two boys. The younger one, Kelton, was holding on to the side of an inner tube.

"We can swim," Betty Sue called back. "I'll go if you will." She looked at me to see if I was willing.

"Okay," I said, though I was afraid.

We sat down and untied our shoes. Then Betty Sue stepped up onto the overhanging bank, reached for the rope, swung out, toes pointed, and dropped between the boys, with the slightest ripple. When she came up, her black curls flat and streaming, Kelton whistled and pushed the inner tube to her.

"Come on, Janet," she said, glowing, looking high up at me on the bank above her.

"It feels great," Kelton hollered.

"You can hold onto the tube when you come up," Bill said.

They all moved in different directions to make room for my plunge so that I couldn't refuse. I stepped out to the edge of the bank, reached out for the rope, and held it, looking down at the glittering, black water.

"Go on the count of three," Bill shouted.

"One, two, three, GO," the three of them chanted.

I had no choice. I swung out, let go, and holding my nose, slipped into the cool, silky water.

When I came up burbling, the boys whooped, and Betty Sue, radiant and laughing, pushed the tube to me. From then on, we took turns swinging out, letting go, and climbing the bank, over and again. Bill cannonballed the rest of us, rocking the inner tube that Betty Sue and I clung to, and Kelton, dunked and splashed him back. When it was my turn with the rope, I let go with my Nyoka yell. In response, Kelton, put his fingers in his mouth and made a whistle so loud and shrill that it dwarfed my jungle girl yelp

"Show me how you do it," I said, as we sat dripping on the bank.

The hair on his upper lip, a faint blond mustache, shone in the slant of the late afternoon sun. I studied how he placed his fingers, pinched his lips, drew his breath, and emitted another shriek, but I couldn't do it.

"Uh-oh, I guess we're chasin' off the fish," Kelton said, looking up. A man with a fishing pole had come from the trees on the opposite bank.

"Sorry if we ruined your fishing," Kelton hollered.

"I just wish you'd kept on scarin' the fish my way," the man said, holding up a string of three or four fish.

Kelton laughed. "Nice catch!" The man walked on down the path on the other side of the river. I watched his plaid shirt and pole disappear into the willows.

"Who was that?" Bill asked, coming out of the water.

"The bum who lives in the lean-to down river."

"The same one?"

"Yeah. He's passing through town again, I guess."

"He's got his dinner for tonight. Somethin' to go with his pint of whiskey." The boys laughed, and Bill asked us if we wanted to be dropped off in town.

"We've got chores," Kelton explained. "We have to leave."

I wanted to leave. The sight of the man had given me a sinking feeling. I followed Betty Sue and the boys down the path and through a row of corn, swathed in dust, to get over to their truck. The sun was low behind the trees along the river, but the bed and the sidewalls of the truck were still so hot that Betty Sue and I sat on our towels.

We were quiet as we were buffeted along toward town. When we passed the boxcar house, kids were playing out front, but Ray wasn't one of them, and I was glad. I didn't feel like seeing him or having to wave or even raise a forefinger. I sat with my knees under my chin, catching my balance with my hands and feeling like I might throw up when the truck jolted.

"Did you see the man with the fish?" Betty Sue asked me.

"Not real good," I said, which wasn't the truth.

We rode the rest of the way in silence because I felt queasy with shame, unable to admit to Betty Sue or even to myself that the man with the fish was my grandfather, Clay Dysart.

***

By the time I got home, it was sunset. The house was hot and deserted. The slanted light coming through the living room blinds made shafts across the roses in the carpet. I could see the tiny particles of dust in the sweltering, still air. It was too lonely to stay inside. I walked through the dusky rooms to the back porch. GranRose was still working in the garden. I could see the white of her dress through the leaves of the grape arbor. I lumbered down the back steps and out the fence gate. There was a rooster making a racket and chickens pecking the dirt. I stepped carefully in and around the droppings in the yard to the chicken house. Inside the coop, I angled along the wall as far away as possible from a nesting hen over to the ladder to the loft. I climbed up through the hole to safety and sat down in the opening that looked out over the garden. GranRose was digging up potatoes in the dim remains of light. I watched the way she held the hoe and raked it over the dirt, at the sureness of her movements, and listened to the soft clucking of the hens until I felt better. After a while I called out to her and she looked up at me, surprised.

"What are you doin', Fiddle?"

"Just got back from the bridge."

Our simple exchange picked me up. I wanted to tell her about the sickening sight I had just experienced, but I couldn't. I couldn't tell her that my grandfather lived in a lean-to on the river, a laughable bum with a pint of whisky and a string of fish.

She stood in the twilight leaning on the hoe, squinting up at me.

"I thought you were practicing with Betty Sue."

"We went... to the river instead." Since my shorts and top had dried, I didn't think I had to tell her we had gone swimming.

"Well, I don't want you down there from now on. Understand?" That was the firmest thing GranRose had ever said to me, but for some reason it came as a comfort.

"Okay," I replied.

And I kept my promise, despite the pure elation of swimming that afternoon and my infatuation with the Cole brothers. Had one of them asked me to go swimming again, I probably would have broken the promise. The allure would have been too much. I would have gone to the river again. And that might have made me reckon with the fact of my grandfather. The fear of running into the bum who lived in the lean-to might have forced me to acknowledge the truth of his circumstances. But I never went back to the swimming hole. Instead, I wound up pretending that my encounter with my grandfather on the banks of the Little Sac had never taken place. It baffles me that I was capable of such a pretense. But I was. I simply blocked the man with the string of fish out of my head. I pretended he was someone else, someone who looked like my grandfather. I pretended I had made a mistake. I looked out of the loft of the chicken house and into the garden and told myself that lie. It was a leap of dishonesty that my child's mind was simply unable to resist.

"Wanna see me jump?" I asked GranRose. From the loft to the ground seemed like nothing compared to the leap into the river.

"Watch out for my lettuce," she said and went back to hoeing.

***

That night GranRose pumped the water in the tin bucket on the back stoop, carried it to the kitchen, and heated it on the stove. It would've been so much easier if we'd had running water for the tub as well as the toilet. The drain pipes were all there. Why hadn't my aunt and uncle seen to that? Why hadn't they finished the job? A year later one of them did, but why did GranRose do without for so long? Why was she among the last to get a hot water heater? For what she was doing for me, my father should have seen to it. My mother should certainly have seen to it. All that water GranRose pumped and lugged to the kitchen stove and heated and lugged to the bathroom and poured into the tub for me, reserving enough to soak her aching feet while I took a bath...

"You didn't tell me you went swimming in the river today," GranRose said, picking up my feedsack shorts, dried stiff with the dirt of river water.

"There were adults there."

"What adults?"

"Kelton and Bill Cole."

"Whoa," she said the way other people say "pshaw." She didn't consider teenage boys adults.

I put on the clean nightclothes that GranRose had tossed on my bed, the light cotton shorts and the camisole top, the coolest things I had to wear on hot airless nights. After I went to bed, I heard GranRose draining my water and pouring her own bath. That's the last thing I remember, the soothing splash of the water being poured from the bucket into the clawfoot tub.

90

The next sound I remember was a door bang that woke me up, followed by another jarring bang and another. The noise, an intermittent, insistent pounding, came from the front of the house. When it ended, there was a harsh slam of a door and a commotion of groaning and shoving in the living room. I couldn't hear voices, just knocking about, a visceral moaning and grunting. The door from my bedroom to the living room was closed, as it always was, and I was too terrified to open it, too afraid of the awful struggling sounds, of the actual sight of what horrible thing was happening on the other side of the wall.

I lay there, flat and immobile, my pillow damp from perspiration, until a deafening crack, the loudest noise I had ever heard, blasted my room. It was the kind of explosion so shattering that it was followed by a bizarre, dizzying silence. Before the silence was up, during the suspension of my hearing and thinking, I rose trancelike from the bed, walked out the open door to the porch and stood with my back up against the side of the house in my sweat-soaked shorts and top.

I thought afterwards that the way I stood there, fixed against the clapboard, was a worse thing than any one of my mother's failures to "do right by" my grandmother. My mother may have been a fool, but she was no coward. I can't believe I just stood there, unbudging, behind the porch swing, but I did. When my hearing returned and I heard my grandmother cry out, I can't believe I didn't run back to my room and through the door to the living room or rush around to the front door and into the house, but I was too unnerved. Only when I heard the slam of the screen door and the departing footsteps did I inch past the swing to the corner of the porch to see who had left. Only after I was certain that the dark figure moving down the road was gone, did I dare turn back to look for my own grandmother.

When I did, her figure appeared inside behind the screen door. A light somewhere in the back of the house blocked out her features so that I could see only her silhouette, mute and motionless, holding a shot gun. The barrel pointed up past her

91

shoulder on one side, the butt protruded from her hip, on the other. The outline was unmistakable and yet mysterious. I've never known what happened to the gun, what she did with it that night or where she put it later. I just remember staring through the dark mesh until the door opened and GranRose, empty-handed, came out on the porch.

"Well, I guess he'll be on his way out of town now," she said. She had on a sleeveless white cotton nightgown that she wore on hot summer nights. When I put my arms around her, the gown was damp, and she was trembling.

"I think I'd better sit down," she said, weakly.

I followed her as she walked beside the balustrade and around the corner to the swing. She let herself down with both hands.

"There's a bottle of aspirin in the medicine cabinet," she said, the words so faint and faltering I wasn't sure I had heard her right.

"Aspirin?" I asked.

She nodded and mustered a weak half-smile.

I didn't know I was trembling, too, until I knocked over the Campho-Phenique in the bathroom medicine chest reaching for the aspirin. When I got back to the swing, GranRose sat shivering with her hands in her lap.

"Open it," she said hoarsely through her wavering breath. I couldn't make my hands do what they were supposed to do. When the top came off, I dropped it and it went rolling. I tried to hand her the open bottle but she just opened her mouth. I spilled half the aspirins out into my shaking hand and set the bottle on the floor. I picked out an aspirin and put it on her tongue and she gestured another and then another. Then I sat beside her holding the aspirins in my fist and waited. When her breathing eased, I moved over by her and put my head on her shoulder. I don't know how long we sat there like that, but after some time, she put her arm around me and said, "Thank you, Fiddle."

I never asked her who had assailed her — who it was that would now be on his way "out of town." That is one time when my reticence paid off. She would have been taxed to answer me. Besides, in my heart, I knew, and she knew I knew. It was better to leave his name unsaid.

As we sat in the swing, a breeze came up. The trees in the side yard rustled and soughed.

"Hear that?" GranRose asked.

"The trees?"

"Listen."

"Where?"

"That was thunder."

"Is it going to rain?"

"I guess we'll know in a minute or two."

I put the tablets in my wet palm back into the bottle and began looking for the cap. I found it on the porch floor by the trumpet vine. The wind was cool. It was the strongest, coolest air I'd felt all summer. A door somewhere inside the house banged close.

"Can you feel a sprinkle?" GranRose asked.

"I can't feel anything," I said stretching my arm out over the porch railing. "Betty Sue and I prayed for rain and did a rain dance. Wanna see the rain dance?"

"Do it for me," GranRose said.

I turned on the porch light, climbed over the railing, and let myself down into the side yard where she would be able to see me.

"You have to pray while you do it," I said spreading my arms out with open palms and looking at the sky. "And then you run around like this." I ran to the far side of the yard near the garage. "And you get down on your knees and bow your head." I knelt and yelled out so GranRose could hear me, "Rain, Rain, come we pray. Take away the drouth today." I stood up and walked around to the front of the house and back up on the porch. "You can do it over and over and say psalms praising God," I said as I came around to the swing.

But GranRose wasn't there. The swing was moving slightly in the breeze. I sat down and picked up Bear de Rowe, who was sitting where I had left him days ago in one corner by the creaking chain. I was played out. It felt like I might doze off, like I might sleep right there in the swaying swing for the rest of the night with Bear De Rowe for my pillow, but GranRose's voice brought me to.

"Well, I guess it works," she said. She was standing by the porch railing with her arm outstretched.

"What works?" I asked sleepily.

GranRose was barely visible in the dim glow of the porch light. "Come here," she said. I got up, drifted toward the rail, and prepared to go back into the house to bed. "Hold out your hand." I heard the pelts on the porch roof at the same time that I stretched my arm out and felt the first drops.

"It's raining…" I said to GranRose, coming alive. "It's RAINING!" I screamed. I began jumping up and down, swinging Bear-de-Rowe into the air, and when the downpour came, I ran back out into the dark yard and did my dance again on the wet, brown stubble in the sweet-smelling rain.

I could hear GranRose call out through the rivulets streaming down the roof, "Hallelujah!"

Chapter 12

Betty Sue came along with me when I went to Oneita Hicks' house to get my Toni. Oneita wasn't what I expected. Uncle Pat had said she was built like a native-stone outhouse, but I hadn't known what that meant. I wasn't prepared for a woman wearing overalls and work boots to cut and curl my hair. "She's strong as a horse and stubborn as a mule." Uncle Pat was right. And yet there was something soft about her, too. She had short brown hair that curled from the Toni she had given herself and brown eyes that sparkled when she "got off a good one," a good one being a punchline, a prank, or any kind of personal triumph. She called Betty Sue "Little Betty," as distinct from her mother, "Big Betty," and me "Little Rose," because I was a "throwback to Rose despite the blond hair, which musta been from George's side."

"First we'll jest chop off some o' these long blond locks where the rats like ta nest," she said, clipping away, "so's you can be short and curly like Little Betty." The long wet strands fell on the floor beside the high stool. "If we have to, I've got some old end papers from when I did the Hogshooter girl's Toni."

"Hogshooter!" I burst out laughing, which made Betty Sue start laughing, too.

"A body can't help what name it gets assigned to it, girls." We fell silent. "She come up here with her Mama in a old car so slow it musta took 'em I don't know how long ta git here. They live out in the country over by Humansville. When they's leavin in that clunker, I could hear the thing a clickin' all the way down my lane. If the motor blowed up between here and Humansville, it wouldn't surprise me. But her hair come out good. Lily Hogshooter." Betty Sue and I started laughing again. And Oneita began laughing, too.

"Them two names jest don't go together. Lily sounds like one thing and Hogshooter is jest the opposite. One's like lily of the valley, all pure as snow and t'other's like a sloppin' trough." We laughed more. "But, that's jest how it goes. You can't have one without the other. And they's both got their points. O' course, they won't tell you that down thar at the Aldrich Methodist Church. Takes Oneita ta tell ya the sloppin' trough's not all bad," she winked and nodded. "Uh huh. Lily Hogshooter," she mused. "I never did see such hair, jest like a horse's tail. But it come out good. They's just barely got a pee pot, the Hogshooters, but the Mama paid me and give me a quarter tip so they's okay with me. Okay, Little Rose, jest lean yer head back here."

When Oneita finished my hair, I had wet ringlets all over my head. Betty Sue said I looked like Shirley Temple.

"She looks like the new version of Rose Dysart. I wish I could take you girls along with me to the beauty shop in Bolivar to show 'em what I can do with nuthin' but a Toni!" Oneita told us she was as good or better than any dang Bolivar beautician. She was known for bragging.

"Youse could walk around the square after I show ya off. How about it?"

"I would LOVE to go."

"I would LOVE to go."

"Well, heck, let's get in the car and go!"

"Should I call my grandmother?" I asked Oneita.

"Ah, heck. Rose won't care. She knows yer with ME, don't she?"

Going to Bolivar was something I didn't expect. That was the big city where Aunt Pansy worked! It was something people talked about—going to Bolivar. It was worthy of the Bolivar Herald.

"Ora Crane, from Aldrich, travelled to Bolivar last week to visit her cousin, Onie, with whom she enjoyed a pleasant visit."

Bolivar was the farthest from Aldrich I had been that summer, twice the distance of Fair Play and ten times the size. We drove on a washboard road until we came to a blue water tower where the road became paved and turned into a boulevard lined with poplars that led all the way to a square in the middle of which sat the largest building I had ever seen: the Polk County Courthouse. It was made of large gray stones, three stories high with a domed cupola on every corner and a tall clock tower on top of which Lady Justice, armed with a sword, held up her scales.

"Have you ever been in it, Oneita?" I was awed by the grandeur.

"Why o' course. I jest walk by them whittlers and right on in."

"What's it for?"

"It's fer filn' a claim, er findin' a deed. The best thing it's fer is gettin' a deevorce." Oneita said, authoritatively. "I did it myself oncet and didn't use no lawyer neither. Jest marched myself right in thar past the deeds recorder and told 'em, give me the paperwork, and I'll do it fer myself."

We turned one corner of the square.

"Look! There's Delarues. That's where Aunt Pansy works!"

"Yep. If'n you girls visit her, tell her hello fer me. Jest because the Fair Play Beauty Shop don't know one end from the other don't mean it's Pansy's fault. Me an' her go way back. I know'd Pansy before she ever worked at Dellyrues. I knowed 'er before she hitched up with yer Uncle Pat. Ya know his name is over there by that statue of Simon Bolivar. See whar I'm talkin about? Right to the side o' the court house? Pat's one o' Polk County's war heroes."

Oneita turned down a side street, pulled up in front of the Spit Curl Beauty Shop, turned off the engine, opened the car door, and turned in the seat and sat with her feet apart on the pavement. "Okay I want each o' youse ta come stand in front o' me and let me touch ya up." She had a brush and a rat tail comb. "Don't wanna look like youse from Fair Play," she said as she brushed out my curls and then put them back in with the end of her comb.

When we entered the Spit Curl, Oneita introduced herself and said she was looking for a job. "These two is my

97

models, Little Betty and Little Rose," she said addressing everyone in the shop. "I coulda done thur hair better but I had ta do it with a Toni, which don't have the best neutralizer in the world, but I know how ta doctor it. What I do is I..." The owner of the shop, a big woman who jiggled when she walked, interrupted Oneita.

"Let's go to the back and talk about it," she said. "You girls look as cute as can be. Are you ready to start school next week?" We said we were, and Oneita told us we could go walk around the square.

"That's ma back-ta-school special I give 'em," Oneita said, to the owner. "I give about ever girl in Aldrich ma back-ta-school special. Theys come ta me with their hair straight as a string and leave curlier than a pig's tail." I could hear Oneita hawing at her own remark as we left.

Betty Sue and I walked up to the square and into Delarues where Aunt Pansy welcomed us. Betty Sue whispered in her ear and Pansy brought out the tiniest brassiere made. It was white cotton with ribbed cups, adjustable straps, and one hook at the back. I wanted it more than any bathing suit, or ballet tutu, or matching pair of shorts and top, or other article of clothing I had ever coveted. Aunt Pansy said we should each have one. That she thought I needed it made me almost as happy as seeing Uncle Pat get out of his Chevrolet at the Fair Play filling station my first night in Missouri.

Betty Sue actually did need it. Her mother had instructed her to consult Pansy regarding the matter, which I never would have had the courage to do. Pansy told us that she could be reimbursed through Pat as she wrapped each item in white tissue, and placed each in its own small size Delarue's bag. We left the store with our prizes and continued around the square, swinging our bags and admiring ourselves in the reflections of the store windows we passed.

"You could easily pass for a Bolivar girl," Betty Sue observed as we paused in front of the large glass window of

Woolworth's. "With your Toni, no one would ever guess you weren't from Bolivar."

We went up and down every aisle of the store, admiring the loose powder, the lipstick, the nail polish, the hairnets.

"Did you find anything?" asked the teenage clerk, tapping her long red fingernails on the cash register.

"We were just looking."

"Come back," she said with a bright red lipstick smile.

"Wouldn't it be fun to work at Woolworths?" I said, once we were back out on the sidewalk.

"I know, but we could never work there."

"We could learn to do it," I said.

"But nice girls don't work in dime stores."

We walked by loafers sitting on the shady side of the courthouse on our way to the WWI monument. When we walked back by them one said, "Didja find who you was lookin' for?"

"Uh huh," I said.

"Who was he?"

"Pat Dysart," Betty Sue said.

"Oh yeah. Pat Dysart, from over in Aldrich."

He spat a big splat of tobacco in the grass. I didn't want to have anything to do with the loafer.

"That's right," Betty Sue said.

I wanted to leave, to get away from the loafer. "We'd better go. Oneita might be waiting on us."

"Have a nice day," Betty Sue said to the loafer as we walked away.

When we got back to the car, Oneita wasn't there, so we got in the back seat and took out our brassieres and inspected them. Four dollars and sixteen cents the receipt read. "A reasonable price," Aunt Pansy had said, but nothing is "reasonable" for something you don't need. What if GranRose disapproved? What if she didn't have the money?

"I don't know if I should have gotten it."

99

"Just tell her Pansy said you should have it," Betty Sue advised.

As a clerk at Delarues, Aunt Pansy had stature. She knew who could wear what—size, color, style—and outfitted people from Aldrich, Fair Play, and Bolivar, from throughout the *partes tres* of Polk County.

"Pansy's as good as anybody in Bolivar retail. Dellyrues is lucky to have her," Oneita told us in the car as we were driving home. "She never spoke a mean word to a soul." Oneita was feeling generous, exultant over the job she had landed, which was NOT at the beauty shop. She told us how the interview with the owner of the Spit Curl had ended.

"'If youse was ta hire me, I could bring in as many a customer as the next,' I says to her nicely. But she says in her high and mighty voice, 'We don't really need nobody right now.' Which anybody could see from all them empty stations was a dang lie. And she says ta me, 'If you got yer own clientele, well then you don't need us, do you?' And she laughs in this fake prissy way and walks outta the back room with her big bottom wobblin' like a wheel with a bad ball joint. And so I follows her outta the room and she goes over to this old woman and unwraps one of her curlers and says 'not quite done, Miss Flossie,' in her whatchcallit... falsetto voice. I could see the old lady's hair was already baked, but I didn't say nuthin'. I jest walk toward the door but before I go out I say, 'Well, I guess yer not interested in the best darn hairdresser in Polk County,' and she says, 'Why you haven't even been to beauty school,' and I says, 'That's because I don't need no dang beauty school ta tell me yer fryin' Miss Flossie over thar.' And the old lady looks at me kindy scared and says, 'Is it time to take the rollers out?' Poor old thing. And I look right at her and say, 'It is lessin you want pure frizz.' Well that threw Miss Wobble Bottom for a loop and she says, 'You better leave now and go back on over to Aldrich.' So's I turn ta leave, and she says ta Miss Flossie pretendin' I weren't ta hear, but knowin' I could, 'Ignorant country trash. You simply don't know what to think. I

100

simply don't know what to think.' And I says, 'Well, if yer brain was as big as yer bottom I'll betcha you could think up something.' Then I says ta Miss Flossie, real kindly, 'I'm Oneita and I'm over in Aldrich if ya ever want a special treatment on yer burnt hair.'"

Betty Sue and I covered our mouths and stomped our feet.

"I guess that showed her we'uns over in Aldrich ain't no slouches. Anyways, that's when I marched out o' the Spit Curl and took myself over to the Nifty Café ta try ta cool off. You know the Nifty Café has the best rhubarb pie you ever flopped a lip over. They always HAS been the best café in Bolivar. So I'm sittin thur at the table, sniffin' and smartin,' and I take a swig o' my ice tea and a bite o' rhubarb when I see the sign, right up thur in the window: 'Help Wanted!' That's what she said, 'Help Wanted.'" She slapped her knee. "Heck, I went ta Bolivar ta get a job workin' for a woman who don't know her butt from a bulldozer and got me a job workin' in the best dang café in town!"

Betty Sue and I laughed and clapped. Oneita had a new job and we had our new brassieres.

We drove the brown rocky road to Aldrich with all of the windows down smelling the wild roses in bloom along the roadside. After a while Betty Sue and I and started singing "Do Lord, oh Do Lord" and Oneita chimed in. When we got to "I took Jesus as my savior. You take him, too," Oneita shushed us.

"Ya hear that thump?" We listened. The thump got faster and faster. "Shoot. We got a flat." The car veered as Oneita brought it to a stop at an entry to a gate which led to a cow pasture. Betty Sue and I offered to help, but Oneita said we'd just get in the way. "Here," she said, taking off her watch and handing it to me. "You kids stand over thur. And don't start timin' me until I start pumpin'. First I gotta see if the spare got any air in it."

"Are you ready?" I asked, after Oneita had opened the trunk and gotten out the spare.

"Yep. Let 'er rip."

In thirteen point nine minutes Oneita stood up and threw her arms over her head.

"Done! she exclaimed. Then she put her foot up on the front bumper, palm on her bent knee, and cocked her head. "How do ya like that?"

"That was FAST!"

"Aw, heck," she said, getting back in the car, "alls ya have ta do is jack it up and turn a wrench." She started the ignition. "But I can do it faster than any dang man. Those boys down at the garage'll tell ya. I oncet worked down thar, ya know. I told 'em thur's nuthin come in here yet I can't fix, and Curley Crane, he's in thur with a broke axel, he says, 'Oneita Hicks yer the biggest bragger I ever seen.' And that's when I stopped Curley in his tracks quotin' the scripture." Oneita waited for one of us to ask her the obvious.

"What passage was it?" Betty Sue asked.

Oneita paused for effect and then pronounced, "She who tooteth not her own horn, the same shall not be tooted." Betty Sue didn't question Oneita's authority. "Yep. If'n you don't have a good opinion of yerself, don't expect nobody else to. Ever time I feel sorry fer myself, I jest think on my own virtues," and then she tooted the car horn. "It jest make ya feel better. You girls remember that. If'n somebody tries ta take ya down, you jest toot yer own horn." She honked the car horn again. "See if it don't make ya feel better."

When Oneita dropped me off at the store, GranRose was standing just inside the screen door. "Here she is, Rose," Oneita called out. "She got herself curls, now." As I got out of the car, she turned to me and said, "You know I popped yer mother in the nose one time. We was jest kids. Next time you talk to 'er you can tell 'er howdy from one ole hillbilly who'll own it to anothern who don't know it."

She guffawed at the rime she'd made. I didn't know what to make of her remark, but later in life I realized that she had taken a crack at Mom. If my mother thought she had risen above Aldrich, she was a fool. That's what Oneita thought.

"Okay, Little Rose," she said as I got out of the car, "Don't warsh them curls fer a few days."

GranRose came out of the store with several folded dollar bills. She leaned down the high walkway and gave them to me, and I took them around the car and handed them to Oneita through the car window.

"Jest you remember," Oneita said, raising up to pocket the money, "Don't let nobody, least of all yer ole lady, put you through the clothes ringer." Then she waved to GranRose and called out, "Guess what happened in Bolivar. I got me a job at the Nifty Café!"

"Good for you, Oneita," GranRose called back.

"And I'll toot my own horn if I dang well please!" Oneita grinned, honked the horn twice, and drove away.

Chapter 13

GranRose and I left Uncle Pat to close up the store and walked home. Usually in the late afternoon we would would have been perspiring by the time we'd passed the stores and crossed the street to where the houses began. But the weather had begun to cool.

"We're stopping for a few minutes at Doc Lawson's," GranRose said, as we walked along. I was glad that when we got there the bees had stopped buzzing in the honeysuckle. In the garden patch in the front yard, Grace, Doc's wife, was bent over in a row of tomato vines.

"Come on in, Rose" she said, looking up. "He's inside." I had never been inside the metal gate. GranRose lifted the latch, and I followed her down the dirt path on big stepping stones that led to the front stoop of the small gray house.

"You can wait out here. I won't be long," GranRose said as she entered the scrolled screen door.

"Marge's girl, are you?" Aunt Grace asked me, standing up. She was shorter than the hollyhock stalks behind her, and if she hadn't greeted GranRose I wouldn't have known she was there.

"Yes, ma'am." I hadn't yet dropped the "ma'am," but it had begun to sound awkward.

"I'd heard Rose had a young lady staying with her."

"Yes, ma'am." It was a hard habit to break.

"You can sit there." She pointed to a rocker on the front stoop and went back to weeding.

The small house had tar paper siding covered with gravel, one of the least homes in Aldrich. Doc Lawson had simple taste and no pretensions. There were two big rocks for steps to the porch. On either side were beds of iris their purple and yellow blossoms shriveling for the night. I stepped between the iris and up the rock slabs onto the porch. The sun was low, and from the rocker I could barely see the outline of Aunt Grace bent over in the

104

shadow of the tall hollyhocks. I watched her as I rocked, troubled by Oneita's remark about Mom putting me through the clothes ringer, on the one hand, and peeking from time to time into the Delarues bag, escaping into a secret delight, on the other.

After a while, a stern male voice from inside rattled my thoughts. "Janet?" I clutched the bag and peered through the screen door. "Come in here," the voice commanded. I rose, entered the house, and walked to the light coming from the open doorway of Doc Lawson' office, which took up one whole side of the little house. Doc Lawson was holding a blood pressure cuff and pump. GranRose turned in her seat beside his desk and gave me an encouraging raise of her eyebrows and a little half smile.

"Hello, Janet," Doc said.

"Hello, Sir."

"I just took your grandmother's blood pressure."

"Yes Sir."

"Now, Janet, there's something you need to know. Your Grandmother has very high blood pressure. Very high. She needs to take it easy. You'll have to help her out when you can."

His words were unequivocal. They made me realize for the first time that GranRose had a serious, ongoing problem. They put pressure on me that GranRose herself would never have exerted. Doc understood that and knew that I needed to be instructed.

As we walked toward home in the lingering light, I tried to think of what I should do to "help out." I had never fed the chickens, gathered the eggs, pumped water for the bath, or so much as peeled a potato. GranRose asked for almost nothing. It was up to me to figure out what and how I was to help. What she needed most was a running car. If only the Pontiac could be fixed. But GranRose did not have the money for the repair. Now the Delarues purchase weighed heavier than ever. I was ashamed. I was selfish. But I couldn't disclose it. With a stiff arm close to my side, I tried to conceal the bag in the folds of my skirt.

105

As we walked along, a new, tan car, the fanciest car I'd ever seen, rolled by us, stirring up the dust.

"Who is that?"

"Nobody from around here."

"Look… it's slowing down…"

"They probably need directions."

We waited and watched as the driver began backing up, wafting the dust our way. The silver bumper gleamed in the last rays of the sun. It made you feel bad that the spotless car would collect a dirty film. It didn't belong in Aldrich. Where was it from? I could see the glint of the license plate, but couldn't read the letters.

When the car stopped, a blond-haired man with his elbow on the window sill said with a sly, amused look, "Can I give you ladies a ride?"

GranRose started, took my hand, and picked up our pace, passing the car without a word.

"Just keep walking," she said, "Don't look at him."

She kept pulling me forward and I kept looking over my shoulder at the car, which had a bright shiny object on the hood that was moving slowly behind us, stalking us.

"They're following us!" I said.

"Just keep walking."

But I couldn't quit turning around. The car kept crawling toward us, like a menacing bird, which could speed toward us at any moment.

"It's still following us."

"Just ignore it."

The next time I turned back, a head popped up in the front seat and called out, "There's plenty of room in here for a couple of hot mamas." It was a woman. She began waving wildly. The car sped up to where we were and then slowed down again in a new column of dust.

"You sure you two babes don't want a ride?" I heard the woman say. The driver blocked my view of her, but after the car

106

crunched by, she turned around and I saw her through the rear window— a mop of brown hair, a big toothy grin.

"It's Mom!" I yelled. "Mom! Mom!" I dropped the bag, held my cheeks, and began jumping. The car stopped and Mom bounded out and around to the front of it. She was wearing a red sundress with a full swishy skirt. She threw out her arms and twirled, on display for us and for the man in the car.

"Hey, you two!" she said beaming. I raced into the road over to her. "Bear hug!" she said, enveloping me in a beautiful scent that was new to me. She rocked me back and forth for a minute there in the middle of the road, held me back by the shoulders to admire me, and then taken over by a deeper steadier emotion, crossed the gravel, jumped the ditch, and stepped up onto the walk beside GranRose.

"Oh, Mama," she said, opening her arms again, "It's so good to see you."

"I don't know when I've been so surprised," GranRose said on the verge of tears.

"I don't know when I've been so surprised," I said, crossing over to them, retrieving the fallen bag.

"I don't know whether to laugh or cry," Mom said, hugging me again. "Oh, you two…"

We were all so glad to have each other. It was one of those ecstatic reunions—preceded by a long separation and accompanied by the unexpected. It was a soldier's return from war, a mother returned from another country. When I look back on it, I wonder if that wasn't one of the happiest moments in my mother's life. It wasn't just the simple joy of reuniting. She was on the cusp of proving herself as she never had before. She had us to prove herself to the man in the car, with whom she was in love, and she had him to prove herself to us.

"All that hootin' and hollerin'. I should've known it was your mother!" GranRose said. For all of my mother's indiscretions, GranRose adored the sight of her prodigal daughter. She was more emotional than I had ever seen her, made vulnerable, perhaps by Doc Lawson's diagnosis.

Even though we were a block from home, Mom insisted we all ride together in the tan car to the house. I sat in the front seat between Mom and Joe, the blond-haired man with the sly expression. I gazed out the windshield at the sparkling jewel on the hood, which turned out to be a sleek, silver bird in flight. Despite the bumpy road, the car glided along. Mom chattered all the way and Joe just drove, blond and taciturn, smelling of cigarettes and aftershave.

Later on that night, Joe rose to leave saying he'd had enough of all the hootin' and hollerin'. Mother howled as if he had made some brilliant quip. The whole time he was there, he sat all lanky and easy in the best living room chair with his arm draped over the antimacassar letting the ash on the end of his cigarette get so long I was sure it would drop on GranRose's floral carpet and singe one of the roses. Mom sat on the floor by his feet, feeling good beneath the skirt of her red dress pooled on the floor, and oohing and aahing every time he uttered a word.

"Oh, honey, do you have to leave?" she said to him in such dulcet tones I wanted to throw up.

Then, when he got up to leave, she kissed him goodbye on the lips right in front of me and GranRose. She might have waited until she was outside seeing him off, but she had to show us how important he was, how he was going to change her life and ours. Seeing her kiss him made me feel awful—for myself, for my father, for GranRose, and especially for Mom herself. There was something about the show of it that was not only embarrassing but demeaning. After they walked out the screen door, Grand Rose whispered, "I can't wait to get out of this corset," deflecting the humiliation of the wanton kiss, trying to make the best of things.

While GranRose went to her bedroom to unlace her corset, I tried, for the first time, to help out. I got the bucket on the back porch, pumped the water, carried it sloshing into the kitchen, lifted it onto the stove, spilling a third of it on the floor, and turned on the burner. I found a dish towel and began sopping up the water before anyone could see my mess. As I threw the soaked dish towel in the kitchen sink, I heard Mom in the living room.

"Well, what do you think?"

"About what?" GranRose asked.

"About JOE."

"He's a nice-looking man."

"Isn't that the truth." Mom was so tickled. Her words bubbled, on the verge of a gentle, little laugh. "We're serious, Mama."

"What... does he do?"

"He's a high roller! You saw that car!"

"It's a nice car..."

"We're thinkin' about tyin' the knot."

"Oh... well... congratulations." GranRose's vague, halting answers cast disapproval, but Mom was oblivious. "I hope... it works out. You know it never hurts to wait awhile... just to make sure."

"I wanted you to meet him," she said.

"From Arkansas, was it?

"Imboden!"

"Oh...uh huh."

"Daddy was down there selling DDT, wasn't he?"

"For a while."

"Anyway, Joe's people are from down there so when I said I wanted to go to Missouri he said, 'That's not far from my people,' so it worked out!"

"All the way from Las Vegas..."

"Marriage Capital of the World!" Mom said. GranRose didn't respond. After a while Mom said, "You look worn out, Mama."

"I've had a pretty long day. I'm awful glad you're here, Marge."

"Me, too, Mama."

I had been listening from the doorway unaware that the water on the stove was boiling over. Just as I turned off the burner, Mom came into the kitchen.

"Good, Lord. What're ya DOIN' back here?" The water was running down the tin bucket making the burner steam and spit.

Mom took over. She carried the hot water to the bathroom and poured it in the tub. "Your bath is ready, Mama," she called into the living room as she returned to the kitchen.

"You could float a boat on this linoleum," she said. "Where's the mop?"

I found a mop and pail with a wringer on the back porch and brought them to her. She began sopping up the water and wringing out the mop as I looked on, glued to her every move. Finally, she stopped and looked up at me, standing helpless beside the Coldspot. I was afraid she had seen my uselessness and was about to call me out.

She examined me, tilting her head one way and then the other and said, "Those curls are cute as the devil. Oneita may be a redneck, but she knows how to give a Toni." She resumed mopping. "This floor needed a good cleaning anyway."

She began singing a tune I'd never heard. "See the pyramids along the Nile de de de de de de de de de de. Just remember, darling, all the while, you belong to me..." I stood there, irreversibly hogtied, listening to her clear, pretty voice. "I'm just glad Mama has such a good helper. There 're plenty of kids that wouldn't lift a finger." She talked and sang and mopped. Her movement was swift and efficient, the braided cords flinging and swirling in and around the kitchen table legs and chairs. When she came my way, I couldn't move so she mopped between and on top of my feet.

"Mom! Stop it."

"What the heck is wrong with you, anyway?"

"Nuthin." I moved so she could mop.

"Are you Lot's wife?"

"Who?"

"I start mopping and you turn into a pillar of salt. What's wrong?"

"I'm not a good helper," I confessed.

"Well you could be if you hadn't become a statue."

"I've never... lifted a finger."

"Well you..."

"GranRose has VERY high blood pressure. Very high," I said, spewing out what I had been holding in for hours.

"What?"

"Doc Lawson says we have to help her so she can take it easy."

Mom stopped, looked at me, trying to take in what I had said, and sat down at the kitchen table with the mop between her legs. She looked forsaken and crestfallen at first, and then she just went blank and silent. She sat staring at the spoons GranRose kept in a jar on the table. I had forgotten how my mother could go into a stupor like that, but it was a familiar characteristic. It was how she reacted to adversity, a way of blocking out an awful reality. Someone else might have thought she was simply concentrating, trying to remember something, but it was more than that. When my mother sat transfixed, she was taking a break from the horror of life, and when she came back she was able to carry on, almost as if nothing had happened. After I told her that GranRose had high blood pressure, the condition that had done in my great grandmother and all of my great aunts when they were GranRose's age, my mother left this world, possessed, and when she came back she said, sad and resigned, "I thought she looked... hollow-eyed." And then she said, changing the subject with a restorative lilt, "Where are we sleeping?" Just like that, she shifted from the calamitous to the mundane.

"You can have your old room, Mom. I'm sleeping upstairs."

"Will you be okay up there?"

"I'm not afraid."

"But what if you have to pee in the night?"

"There's a chamber pot."

"Okay."

"I found it in the upstairs closet where GranRose said."

"Hmmm. Well, let's check out the bed up there. Do you know how to play feather bed flop?" she asked blithely.

Every bed in the attic had a feather mattress, each of which Mom shook out and placed, one on top of the other, on one bed. When she finished, the pile of mattresses, was as high as the tall iron bars between the posts of the bed.

"Okay, so now you get up on the foot of the bed facing me…" I held onto her as I climbed from the lower bar to the higher, "and now, you ready? Raise your arms and Flop!" I let go of her, raised my arms, and fell backward.

Falling into a huge pile of feathers is euphoric. I have no idea why. The falling is so soft, for one thing, and there's something about the way all that ticking rises up and envelops you. It is a disappearing act from which resurrection is certain. I wanted to do it again and again.

Mom refluffed the mattresses several times. After the fourth or fifth time, though, she refused.

"I'm not fluffing the dang mattresses."

"Fluff them," I begged. "Just one more time."

"Who am I? Your personal fluffer? This is the last time. Right?"

"Right."

"Fluff and re-fluff…" she grumbled. My mother could be so much fun.

Chapter 14

The next morning GranRose left on foot for the store, and I sat with Mom on the front porch while she drank coffee and waited for a car to pass so that she could wave down. She was dressed ready to go with her purse by her side and had made me get dressed, too.

"Half of luck is preparation," Mom said. "Some old Roman guy said that. I'll bet you didn't know I knew that. I'm not just some hick from the sticks."

"Why don't we call the garage?"

"Somebody will come along. Let me listen to the birds and finish my coffee." The morning birds were babbling in the maples.

"I don't want to go to Aldrich School." I kept complaining about the school and she kept defending it.

"Look at ME! A proud graduate of Aldrich High School. I can still remember my Latin. Listen to this: *hic haec hoc, huius huius huius.*" She made funny, hissing bird sounds and exaggerated movements with her lips. She was on a morning high from the coffee. "*Hunc hanc hoc…*"

"Mom, I hear a car." Mom clunked down her coffee on the porch rail.

"Keep your fingers crossed that it's a man." She stood, poised to pounce.

A green truck came around the corner.

"It's Bill Cole!" I said, jumping up. Mom ran down the walk to the road.

"Hey Bill, can you give us a push?"

GranRose's Pontiac lurched as the truck knocked the back bumper—once, twice. Then the engine turned over "smooth as a ribbon," and we took off for the garage. For the rest of the morning, Mom was on a roll. "I waved down a mechanic on his

113

way to work. It doesn't get any luckier than that!" she chortled on the walk home.

"You were prepared."

"That's right," she said, nudging my shoulder in approval. "As soon as they get the car fixed, you and I can go to Delarues and get you some new clothes. You've grown like a weed."

I told Mom about the brassiere, and she hooted and told me she was glad I had made an "investment in the future," which "was always a good thing."

"But for now, I owe Pansy five dollars and sixteen cents," I said.

"I'll take care of it, kiddo!"

When we got back to the house, we gathered the eggs and made scrambled eggs. After breakfast, I divulged to my mother my gnawing thoughts of the brushes with my grandfather —I told her about the banging on the door, the visceral struggling and grunting, and the horrible blast of the gun.

"Well, he was drinking, and he wanted his way with your grandmother" was her matter-of-course reply. "I wouldn't worry about him. He won't be back here for a while. He's probably in a hotel up in Kawf ul silent City somewhere. Clay is Clay."

Some might think my mother's response to my troubled confession was insensitive, but her dispassion relieved me. It made what had happened less remarkable. I was just another kid with a grandfather who had hit the skids during the Depression. Her nonchalance helped me accept what she had long since accepted about him.

"Let's change the subject to something pleasant," she said. "I have something to show you." I followed her to the bedroom. She walked to a chair on which sat her open suitcase. The lid had a pink satin pocket that was gathered with elastic. From it she pulled out a photograph. "Look at this," she said. It was a shot of Joe. He was sitting at a black jack table with a cigarette dangling from his mouth holding up an Ace and a King in

114

one hand and a whiskey glass in the other. "Isn't he a looker?" she said, wedging the picture under one of the clips that held up the big round mirror of the vanity. "And he's crazy about me."

"What happened to Dingbat?" I said, which seemed to take her by surprise.

"Dingbat... Oh, he was just a friend. I'm serious about Joe. When you get to know him, I think you'll like him. If it all works out, you could come and spend Christmas with us. And maybe you could just stay on with us if you like it there. That's what I'm hoping."

I guess Mom could see how sad I was because she just kept on talking. "When we get a place together, I'm gonna make sure it's big enough for you to have your own room." But the more she talked the lonelier I felt. "I'd take you along with us right now if I didn't live in a hole in the wall." She faked a laugh. I was determined not to cry.

"Are you going to marry him?"

"Well," she hesitated, "not if you don't want me to."

My eyes were blurred and I couldn't see her face, when she answered me, so I didn't know if she was telling me the truth or not.

"I don't want you to!"

"You don't know him. I don't think you're giving him a fair shake."

"He's not a man you can count on. He's not a Rock of Gibraltar."

"How would you know?"

"Look at the picture, Mom." I snatched the photo from the mirror. "Look what he's doing. Who does he look like?"

"He looks like himself. He's a handsome man. I could do a heck-of-a-lot worse." Give me that." She reached for the photo, but I pulled it away and shook it at her

"He's a gambler; he's a drunk; he's a... he's a piece of shit."

115

She reached again for the photo but I spun in the opposite direction and when I turned back, I tore it in two and threw it on the floor. My mother sat down on the bed and stared at the torn photo on the floor in a stupor and when she came out of it, she stood up, walked straight toward me, drew back her hand, and slapped my face so hard and so deliberately I went numb.

I knew then that what I thought would not, could not stop her from going with Joe, that wild horses could not stop her from her determination to have him. I pulled open the dresser drawer where I kept my letters from Daddy, grabbed them in one hand and ran upstairs holding my cheek with the other. I stayed in the attic on my featherbed with my letters hidden under the pillow up until I heard the slam of the screen door late that afternoon, which meant that GranRose had come home.

By then my mother had wrung and plucked a chicken; dug up, peeled, and boiled potatoes; picked, washed, and seeded some cherries, and rolled out the dough for a pie. I could hear her coming and going from the chicken house, the garden, and the orchard. At one point she hollered up the stairs, "Janet, are you up there?" I didn't answer and had decided if she came up the steps to climb out the attic window and onto the roof. I had done that several times before when I was fiddling around and the window screen was still out of the window, in case I had to make an escape. But she didn't come up the steps or call to me again. When it was almost dark, from the open window, I heard the spring of the front screen door expand and snap back, and I knew GranRose was home. I sneaked half way down the steps.

"Mama, is that you?" Mom said from the kitchen. "I've made this and that..."

"Where's Janet?" GranRose said, coming into the kitchen.

"She's upstairs. I guess she doesn't feel too good...We got the car down to the garage. I think it'll be fixed by tomorrow.

"They called me at the store. Said it would be Saturday before they could get the part from Fair Play."

116

"Oh, dang it. I wanted to go to Delarues before Joe comes to get me."

"When will that be?"

"Sunday, Mama. I told you..."

"This Sunday?"

"Not until after we go to The Ridge. I wouldn't miss that! But now I won't be able to get something for Janet to wear back to school. I wonder if Pansy could pick out some things and send them over by Pat."

"I imagine so. And Betty Miller is finishing up a dress for her." I edged further down the stairs.

"Well, I'll pay for it. Oh, Mama, something awful has happened." I leaned around the corner of the staircase and watched my mother collapse on a kitchen chair. On both sides of her face strands of hair had fallen out of the band she'd used to hold them back. She looked horse faced and hopeless.

"What is it?"

"You don't know what I've done. I can't even tell you." I was afraid she was going to start crying. "I've made some awful mistakes."

"Well, you've done something right. You've got that girl upstairs."

"I HAD that girl upstairs. Now I've ripped it."

"Whoaaa."

"I'm a lousy mother." As she put her head in her hands, the rest of her brown hair fell down and covered her face.

"Now Marge..."

"I am. You don't know what I've done."

"It can't be that bad."

"It's not just Janet. I'm unfit to be a mother."

Though I have since speculated on the implications of my mother's words, what she might have meant beyond her having "ripped it" with me, I only understood at the time that she was suffering in a way I had never before seen, and for all of my wounded feelings, I walked down the last steps of the staircase into

117

the kitchen, and standing before her abject, hunched-over back, feebly apologized.

"I'm sorry I tore up the photo," I said, clearing my throat.

She sat up, seeing me for the first time. Her nose was red and mascara was running down her cheeks.

"What?" she asked, wiping her eyes with her apron.

"I'm sorry I tore up the photo," I said.

"Come 'ere, kiddo." I walked closer. Mom ran her fingers through her hair and tied it back again. "Let me see." She turned my chin and examined my slapped cheek. "You're sorry?"

"Uh huh."

She hugged me and said, "Do you forgive me?"

"Uh huh."

"Could you say that one more time?" She hugged me again. "I couldn't hear you. You have to say it louder." Mom was initiating what she called the Bear Wrestle. "Otherwise, I won't be able to let you go."

"No," I said, playing into the game.

Now Mom held me in a lock. "Say 'yes' or I'll never let go."

"I won't say it." I pulled away to free myself and the chair Mom was sitting on scraped the floor, but she kept her hold on me.

"Give up or take me down," she said. I pulled and twisted and Mom came down off the chair and we were grappling on the floor.

"Let me go!"

She had me in a grip, now with her arms and legs around me. She started pecking my cheek. "I won't stop kissing you. You have to say it."

"You might as well forgive her, Fiddle. She's bigger than you," GranRose said. We rolled back and forth in a hold. "I don't think it ought to be up to me to break you two apart."

"Ya hear that, kiddo?" She resumed pecking on the cheek that she had slapped. "You could do worse than get kissed to death." Peck peck peck. It was all part of the game. She wouldn't stop.

"Okay. I forgive you."

"Louder!"

"I forgive you!"

"Whew!" Mom let me go, and we fell apart panting on the linoleum. "I thought she'd never give in. Where'd she get that stubborn streak? Not from our side of the..." She stopped short and sat up on the floor: "Mama, the pot's boiling over!"

"I can't referee you two and keep up with dinner at the same time!" GranRose said, swiveling toward the stove. She rescued the chicken and dumplings and mashed the potatoes while Mom fried tomatoes and finished the pie. It seemed like the best meal I had ever eaten. Of course, I hadn't eaten since morning, but I was famished for more than food. After my act of forgiveness and my mother's as well, there was a special communion to our meal, over which GranRose quietly presided.

I have since thought that my mother suffered more that day than I. My challenge to her relationship was more virulent and defining than the slap I received in return. The torn photo was an attack not only on Joe, but on her most instinctive predilections. But despite the agony I had inflicted, she was undeterred. Just as she had won the bear wrestle, she had won the day. She chose Joe, and it was I, who without being asked, searched through GranRose's buffet and proffered the scotch tape she used to tape together the torn photo. Even then, I realized that wanting to be forgiven has little bearing on the capacity to change. At least that was so in the case of Mom.

After our feast of forgiveness, when I was brushing my teeth, I panicked at the sight of myself in the medicine cabinet mirror.

"Mom! There's something wrong with my eyes." Mom came into the bathroom with cold cream on her face.

"That's what happens if you cry all day, kiddo. They get all puffed up."

"I look funny."

"Be thankful you don't have to use eye make-up. There's nothing worse than trying to put on your mascara when you can't find your eyelashes."

"But I have to sing on Sunday."

"By then they'll probably be okay. Castor oil will take the swelling down some…"

Mom had had experience with swollen eyes.

Chapter 15

On Sunday morning when I woke up in my attic bed, it was barely light. There was a cool breeze coming through the attic window. Outside the birds were skittering in the trees. One said "Srose, srose, srose," my grandmother's name preceded by a slight sibilant. The window screen was still on the floor from where I'd positioned it weeks before. I stepped up on the wood frame and climbed out the window and onto the roof. The air was cool and damp. A mist was wafting through the gray treetops. "Srose, srose, srose." The bird was somewhere in the branches of the maple right before me. I could see the leaves flutter, but I couldn't see the bird.

It was that kind of soft, blurry morning, that lets you drift into another sphere. I imagined myself as a bird, flying above the trees, alighting on a branch, trilling "srose, srose, srose." I don't know how long I sat there, chin on my knees, in a rapture with the chirping and twittering, long enough to get cold in my damp nightgown, but I wouldn't have left my perch on the roof if Mom hadn't started calling me. "Janet Stephens, Wake up!" It was Sunday, the morning of the afternoon that she would be leaving, and I wanted to put off going downstairs for as long as I could. I wanted to stay in the trees with the birds, but a flight of fantasy is a delicate thing, a kind of intricate wish, and once it is broken in upon, no matter how you might try, there is no recovering it.

When I finally descended the staircase and ambled into her bedroom, she was packing her suitcase. Alongside the stack of folded clothes was the torn, taped photo. She picked it up and looked at me.

"When he comes this afternoon, I want you to make an effort. Okay, kiddo?

"Okay."

"You'd better get ready. It's late." She put the photo into the satin pocket of the suitcase. "It'll take us a good twenty minutes to get to The Ridge."

I had never been to the church and the cemetery that was known as The Ridge and was located at the top of the hill on the other side of the bridge. Everyone from all of the churches gathered there every few months and afterwards had a covered dish dinner on the lawn in back of the church. My mother and grandmother would get to see a lot of people who came in from the country. Some of them were relatives and others they counted as family. People marked time by these occasions. They wore their best and prepared the dishes they were known for. GranRose was exhilarated but worried. The Pontiac, though it now started up, might still stall out on the steep terrain en route to The Ridge.

Despite the build-up to church and dinner at The Ridge, I wasn't aware of the importance of the occasion. My only interest was that Betty Sue and I were supposed to sing, but even that prospect was dulled by what the afternoon would bring. All I could think of was that my mother would be leaving, leaving with Joe for Vegas, leaving me behind, indefinitely. Instead of getting dressed to leave, I sat at Mom's vanity, and dawdled with her makeup. The odor of the soft round powder puff, stained flesh pink was uniquely Mom. If I could smell it today after all of these years, I would feel her presence as persistent and affecting as ever. From outside the open door to the porch, I heard the bird again: "Srose, srose, srose."

"It's still dark," I said to Mom as I rose and went out on the porch. The clouds were a deep blue and lower down the sky was violet.

"I know, but it's almost nine. It's going to rain."

I looked up into the tree. From below, I thought I might be able to see the nest.

"Come on, kiddo." I could see Mom through the screen taking the feedsack dress Betty Sue's mother had made for me off the hangar. She tossed it on the bed. I kept idling as if my distraction could keep the day from taking place.

Finally, GranRose called me from the kitchen. "You should eat a little something before we go." She gave me one of the fried pies she was packing in her basket. It was a half moon turnover of pastry filled with apricots, fried in lard, and drizzled with powdered sugar. It was so good I almost came out of my pout, but when Mom pulled the dress over my head and began carrying on about how cute it was and wasn't I the berries, I went back into my sulk. A new dress, even a pink one with puffed, elasticized sleeves trimmed in eyelet didn't fix things.

In the back seat of the Pontiac on the way to The Ridge, I sulled up in a snit and refused to speak. I knew that was "no way to be," but I couldn't reconcile myself to being stuck in Aldrich, which my mother herself had deemed "a fate worse than death." As we drove along in the half light, it began to sprinkle.

"Dang it. Here she comes," Mom said, turning on the windshield wipers. I sat up to look out the window at the long, dark line of rain clouds. When we passed Ray's boxcar, Eudorrie came racing through the yard barking at us. I rolled down the window to look at her and let her see me but some drops splattered my face, so I rolled it back up and turned to look at her chase the car and then stop in the middle of the road and watch us.

"Just because it starts up doesn't mean it will make it up the hill," GranRose said nervously as we neared the bridge. "The last two times it puttered out half way up and I rolled back down."

"I know, Mama. But we'll make it this time. I didn't do all that rolling and crimping for nothing. I'm showin' off those cherry cobblers if it kills me." Mom was vain and competitive about pie crust. She refused to entertain the prospect of an aborted effort.

"After packing up all that food, I had to turn around and go back home," GranRose said.

"Well, my money says we're gonna make it."

"If we have to turn around and go home, we'll just make the best of it." GranRose was preparing for the worst. The rain pelleted the windshield. "I'll swan. It looks like the dinner may get rained out anyway."

"I have to sing!" The words popped out of me. "The whole Sunday School class will be there."

"I'd forgotten you were back there, kiddo." Mom took her foot off the gas and the car came to a near stop.

"Oh, my Lord," GranRose said, thinking the car had already failed.

"What is it, Mom?"

"I'm just getting charged up. Two bucks says I can make it to the top of that hill in one minute flat. Any takers?

"We WANT you to make it," I said.

"What would you say the odds are, Mama?"

"I don't know."

"We've only got one chance," Mom said. "Shall we take it?" Mom liked the drama of our plight. She wanted to clarify the stakes for the fun of it, the fun it would be if the three of us and the Pontiac beat our opponent—the hill. "It's an awful steep hill. I don't know if we should take it. What do you think?"

"Just take it, Mom."

"Okay. Ya ready?"

"We're ready," I said.

"What's that? I've got a banana in my ear."

"We're ready!" I screamed.

"Okay. Hold on. We might hit a bump or two. Ya still ready?"

An expression my mother used when she played cards came to me. It was something she said just before making a play against the odds. I said the magic words that I knew would trigger her.

"Bid 'em high and sleep in the alley!"

Mom hit the accelerator. The bet was on. It was us against the forces of the hill. Root hog or die. The tires squealed, the car sped through the bridge, jolting as it came off the abutment on the other side, and began the climb up the hill. The higher we got, the slower the car went until we'd fallen back to half the speed. As we neared the top of the incline, the car was scarcely

124

moving. At any moment the convulsing engine would sputter and die. I closed my eyes, folded my hands, and invoked Jesus using the words I'd memorized from the hymn Betty Sue and I were to sing.

"Fairest Lord Jesus, ruler of all nature, oh Thou of God, let the car get over the hill..." I prayed, hands clasped, not daring to open my squinched eyes. Near the brink of the hill, praying in time to the pulsating groan of the engine, "Thee will I cherish. Thee will I honor...," the car kept crawling, crawling, slower and slower, until at about five miles per hour, it must have reached and surmounted the crest, because Mom interrupted my prayer hollering.

"Hurrah! Hurrah!"

I opened my eyes. "We MADE it!"

"Dysart luck wins again!" GranRose cheered.

"One minute flat, I'll wager," Mom said, cinching her bet.

And then I'm not kidding, this is the truth, the sun broke through the clouds. I remember rolling down the window and sticking my head out to look at the sunlight shooting down over the fields. It was a heavenly light, a backdrop worthy of a biblical conversion. As the Pontiac resumed speed, I began singing the second verse of the song: "Fair are the meadows, fairer still the woodland." I was singing softly to myself but Mom and GranRose joined in and I switched to alto, and the three of us sang in harmony as we rolled along the fair, sunlit meadows of the ridge. When we came to "Jesus is fairer, Jesus is purer," we crescendoed with triumphant, unfeigned praise, and when we came to the last line we slowed to a grateful, heartfelt adagio: "Who makes the woeful heart to sing."

I have always loved that last line of the second verse of the hymn. To me that is Jesus at his fairest—making "the woeful heart to sing."

Chapter 16

Betty Sue and I were early on the program. It was the biggest crowd I'd ever sung before, but I was calm. The emotions I had already experienced that morning had deadened my nerves. Afterwards, everyone bragged on us, how we had memorized the hymn and didn't need a hymnal and how cute we looked in our feedsack dresses. When the service was over, there was no Sunday School. The kids were turned loose to play outside while the women set out their dishes on the long tables behind the church. Betty Sue and I filled our plates, walked into the cemetery, and sat on a little stone bench.

"That's a baby's grave," Betty Sue said pointing with her drumstick to a small nearby stone, across the top of which lay a lamb.

"It was two years old."

"What was it? A boy or a girl?"

"You can't read the name." Betty Sue had explored the cemetery. She knew the particulars of the headstones that captivated children.

"I wonder how it died."

"A lot of babies died back in the old days."

I squatted down close to the letters, blotched with lichens and algae. "It says L-A- something-B."

"Lamb! It's probably 'Lamb of God!'" Betty Sue said, kneeling beside me. She ran her fingers across the indentations so flattened they were illegible. "There is the G! That's a capital G. I can feel it!"

"Uh huh."

"That HAS to be 'GOD!'" Betty Sue proclaimed the word as if she had discovered indisputable proof of the Almighty and life everlasting.

We walked to a tall, slender obelisk that GranRose had pointed out to me on the way from the car into the church. The freshly mown grass was still wet and little cut blades stuck to the sides of the pedestal.

"Kirby," I said, reading the name. "Those are my great-grandparents."

Betty Sue showed me the stone of her own great-grandparents nearby.

"I wonder if they knew each other," I said, musing for the first time on my ancestors and their connections to others.

"Oh yes. They were all part of one big family here in Aldrich."

Betty Sue's reference to the "big family" was something she had probably heard in Sunday School, but her borrowed words were not empty. As young as she was, she grasped the larger idea of family, and it was that widened sense of family, which I was only beginning to learn about, that made it possible for me to open up to her, as if she were a sister or at least a cousin.

"My mother is leaving today when we get home," I told her, as we wandered through the cemetery.

"Where will she go?"

"To Nevada. She has a job there, but it isn't enough yet to get a house for us to live in. That's why she can't take me now."

"Until then, you'll always have a place in Aldrich," Betty Sue said.

She had an opposite opinion of Aldrich. Always having a place in Aldrich had never occurred to me as a consolation.

"Want to see the Unknown Man?" she asked.

I followed her between and around the graves to a sparser section and on to the empty, far back corner of the cemetery where there was just one stone.

"Look" she said, stopping in front of the plain, homely cement marker.

"Unknown man who fell under train, 1934," I said, reading the irregular script. "Fell under train…?"

127

"He was riding the rails," Betty Sue said, wistfully. "Somebody found him by the tracks."

"But... who was he?"

"No one knows..."

"He's out here all by himself."

"His family will never find him."

"They'll never know why he disappeared..."

"Or where he disappeared to..."

"All those years ago..."

"He found a home here in Aldrich..."

Betty Sue and I picked the yellow and pink milkweed in the pasture outside the back gate of the cemetery and put it on the Unknown Man. We made a pact always to remember him. We would decorate his grave whenever we came to The Ridge. We would say a prayer for him. It gave us a kind of reassurance, as if our ritual would make him less anonymous. WE would be his family.

As we were walking back to the church, my mother came walking toward us. For the first time I noticed that she was wearing a pretty pink and purple floral print. I always think of her in that dress. It expressed my mother at her best—bright, playful, romantic. I think of her swaying brown hair and lissome step midst all the tombstones as she made her way toward us.

"Hey, you two. What're you doin' way out here in no man's land?" My mother's voice was alive and nuanced. She surprised and pleased me, coming unexpectedly from a distance, seeing her from a new vantage, an angle widened, perhaps, by the presence of a friend.

"Do we have to go?"

"It's time, kiddo."

As the three of us walked back to the church, we passed Oneita Hicks who was on her knees clipping back the peonies that had grown up around a headstone. "Well, if it isn't Little Betty and Little Rose. You girls was the best thing on the program, and the best lookin' in yer matchin' dresses with them curls I give you."

128

When Oneita saw Mom, she stood up and whisked her skirt. "My Lord, is that you Marge? How are ya, ya old fool."

"Not bad. Not bad. How's Oneita?"

"Tendin' ta Daddy here." She cocked her head toward the grave stone. "Whad ya think of them girls this mornin'? Quite a pair. Almost as good at singin' as we was at fightin'." Wanda hawed. "They's cute as buttons. You done good with that one." Wanda pointed the clippers at me.

"I like her curls," Mom said.

"Yeah. They come out good."

"I wish I could visit but I have to get back to the house," Mom said.

"Well don't let this ole hillbilly stop ya."

"I don't want to miss my ride. It's important."

"Sounds like there's a man involved." When Mom shrugged, Wanda grinned and said to me, "Where he's a goin', she's a goin'."

"But I'll be back to Aldrich in not long," Mom said. "See ya around, Oneita."

"If'n the Army Corps of Engineers don't drown me out first," Oneita quipped. "They's comin' after all o' us, ya know. Before long there won't be no Aldrich. You know about that, dontcha?"

Mom waved a hand and walked away, which was abrupt and which GranRose would have deemed "highhanded."

"Well, idn't she somethin'," said Oneita.

"She's in a hurry," I said, feebly.

Oneita turned on me and said, "You have this ole hillbilly to thank for more than you know," and then she knelt down and went back to clipping. Her reproach stung me. I had been scolded and god knows rejected, but I had never before endured an adult taunt. It took me aback. How had I been thankless? Was I to blame for my mother's snub? Was I the same as my mother? Betty Sue took my hand.

"Come on, Janet," she said, leading me away.

129

When we came through the gate to the church, GranRose was holding her basket ready to leave, talking to several women with their baskets of leftovers.

"I don't see how the county can take away the rest of the school without our say-so," she said, provoking a volley.

"Well, they did it before."

"Losing the high school was hard enough."

"Aldrich High School was a fortress of learning!"

"Once we lose the elementary," one woman said, shaking her head, "that would be the beginning of the end."

"Once we lose the elementary" I repeated the words to myself, latching onto the possibility. If there were no school, I thought, Mom would HAVE to take me with her to Vegas. I wormed my way over to GranRose. "We wouldn't go to school?" I asked her.

"You'd have to go to Fair Play," she said, looking down at me, "but that's not going to happen for a long time, maybe never," and then addressing the many who had now gathered, she said, "Aldrich School is the heart of the community."

Mom was rearin' to go. "Let's go, Mama," she said raising her voice. "I don't want to miss my ride to Vegas!"

"I don't want to go to Fair Play school," I said.

"We'll talk this over on the way home," Mom said, walking toward me and taking my hand with a jerk.

"The school board is one thing," Betty Miller said. "They'll just do as they're told. What we need is someone who can speak up to the County Council. I would ask Pat, but now that he lives in Fair Play... It has to be someone from Aldrich. Rose would be the best to..."

"Mama has no business getting involved!" Mom said, horning in. Her loud interruption and sharp tone was that of an outsider, someone from Vegas.

"I'm not going to stand by and let the government decide the fate of Aldrich," GranRose said, not only as a clarification of her position but as a rebuke of my mother's acerbity. I had never heard my grandmother take on my mother or anybody else, verbally. "They want to put in a dam, Marge. That's what this is all about."

"The school is only the beginning," Betty said, trying to explain and smooth over the slight. "If the government has its way, Aldrich will be under water."

Now others, who had stopped to listen began to speak.

"Up in Ozark they flooded out all of the farms in the bottom. Everybody scattered like dust. It'd be the same thing here. They'd take my farm and everybody else along the Little Sac River, all the best farmland..." a man said.

"They'll take everything half way up the hill, including downtown," said another.

More people congregated. Everyone got into the discussion of the dam project that had been proposed. I didn't understand all they were saying, but I took in the gist of it. The dam posed a threat to all of Aldrich and the surrounding countryside. The dam would mean the wrecking of all the downtown buildings. It would destroy homes, churches, schools, and bridges, and then it would flood the whole area, swallowing roads and creeks and all of the low-lying farms up and down the Little Sac River, even swallowing the river itself. There were no dissenting voices. From all who spoke, I learned that the flood was imminent, that it was driven by an indifferent, all-powerful and ruinous force, and I learned that afternoon to name its evil origin: The United States Corps of Engineers.

But Mom was unmoved by the upheaval. She tightened her grip on my hand and began walking to the car.

"Mom!" I protested as she dragged me along. "Stop it." When we got to the car, she finally let go and I got into the back seat angry. We sat in the car without speaking, with the car running. When GranRose arrived and got in, before she had closed the car door, Mom began backing up.

"I hope Joe isn't sitting outside waiting on us!"

Beside the apocalyptic discussion she had pulled us away from, her rush seemed selfish and paltry. So what if Joe had to wait awhile? What about The United States Corps of Engineers? But in the course of the drive I forgot the larger foe and began dreading the immediate one. I imagined him on the front porch leaning up against a baluster smoking a cigarette or lounging in the tan car flicking ashes out the window. Mom flew down the hill, over the bridge, and through town jarring the Pontiac on the washboard road so that I had to hold onto the arm rest. When we screeched up to the house, Joe wasn't there.

"Whew!" Mom said as she rushed into the house and into her room to finish packing. "Come in here, will you, kiddo?" she said.

I followed her into the room. "I've never known him to be late, but this is one time I'm glad he is!" she said, throwing into her suitcase a pair of underpants and a bra that had been drying on the back of a chair. "I'm sorry about that back there, dragging you to the car." I sat down on the bed, brooding, and watched her hurriedly powder her nose and put on her new Persian Melon lipstick.

"Oh, crap," she said, having smeared the lipstick. "Would you get me some toilet paper?"

I brought her the whole roll sitting by the toilet in the bathroom.

"Thank you, kiddo," she said, repairing the smear with a piece of the tissue. "I don't want to turn up with crooked lips." She turned and made a funny face with her lips all scrunched up to one side. "Just call me Crooked Lips," she said, like a gangster, forcing me to laugh. "Okay. I've got my cologne." She dabbed behind each ear, closed the bottle, wrapped it in the dried underpants, and closed the suitcase. "Mascara, comb, lipstick, powder..." she muttered to herself, as she dropped each item into her purse. "Oh, and the map." She opened a drawer of the vanity, pulled out a new road map, and said waving it a couple of times, "Is Joe ever going to love THIS." She took off her flat shoes and put on her new high

132

heel patent shoes with the toe out. She leaned over, slipping one shoe on and then the other. "What do you think?" she said. raising both legs straight out admiring the shoes. "Did I ever get a great buy? They're a half size too small, BUT because the toe was out, guess what? It didn't matter!" She stood up and turned this way and that looking at the shoes. "Luck of the draw!" She picked up her purse in one hand, her suitcase in the other, carried them to the front porch, and plunking them down on the top step, heaved a sigh. Then she sat down beside the suitcase and took me into account. "We want to make it to Albuquerque before dark, so we'll have to run when he gets here, kiddo."

"I dread Aldrich School. I'd rather go to Fair Play. I'd rather be a Fair Play girl."

"Oh crap. Quit sulking. You'll have teachers as good or better than you've ever had right here in Aldrich. Wait till you meet them."

"I already have." That was partly true.

"You've met Lila Bauer?"

"No, but I know Solomon Sharp well."

"Is that so. I can't believe the old geezer is still teaching."

"I might get to take Latin… if my grades are good enough." Mom raised her eyebrows and tilted her head in approval. "He said YOU didn't live up to your potential," I added.

"He did, did he. Well, you tell him, I can still recite Seneca." She screwed up her nose, showed her front teeth, and repeated with mock superiority and an extra heavy accent on the first syllable: "SEN e ca."

"Who's he?"

"I don't know… some Roman who said wise stuff."

"Is it true? You can still recite SEN e ca?" I was thinking that Mom was leading up to some joke. I was going to have to say "Seneca Who," or play along somehow.

"Of course, it's true."

"Recite it then."

133

"*Ducunt volentem fata nolentem trahunt.* So there."

"Wow. What does it mean?" I was still expecting a punch line, but Mom had become sober. Not very often, but sometimes, she would do that—start out silly and then turn serious.

"Just tell him I've remembered my Latin." She was practically somber now.

"But I want to know what it MEANS."

"It means that neither your grandmother, nor Betty Miller, nor Uncle Pat, nor Solomon Sharp, nor the whole of Aldrich can save the school."

"Mom!"

"They're all wasting their time and their energy. It isn't worth it. It isn't worth spending your declining years in a losing battle. Your grandmother needs to have a little fun." Mom looked like she might explode, but then she calmed down. "She doesn't need to go politicking all over the county. She needs to take it easy."

***

When I decry my mother's superficialities, I try to remember that she quoted Seneca to me. In Latin she had said, "The fates lead the willing; the unwilling they drag." My mother foresaw the inevitable end of the school, not to mention the end of Aldrich and the toll that would take on her mother—how GranRose might be dragged by the fates to her end. Part of a daughter's mission is to ease the later years of her mother. Mom felt that. It was an important dimension of "doing right" by one's parent. But she wasn't willing to make the sacrifice that would entail—she might not have been able to imagine what that sacrifice might be—and so she bore the burden of guilt instead.

***

134

While we were sitting there on the front steps waiting for Joe, several cars came around the corner and passed the house. When we heard the first one, Mom got up.

"It's about TIME he got here," she said, but it wasn't Joe's fancy tan car with the silver bird. She sat back down. "Shoot. We'll be lucky if we get to Tucumcari."

Each time she heard one approaching, Mom rose expectantly, and each time she'd sit back down and say, "Where IS he?"

After an hour or so, GranRose got up from her rest and came out to the porch to join us. "I guess he got held up," she said.

"Well, why hasn't he called?" Mom said, irritated.

"He could be on the road. His car could have broken down."

"Does that brand new Studebaker look like a car that could break down?"

They were doing that kind of reversal dialogue when you say what the other person wants to believe, though you don't believe it yourself, and the other person says what you are thinking, which is likely the truth.

"You don't know that he didn't have a flat," GranRose said, providing my mother with what she wanted to believe and with a rationale to fall back on.

"Then why hasn't he phoned me?" Mom said, knowing that that was exactly what GranRose and I were thinking.

At some point, after dark, the telephone DID ring, and Mom stumbled over her suitcase on the way into the house, but it wasn't Joe. It was Uncle Pat. While they were talking, GranRose told me she had the feeling that Mom wouldn't be leaving that night and that to make it easier on her I should go ahead and turn in and that she would come to get me if Joe happened to turn up. I kissed her goodnight and went upstairs, but my heart being heavy for my poor mother, I climbed out on the roof and sat there right above where she was sitting on the front steps. I looked into the dark branches of the tree and pictured the "rose bird" asleep in her

135

nest. In my half-sleep, Uncle Pat was singing "Somewhere a bird that is bound to be heard is throwing its heart at the sky," which made me happy, but when I nodded and came to with a start there was not so much as a solitary chirp coming from the tree, just the empty whisper of leaves. As if in a dream, I climbed back through the window and onto my feather mattress and went to sleep in my feedsack dress, Daddy's letters tucked under the pillow.

Chapter 17

When I woke up in the night a few hours later, I was shivering. The cold air was drifting in through the attic window. It took me a minute to remember Mom. I wondered if she was still on the front steps waiting. I tripped on a step and caught myself by the rail hurrying in the dark to get down the stairs. I felt the wall for the kitchen switch at the foot of the stairs, turned on the light, and called out, but there was no answer. I ran from the kitchen through the dining room and the living room to the front porch. There was no one and no suitcase, there or in my mother's bedroom. The house was empty. I ran out the back door past the smokehouse and looked in the garden, calling for GranRose, then through the gate past the outhouse and into the chicken house. The chickens were still sleeping. It was too early to gather the eggs. GranRose was nowhere. There was no point in calling to her. I lumbered back out the low door of the chicken house and into the far corner of the field and sat down on the smooth dirt under the pear tree. I had missed saying goodbye to my mother.

Why hadn't GranRose gotten me up as she had promised? Why had she gone so early to the store? I sat, hugging my knees, my feedsack dress hitched up under my bent legs. In the distance below the ridge on this side of the river, I heard the remote whistle of the train. Only one train came through town, and though I had often heard it from the attic, ensconced in my feather mattress, I had never seen it. Crouched under the tree, I listened to the approaching cry of the whistle, then the low moan of the rails. As the train neared, there appeared a single, barely perceptible light which grew into a small, opaque orb. I watched the steady, glimmering haze as it moved through the black field and receded out of sight. If it hadn't been for the whistle and the moaning and the faint clacking, you wouldn't have known, from the light alone, that a train was passing through. It might have been an apparition. That's how dark it still was.

Sitting under the pear tree, my arms tight around my legs, I was cold for the first time since I had come to Missouri. When I went back into the house, I found an old flannel robe in Mom's bedroom closet. I put it on over my feedsack dress and began looking for a note from her, but I didn't see one on the bed or the vanity, or on the kitchen table or the dining room table, or on the buffet or anywhere on the porch—on the steps or the swing. I decided to call the store.

"Dysart Brothers, please."

"I'll try, but it's too early for anyone to be there," Nola said, drowsily. She rang the store, but no one answered. "Your grandmother oughta be along about dawn, failing a flat tire on the way back from Fair Play."

"Fair Play?"

"She probably took your mother over to Fair Play..."

"Oh."

"... to catch the 6 AM bus... on down to Oklahomie."

"Oh."

"Pat helped 'er out on the ticket, don't you know." I didn't know. I had no idea. But Nola knew and all those on our party line probably did, too. "Are you down there by yourself?"

"Uh-huh."

"Well, she'll be along. Marmalade had her kittens last night if ya wanna walk on down here to see."

"Okay."

I hung up, not really knowing what it was I was saying okay to. In a way, I was acknowledging all Nola had said—about my grandmother's drive to Fair Play, my mother's departure on a bus en route to Oklahoma, and Uncle Pat's financial assistance—but none of it made sense to me and none of it was "okay," with the exception of her last bit of news regarding the kittens. I wanted to see Marmalade's new litter.

138

I took off my mother's robe and put on a jacket I found in the back of a closet. It was deerskin with fringe, a present that someone had sent my grandmother from a trip out west. And though it was heavy and hung below my dress, it was warm, something to wear on the walk to Nola's two-room house at the edge of downtown. I was thinking that if I went to see the new kittens, I would pass the store and maybe GranRose or Uncle Pat would be there opening up.

But neither was there. None of the stores in town were open. Two long rows of dark storefront windows flanked the deserted road. There wasn't a car or a truck anywhere in sight. The whole area was lit by a solitary street light that I had never noticed before. It was in the middle of town by the post office at the top of a tall wooden pole that had a metal hat over it. I was the only person anywhere. I felt tired as I plodded along under the lone light, my deerskin jacket with the fringe weighing me down.

After I passed Dysart Brothers, I could see a dull glow coming from Nola's house at the far end of the street. It shone from the one little window of her front room. As I approached, I could see her inside at the switchboard. She was listening in on someone. When I knocked on the screen door, the whole door rattled. Nola put her hand over the receiver, hurriedly whispered to me that the kittens were in the shed, and went back to listening. I followed the path around to the back of the house and found the kittens, a black and white one, two with orange and brown spots, and an orange striped tabby, nestled on an old rug. I tried to pick up the tabby, but Marmalade, my favorite Aldrich cat, hissed at me and wouldn't let me get near.

I left Nola's and walked back past all the forlorn businesses and sat down on the loafers' bench in front of the store. It was odd to be in the town with the somber street light and no people. My mother's words about the impossibility of saving the school, "or Aldrich for that matter," came to me in a ghastly, inchoate way. I didn't comprehend the circumstances of the demise she was certain was to come, but as I sat there in the gloom, alone, I felt a part of it.

That may have been the first time I ever associated myself with a larger human loss. If Aldrich were no more, what would happen to the people? To the one big family? And the question of the inevitability of loss—was my mother right that Aldrich was a lost cause? All of those questions, vague and unintelligible though they were, bore down upon me. And they, along with my rising fever, induced my vision of the deluge of Aldrich.

The vision occurred sometime during the remainder of that night or after dawn, either on the loafers' bench or on Uncle Pat's cot, before or after he arrived and carried me from the bench to the cot in his office. I can't be sure, because after I had it, I was delirious and pretty much bedridden for a week.

In my vision (I call it that because it was different from a dream or a nightmare—less absurd and unlikely and more apocalyptic), I have lain down on the loafers' bench in front of the store. It is a chilly night. I am covered with a deer hide. The town is deserted and silent. As I am about to go to sleep, I hear the lapping of water. At once, I know the Little Sac River has overflowed, and when I jerk myself upright I see a low wall of water rushing down the street from the direction of the bridge. I am sure it will ebb before it reaches me, but it keeps getting higher, babbling up and slapping against the high concrete walkway in front of the store. I run up the gradual incline of the walkway past the café to Nola's house, sure that the water will level off, but the water furiously follows me, rising close behind. I begin climbing the hill to Betty Sue's. The water is growling and splashing, advancing quicker than I can climb. I slip and fall on the rocks. The water keeps coming faster and higher, slushing up over the rocks. When I get half way up the hill, when I can no longer breathe, it finally ebbs. I can see that I have reached a level beyond which it can rise. Breathless and wheezing, I collapse on a large flat outcropping. I look at the town below me. The water has now covered the loafers' bench and all but the upper portion of the storefront window. I watch as it ascends and engulfs the Dysart Brothers sign. It lashes against and knocks off the metal canopy and surges above the red bricks up to the roof. For a moment just beneath the water, I can see the top of the store, and then in a precipitate swell, like all of the other buildings, it too vanishes beneath the inevitable rush of black water. Now there is silence except for the ripple of the vast, undulating body of water and the lap against the rocks just below me. I lie down on the rock trying to keep warm under the deer hide. I am barely safe just above the water line where it is freezing cold. Aldrich is under water.

As I lay there quaking, the rock turns into a cot and the deer hide an army blanket. I am no longer on the hillside. I don't know where I am. I lie on my back, quaking, looking at squares in a tin ceiling high above me. There are noises—the tearing of butcher paper from a roll, the ring of a cash register. A loud clanging wakes me up. Mercifully, the vision comes to an end.

***

I don't know how long I remained on the loafers' bench in a delirium, but when I came to I was in the back of the store in Uncle Pat's alcove, lying on his army cot under his army blanket. I still had on my feedsack dress. GranRose's deerskin jacket was hanging over the back of Uncle Pat's desk chair. Sitting up made me dizzy. There was a scraping sound I couldn't identify. I stood up, caught my balance, and made my way down the aisle of the store. Uncle Pat was shoveling coal into the open door of the stove. GranRose was tying up a package with string. As thankful as I was to see them, I was too shaky to speak. I tried but I couldn't eke out a sound. I just stood there willing GranRose to look up until she finally did.

"Fiddle?" GranRose dropped the package and came from behind the counter. She hurried toward me in her white apron, reaching out and putting her hands on my upper arms to steady me. "Come here, Pat!" she said. After the clang of the stove door

141

closing and Uncle Pat rushing toward me and GranRose's grip, holding my arms tighter and tighter, I went blank.

***

How I got from the store home I do not know. All I remember is Doc Lawson standing by my downstairs bed, instructing GranRose. After a few days, when my fever was gone, GranRose went back to work and took me with her to the store wrapped up in a quilt.

"She's lost the roses in her cheeks," Miss Sunbonnet said to Uncle Pat, leaning down in front of my rocker by the stove and inspecting my face.

"She'll be all right," Uncle Pat countered. "School's starting in a couple of weeks. The carnival is right around the corner. She's GOTTA be all right!"

It was an early autumn, which had Uncle Pat in fine fettle. "Shine on, shine on, harvest moon, up in the sky," he sang as he moved around the store from one job to the next. For the next week the melody played over and over in my mind. "I ain't had no lovin' since January, February, June, or July…" The line made me think of Mom.

I never fully understood what had happened the night she got jilted by the high roller, the man she considered to be her fiancé. The ticket to Oklahoma was just the first leg of her bus trip back to Las Vegas, the portion that Uncle Pat helped pay for. That I do know. But whether or not she ever saw the high roller again or even talked to him on the phone, I don't know. In a letter, she did tell me that "things had fallen through" but that she still wanted me to come live with her as soon as she had the "moola." But who knew when that would be? A month? two months? As badly as I felt about my poor mother's disappointed love, as much as I wanted to believe in her, I had lost faith in her capacity to fulfill her promises. Oddly, scarlet fever, which dulls the emotions, made that loss more tolerable.

142

Once I got to feeling better and could be on my own, GranRose stopped taking me along to the store. In my half sleep I could hear her going out the back door to feed the chickens, moving about in the kitchen, starting the car to leave for the day— to the school board meeting in Fair Play or the county council discussions in Bolivar with the representatives of the United States Corps of Engineers, or just to the store.

"You feeling all right, Fiddle?" She'd crack my door and ask me before she left.

"Uh huh."

"Okay. Well, take it easy. Your breakfast is keeping warm under the dish towel."

I stayed in bed all morning because it was warmer there than any other place in the house. Afternoons I sauntered out back beyond the chicken house and sat in the warm air under the pear tree where I had a good view of the foreboding, two-story Aldrich School, the largest building in town and "the heart of the community."

Mom had praised the teachers, but for all her touting of Aldrich School, she had not been happy there. She had been unstudious and contentious, prone to a schoolyard fight. Why? I asked myself. "I was buried alive in a one-horse town," I had heard her say a million times. "Buried alive" That is how she described those school days before she made her escape out of town at the age of seventeen with my father.

Under the pear tree, I took in the sheer size of the "fortress of learning" with its high windows and its amber brick walls and tried to absorb my fears. As my health improved, I fiddled around resigning myself to school. Aunt Pansy sent over a pale green sweater and a pleated skirt from Delarues. I stuffed my brasierre with socks, pulled on the sweater, and admired my bosom in the big round mirror. By the time school started, just as Uncle Pat had predicted, I was well enough to attend, and the morning of that day I donned my new outfit, minus the socks which were too lumpy to pass for real, and headed out to Aldrich School.

143

Chapter 18

As it turned out, the "fortress" was four or five times the size needed for the number of students, which kept dwindling each year. I could get there by sidewalks and paths through neighborhoods of clapboard houses or by cutting through the field behind the house, which was much faster. The first week I took the sidewalks, but after that, in the mornings, I crossed through the field, though there was no defined path. The main thing was to avoid the cockleburs, which I could do if I stayed away from the clumps of weeds. Once I got to the railroad tracks, the way was clear to the schoolyard.

For all its many rooms, the building actually functioned as a one-room schoolhouse, for all but one room had been abandoned. The upstairs was a ghostly corridor of forsaken rooms on either side. Downstairs only my classroom was in use. In it were seven rows, one for each grade. Betty Sue and I were in Row Seven.

I was the one on the first day of school who said, "Let's sit there," pointing to the last two desks in the row.

We sat and whispered as we watched the teacher, Lila Bauer, organizing the little kids—Row One, Row Two, Row Three. She was thin as a zipper in a blue dress with a narrow belt of the same fabric and a white collar that looked like a doily. With paper and pencil, she walked by each row, quickly recording the names on her chart. Her straight white hair was parted down the middle, and when she looked down to write, the fine hair fell forward on either side of the pink part.

"Good morning, seventh graders," she said, arriving at Row Seven.

"Good morning," we said in unison.

144

She paused thoughtfully with her pencil raised, rapidly scanning the row. Her eyes were the same light blue as her dress. Instead of arching up, her eyebrows slanted downward like parentheses, giving her pale eyes a sad, disappointed look.

"Seventh graders hold a special position at Aldrich School," she said neutral and unsmiling. "They are responsible for setting an example for all, which means they must make wise choices." She began walking down the row and looking directly at me and Betty Sue. Up close her face was soft and lined like a dried apricot. I thought she was going to walk by us to the big windows at the back of the classroom, but she stopped at my desk and in a confidential, lowered voice said, "I've heard some whispering back here. Can you girls sit one in front of the other without talking?"

"Yes ma'am," I said, clearing my throat.

"Yes, Miss Bauer," Betty Sue said.

"Well, we'll see. You may be tempting fate. If you change your mind, tell me and we can seat you a desk or two apart."

"Yes, Miss Bauer," we said together.

She turned and walked back down the aisle, placed the pencil and chart on her desk as if the matter were settled, and began writing on the board. First, she printed her name in large letters, her skinny arm moving decisively with each tap of the chalk. Then she wrote it again in a free, graceful cursive, not too frilly or round or perfect.

"I am Miss Bauer," she said, turning back to the class. She spoke in a low, unaffected purr. "I'll be your teacher this year," she said, panning the room. "Today we will all get to know each other." Then, smoothing the back of her skirt so that it caught up in the bend of her knees, she sat on a chair to the side of her desk as we each stood and said our names.

On Row Seven were three boys: Percy, the bully from Sunday School, who lived in a red brick two-story house, the nicest in town, and whose father owned the bank; Paul, who lived in the country and rode to school on a horse, which he fed and

145

watered at recess; and my friend Ray, who lived in a boxcar and
came to school barefoot because he had no shoes. Besides me and
Betty Sue, there was one other girl on Row Seven, a withdrawn
country girl named Agnes who wore a faded hand-me-down, a
spare, shapeless dress without trim or gathering or pockets.

After all of the introductions and after Miss Bauer led us
in "Good Morning to You," the girls on Row Seven were given
their first reading assignment. Miss Bauer wrote the name of the
poet we were to study on the board. I was listening to the cool taps
of the hard chalk on slate and dying to write on the board myself
when Betty Sue leaned forward and whispered in my ear.

"Agnes' father is the man in the black truck."

My gasp was instant and audible. Betty Sue and I were
afraid of the man who appeared from nowhere, driving through
town in a rusted, mud-splashed black truck. He had only one arm,
the one on the steering wheel. The other, a stump of the upper arm,
he propped on the bottom of the open window, a grotesque
protuberance for all to see.

"He's her FATHER?"

Miss Bauer's back stiffened and the chalk stopped
moving. "Henry Wadsworth Long…" was frozen on the board.
After a few tense seconds, the soft sound of the chalk resumed and
I resumed breathing. I watched the smooth strokes, the looping up
of the "f" and the "l's" and the small curling vowels of "fellow"
and longed to write on the board myself, which seemed like a form
of ballet.

I had thought that Betty Sue and I were in the clear but
when Miss Bauer finished writing, she addressed the two of us in
front of the whole class.

"Do you girls have something to ask me?" she said with
a despondent gaze in our direction.

"Yes, ma'am," I said, automatically, without thinking.

"What is it?"

I thought maybe I should ask about fate, about tempting
it, but I couldn't think how. … I'm not sure…"

146

"Should one of us trade desks?" Betty Sue said, shame-faced.

"Yes," Miss Bauer said with her sad blue eyes. "A wise choice, Betty Sue."

I agreed to switch desks with Ray, who sat in the first desk of the row, and that's how I wound up under Miss Bauer's nose and right in front of Agnes.

***

In the weeks to come, Betty Sue and I made friends with Agnes despite her father. Miss Bauer, with the help of Longfellow, saw to that. For our first assignment, she sent the three of us to an empty classroom to read and discuss "Evangeline."

> *"Where is the thatch-roofed village, the home of Acadian farmers, men whose lives glided on like rivers that water the woodlands?" Longfellow asked. "Waste are those pleasant farms and the farmers forever departed! Scattered like dust and leaves…" he lamented.*

From the opening lines, Longfellow had me in thrall. I couldn't help but link the demise of Acadia to the future of Aldrich. We divided the poem and read aloud to each other, Betty Sue and I emoting between passages upon the tragic romance of the young heroine, who was not much older than we. Agnes, too, was entranced, though she rarely uttered a word. She looked up from her turn at reading, her eyes wide or misty, on the verge of speaking, but always retreating as if words would dispel or cheapen the emotion. Still, the poem united us. Together the three of us fell in love with Evangeline's Gabriel and championed the people of Acadia.

> *Neither locks had they on their doors, nor bars on their windows;*

147

But their dwellings were open as day and the hearts of the owners...

In the spirit of Acadia, Betty Sue and I took in Agnes, daughter though she was of the disfigured, repugnant man in the black truck. We were determined that in Aldrich as in Acadia, "the richest was poor, and the poorest lived in abundance." That was a line that Agnes, a poor girl from the country, might well have clung to, a line to remember and fall back on, a line to recite if only to oneself. Soon after we finished "Evangeline," however, our new friend, without explanation, dropped out of school.

"There is a great deal to do on a farm," Miss Bauer said, "but we will all miss Agnes." Those were the final words granted Agnes.

We pictured her milking the cows, slopping the pigs, gathering the eggs in her baggy threadbare dress.

Later that year, we saw her at church, sitting alone on a back row. After the service we clamored back to the last pew.

"Hi, Agnes. How ARE you?"

She said nothing so we did the talking for her, the way we had at school.

"We miss you, don't we, Janet?"

"We sure do. Everyone does."

"You should come back to school and pay us a visit."

"Carnival is right around the corner."

"Yes. Come to Carnival!"

But she wouldn't speak. Instead she stood up to leave. It was impossible to think she could just walk away. What about *Evangeline*? I wanted to ask. What about Acadia where all are one?

As Agnes began to exit the pew, Betty Sue said, "Would you like to come with us to Sunday School?"

"The teacher has a flannel graph story!" I said. "Her name is Charlene and she..."

148

And then without looking up, in a clipped murmur, she said, "My father'll be pickin' me up," and she walked out of the pew, down the aisle, and out the back door of the church.

Her denial of our bond made me feel weak. I couldn't believe our special tie could so easily be broken or worse that it had not existed. How could a friend simply walk down the aisle and out the door? It was a form of death, a divorce I could not accept, just as I could not accept the breaking of my parents' union.

As Agnes was leaving the church, Charlene appeared, urging us to come along to Sunday School. We were late, she said, but her real motive, I have since thought, was to draw us away from Agnes. Some time later we learned what the adults had known all along. Agnes had given birth to a child by her maimed father. After that, when we saw her alone on the back pew, we didn't approach her. Agnes came and left church, most every Sunday, without speaking and without being solicited.

Even now I have difficulty understanding Agnes—her silence, her self-persecution, if that's what it was. Many years after the fact, I asked Betty Sue if we were remiss in our treatment of her, and she thought not.

"She didn't WANT us to make an overture."

"She didn't want us to think she wanted us to, but she did."

"I'm not so sure."

"Then why did she come to church? Wasn't it to see if we or someone would talk to her?"

"It could have been for penance. She thought of herself as tainted."

"But she'd done nothing wrong."

"But she didn't know that; she couldn't let herself realize that."

"Why not?"

"The child."

"You mean she might have been capable of realizing her own innocence, if there'd been no child?"

"Yes. You might take on the guilt to make sure it isn't passed on to the child."

"Oh, Betty Sue, I love you for being so complicated."

I meant it. The great thing about Betty Sue was that she could delve where others of her religious conviction dared not.

"That's where Christ comes in," she added, just as I thought our quandary had come to rest.

"Oh?"

"Christ relieves you of the burden of guilt."

"Whether you deserve to feel guilty or not?"

"Oh yes."

Christ always hovered in Betty Sue's thinking, but never seemed to prevent it, never intervened with a hard-line agenda. I asked her if she knew whatever happened to Agnes' child.

"I don't know. I don't know if it was a boy or a girl."

"Maybe her mother raised it as her own."

"Probably."

"I still wish we had tried again... to befriend Agnes."

"Me, too."

"But you know what I think?"

"What?"

"I think our folks wouldn't have let us."

"Maybe not."

"She was 'common.' That's what they all said. I heard them say it. They didn't want us around her. Charlene steered us away from her. They all shunned her, and we were expected to do the same."

Betty Sue didn't reply. She wasn't willing to place blame, especially not after the fact.

I kept pressing the matter. "They didn't like Ray either. They didn't want me around him. Aldrich was no Acadia."

I wanted her to admit to the past biases against the innocent and the poor, but Betty Sue just tilted her head and pressed her lips together in sympathy. That was Betty Sue.

***

She was surely our teacher's favorite. Not that Lila Bauer ever showed bias. Lila was stern, reserved, and preeminently fair. She had ways of observing and developing her students' talents with few words, softly spoken. She saved her voice for rows one through six. Seventh graders received their assignments quietly and carried them out independently. She walked down our aisle, thin and unobtrusive, pausing to inspect our writing and walking on. Sometimes she stooped to ask a question or make a remark, her fine white hair falling forward, a sign of her attentiveness, which was methodical and unbiased.

Only in music class was I ever able to read her preference. One day as everyone was singing our morning song, she looped through the rows, stopping and leaning down at each desk, ear bent to listen.

"I'd like to hear the song again," she said when we finished it, the first time and the second and the third.

"We're all in our places with bright shiny faces," we sang, as she tilted her head toward each of us. "Oh this is the way," we sang up the scale, "to start a good day," and came back down.

She knew in a moment who among us, youngest to oldest, could hit the notes of the elementary song, but her face was expressionless, her pale eyes unmoved. By the time she got to Row Seven, however, I had detected a telling irregularity. The longer she listened, I was certain, the better the singing she heard. When she came to my desk, sitting upright and looking straight ahead, pretending she wasn't bent over me with her ear cocked, I sang out the words, hitting every note. And she listened and listened. So far, with the possible exception of one little third-grade girl, I was sure I was the best. When she stooped beside Betty Sue, however, she didn't raise her head for what seemed forever. But for that, I would never have known her preference of Betty Sue's singing over mine.

As the weather cooled singing class took place in the gymnasium that took up one half of the building. Music was Lila

Bauer's means of bringing us together, first grade through seventh. Twice a week she moved the class to the gym, lined us up on stage, and took her seat at the piano on the gym floor. We learned every song in our songbook: "My home's in Montana. I wear a bandana," "Home, home on the range," "From this valley, they say you are leaving." Most of them had a Western slant and a male point of view. But there was "Sweet Betsy from Pike," which Lila Bauer said should be dramatized.

For the fall carnival, I played Betsy, and the boy who rode his horse to school played my "lover" Ike. Together the couple travels west from Missouri. After great hardship crossing the Plains, during which Betsy gets drunk, fends off the advances of Brigham Young, and dances with another man, the two marry. But soon thereafter Ike gets jealous and divorces Betsy. I told Lila Bauer that the waltz clog went with the song and she incorporated a tap dance into one scene. The play closed with Betsy's retort to Ike: "Goodbye you big lummox. I'm glad you backed out!" which I sang out as loudly as I could. The audience laughed and clapped, but when I took my bow, a voice from the back of the gym shouted out "Betsy from Pike was a floozy!"

It was Percy. After my performance I worried that he had the power to brand me publicly based upon some special insight, some knowledge of my innate inferiority to which others were blind. If I had dared to talk about it, GranRose would have said, "There's a Percy in every bunch," or "Sweet Betsy wouldn't let him bother HER," but instead I harbored that silly, painful fear. Otherwise, Aldrich School was pretty perfect.

Chapter 19

When Betty Sue and I finished our work early, we helped the younger ones with reading, or we were allowed to work on some project in one of the empty classrooms that used to be occupied by the older students who now went to Fair Play High School. We talked about what it would be like if the older kids were still there, but we never discussed the ominous future of the school or of Aldrich.

I never told her or anyone else of my vision of the flooding of Aldrich. In a way I was ashamed. It made me complicit in the extinction of the town, as if I had wished it. But surely, I wasn't the only one whose fear and dread triggered images of a deluge. There must have been many troubled by similar imaginings. How could such a threat escape any of those who would be affected, especially the most defenseless?

What did Ray think when they talked about how all the places near the river would be the first to flood? What would happen to his boxcar house? Where would his mother and all of his brothers and sisters go? Those thoughts surely troubled him throughout that October and November as the Corps of Engineers pressed forward, churning up everyone in town.

Each day when we got out of school, Eudorrie would be waiting for Ray. If I came out before him, she would let me pet her. The day before Thanksgiving, Lila Bauer asked Ray to stay behind. When I came out the door, behind all the rest of the students, Eudorrie was sitting on the front walk watching for Ray.

"Hi, Eudorrie," I said. She wagged her tail and looked at me, her dark eyes, liquid and glinting. "You're a good girl, aren't you?" I said, stroking her head. "What have you been doing all day?" When Ray appeared, she bolted toward him. He came down the school steps carrying a bulging feedsack and wearing shoes for

153

the first time. The shoes were too big, like a clown's, but he was smiling.

"What's in that feedsack?" I asked.

"I don't know. It's for my mother."

He was spirited, not his usual quiet self.

We walked together as far as the Christian Church where I always turned and headed for the store and he and Eudorrie went their own way, but that day Eudorrie dashed unexpectedly into the field behind the church.

"Eudorrie!" Ray called out. "She's chasing a squirrel or a rabbit."

He set down the sack, which sunk on the walk.

"Is it heavy?"

"Nah."

"Let's see in it."

Ray untied the opening, and we pulled out the items: a homemade child's dress with ruffled sleeves, a faded pinafore, baby's shoes and socks, two pairs of mittens, a woman's black wool coat, nubbed and frayed. Ray wasn't the least bit disappointed by the used, female clothing.

I said, "Your mother will be glad to get these."

"Do you like them?" he asked.

"Yeah," I said, which pleased him so I added, "I like them, a lot."

Ray held the sack open as I folded each item and placed each back in the sack.

"Eudorrie!" Ray called out, and this time the dog surfaced, bounding through the orange and red leaves on the lawn of the church.

"Happy Turkey Day," Ray said, smiling, picking up the sack, glad to be going home.

"Happy Turkey Day," I replied, "to you, too, Eudorrie." I smoothed the blond, flecked fur on her head.

"You know what you are, Janet Stephens?" Ray said. His question was abrupt and uncharacteristic. I thought he must be cracking a joke

"What am I?" I said, setting up the punchline.

But instead of a joke he lowered his eyes and said, "You're the berries."

He swung the sack around over his shoulder, and began walking and then almost skipping in the opposite direction. It was about as nice a compliment as I had ever been paid. I watched him hurrying for home in his clumsy shoes with his prized bundle and thought of the crayon I had sent Mom—a turkey with yellow, brown, and orange feathers splayed—and wished instead of the card, I were on my way to see her with a sack of valuables, things that I could provide my mother with that would change our lives for the better.

***

I can't recall when or from whom I next heard of Ray. Unbearable news, I have been known to block out. A child can only tolerate portions of the truth. But I remember the day before Thanksgiving whenever it rolls around, because that was the last time I ever saw Ray.

The day after Thanksgiving a terrible rumor began to circulate. It came first through the shared phone lines and spread to the stores downtown. From the businesses, it spread to every family and then to the children, the ones who only knew Ray as one of the Parsons brood, and the ones who knew him from school, who like me didn't really know him, didn't really call him a playmate or exactly a friend, but who sat in the classroom of which he was a part. What they said was this: Ray had fallen in the well behind the Christian Church and drowned. Some said that Ray stumbled and fell and Eudorrie jumped in to save him but drowned him instead. Others said that Eudorrie chased a rabbit into the well and that Ray jumped in to save Eudorrie, who drowned him. What we learned for sure was that we could never know what had happened. We could only know this: Ray died and Eudorrie survived.

A childhood reckoning, which is both baffling and crushing, is also indelible. My recollection of Ray's death comes to me in vivid, elliptical fragments of the aftermath. I remember his mother in the black wool coat below the altar of the Aldrich Methodist Church, flinging herself across his body and refusing to let go until the elders pulled her away. I remember the pallbearers, four boys no bigger than Ray himself, carrying the small wooden casket through the cemetery on a bleak winter day at The Ridge. And I remember Eudorrie. For weeks after school restarted, she would be outside waiting for Ray when school let out, and when all of the kids had left the schoolyard, she would wait and whine and bark.

***

During the weeks of December, after Ray died, I walked every afternoon after school to the store. It was a lonely, dismal fifteen-minute trudge that I dreaded. At the beginning, when Eudorrie was waiting for Ray, I would pet her but she wouldn't walk with me, and I would have to tug myself away from her, yearning like my mother before me, to be delivered from Aldrich. When I got to the store, I sat by the stove where it was warm and did my homework on my lap.

I spent the dreary winter afternoons with Uncle Pat while GranRose was attending meetings and going from house to house to get signatures on a petition. Uncle Pat was a good tutor, especially when it came to Latin, which he had taught for several years before my grandfather talked him into becoming a businessman. Because of him, I never made less than an A in Solomon Sharp's class. He drilled me on the cases and the tenses, and I could recite the ablative absolute in my sleep. I brought all of my graded papers for him to see so that he would say, "Hmm.

Pretty good," and walk away crowing under his breath, "a scholar in the making." Latin became my escape. Uncle Pat knew the famous Latin quotes, which he translated for me, including the one about fate, which my mother had touted.

His take on fate was less dreary than Seneca's. "Well, you can't change the fiddle you're given, but you can choose the tune you play," Uncle Pat said, optimistically. I, the "Fiddle," had been told to change my tune more than once, and I knew it wasn't easy, but if Uncle Pat was right, and I had the power to change my tune, that seemed to mean I could change my fortune, too. "Applying the bow," he said was the important thing. I didn't fully understand his philosophical position, but in the wake of Ray's death, his attentions made the long afternoons sufferable. He was interested in all my school subjects—math, English, and history. Between customers, he would ask me if I was still "applying the bow." During that dreary winter, homework became its own reward. From Uncle Pat, I learned the value of study as a distraction from woe.

When he saw the mail hack go by, he would exclaim, "*Hermes adest!*" That was my cue to go pick up the mail. Often I would receive one of my father's one-page letters. They were printed, and the letters were large enough for a first grader to make out.

"What's your Dad have to say?" he would ask, and I would read aloud the few sentences my father had written.

The first letter I received in December, I can recite. It said in enormous black letters, "Guess what, Pal. I have gotten leave. I am coming to Aldrich for Christmas, and I have a big surprise for you!"

I raced from the post office to the store waving my letter. "Uncle Pat, Uncle Pat!"

When I came in the back door, GranRose was standing beside the stove in her best, warmest coat, which my uncle had sent her from Germany. It was black wool with a fur lining and a fur-lined hood, an elegant, smart coat that Mom said was "way too

157

good for Aldrich." She wore it to church or funerals or meetings to decide the fate of the school. Probably, she had just come back from Bolivar; probably, she was trying to warm up because the heater in the Pontiac was on the blink. All I remember is her standing there in the coat with the hood still up looking formidable.

"GranRose! Daddy is coming for Christmas!" I handed her the letter as proof.

"Well isn't that a nice surprise," she said. "Did you hear that, Pat? George is coming for Christmas."

I embraced her, never once considering how my news might inconvenience her or how she was coping with school board politics, which were surely vicious.

"My father is coming all the way from the Philippines to see me," I said to Uncle Pat as he emerged from Hardware.

"Did you say your father's coming?" he asked, knowing very well what I had said.

"He's coming for Christmas! And he has a big surprise for me."

"Father is coming for Christmas…" Uncle Pat said and added, *"Pater Christmas venit."*

"Pater Christmas venit!" I shouted.

Chapter 20

When I told Mom that Daddy was coming to Aldrich, she wanted to know when he was leaving, and after I said Christmas morning, she said she would arrive later that same day "for a week or so." But I wanted her to come sooner. I wanted her to see Daddy, so I ignored her. The idea that I could get the two of them together I couldn't get out of my head. At first, it was a longing and after a while, it somehow morphed into an expectation. I awaited Christmas with the excitement and obsession Santa Claus had once evoked. Now Mom and Daddy had replaced Santa. Just as I had once believed in him, I now believed in them, in the possibility of them, us, together again.

A few days before Christmas Uncle Pat and I met Daddy at the gas station in Fair Play. I hadn't seen him for six months. When he stepped off the bus he was bigger, more handsome, and stronger. If my mother had been there, she would have had to fall in love with him all over again. The moment the bus door gasped and Daddy appeared in his uniform with his duffel bag, she would have had to take stock. I was sure of it. I was obsessed by the thought of it.

On the way to Aldrich, I sat between Daddy and Uncle Pat, happily ensconced in their easy conversation. They talked about the Philippines, baseball, quail hunting, my Latin studies, my performance as Betsy at the school carnival, whether or not we would have a white Christmas. Daddy's plan was to spend a few days in Aldrich and then leave to visit his parents in Oklahoma. My plan was to keep him there until Mom arrived on Christmas Day. I pictured the three of us sitting in the lambent glow of a Christmas tree, singing and bantering.

Two days before Christmas the predicted snowstorm came through Aldrich, snowing lightly at first and rapidly developing into a driving blizzard. The morning after, the yard and

159

the road were soft white and every branch and twig of every tree and bush glistened. I had never seen unbroken, twinkling white like that. I went out on the front porch into the cold, bright air in my pajamas. Daddy had shoveled the front sidewalk and was now bent over at the end of the walk under the hood of the Pontiac.

"Hey, Daddy!" My breath misted. "Merry pre-Christmas!"

He waved a hand at me from under the hood. I wanted to run down the walk through the trough of snow and look with him under the hood, but the phone rang two shorts and a long inside the house, and it was Mom.

"Wait till you see Daddy! He's so handsome 'every woman in Aldrich has her eye out for him,'" I said into the phone, quoting Miss Sunbonnet

"I told you. I can't make it any sooner. I'm moving heaven and earth just to get there Christmas afternoon."

While I absorbed the blow, she talked on about how she'd won the confidence of the doctors she worked for and become "a person of importance that patients and nurses alike had to listen to." She went on about the doctor who had first hired her and "seen to her promotion." He was "going through an awful divorce," and his wife, who was "big as a house," was "taking him to the cleaners." As my hope shrank, a fear arose that she might be "seeing" the doctor. She told me that he and others from the office went to a show at a big casino and that there was a "gorgeous babe" in the chorus who looked like the grown-up me and carried a fan "as big as a horse." She said there was a different show at every casino and you never got bored. Before we hung up, she said she had a surprise for me, but she didn't want "to lay me among the sweet peas," not just yet. I tried to get out of her the nature of the surprise.

"Give me a hint."

"Nope. No hints, kiddo. You'll just have to gut it out until Christmas."

"Well, is it something to wear?"

160

I was trying to get her to rule out the usual kinds of presents. It was a game we had played since I was four years old.

"I told you. NO hints."

"Well, how big is it?" I was thinking of Daddy's promised "big" surprise.

"You can't worm it out of me."

"Daddy has a BIG surprise for me."

"Is that right? Well, I'll bet it isn't as big as my surprise."

Bingo. Mom had bitten. "How big is yours?"

She began to laugh. "You're a clever little skunk."

"As big as a horse?"

"No!"

"No?"

"No."

"Bigger?"

"What do you mean?"

"I m-e-a-n," I said, stretching out the word, "Is it as big as a...HOUSE?"

"Stop! That's it. We're not playing this game." She was serious. Her reversal was too sudden, too final. I had unwittingly guessed the surprise.

"It's a HOUSE?"

"I said STOP."

She was mad at me now, and that's how I knew I had guessed right. She was getting a house. The only thing I didn't know was when I was going to join her, but if it was a Christmas surprise, as she said, I had every reason to believe that I would be leaving with my mother for Las Vegas in a matter of weeks.

Now I was confused. I wanted my parents to reunite more than anything. For weeks I had nursed the idea. And so, with this news from my mother, which would have elated me just days ago, I was hesitant and torn. But as I considered the wonders of Vegas—the musicals, the lights, the dancing girls with their fans who looked like me—I wanted to know more. I wondered what GranRose knew about the house.

161

While Daddy was outside and I was helping in the kitchen, I tried to find out.

"I guess Mom has gotten a house in Vegas," I said to GranRose.

"If she did, she didn't say anything about it to me." I didn't know if GranRose was keeping Mom's secret or if she really didn't know, but she tried to change the subject: "Your father certainly is handy," she said, but I wasn't to be diverted.

"That means I'll be leaving with Mom after Christmas."

"Well, I haven't heard anything about it." GranRose seemed vague and evasive, which I found suspect. That was just how adults kept their Christmas secrets.

"I guess only Santa knows," I said, thinking she might wink and say something that would confirm my idea, but she just kept right on beating the egg whites for Daddy's angel food cake. I found a paring knife and picked up a large bumpy potato from the colander of washed ones waiting to be peeled.

GranRose's silence had corroborated my suspicion, and as I peeled I began to think that I would soon be leaving Aldrich for Las Vegas. It was not my dream come true, which was the preposterous notion (and occasional conviction) that I would soon be leaving Aldrich with both of my parents for some unknown destination, but it was my next-to-best dream, a temporizing dream to fall back on until my parents came together again. The important thing was that I would be leaving, that I mattered, that I was not to be left behind in Aldrich.

Being stuck in Aldrich was my worst fear. Mom had planted in me the idea that Aldrich was fated, and I believed she was right. The apocalypse was just a matter of time. The dread of being present when the school failed, when the store was torn down, when the houses were removed, and the place went under water preyed on me. The rising water. The vision of it made me woozy. I hated the idea of the slow demise, the dragging out of the inevitable, the endless undulating water. I did everything I could to put it out of my mind, but I was a born worrier. Like my mother, who had once felt she was "buried alive" in Aldrich, I too needed to leave the place behind. Vegas was my escape from Aldrich. But I worried that my mother wouldn't keep her promise to take me there. What if she found some distraction? What if she struck up a relationship with the doctor she was working for? I half expected her to show up with him on Christmas Day.

"Do you think the doctor will come with Mom?" I asked GranRose, picking up another potato.

"The doctor?"

"The one she's working for who's getting taken to the cleaners."

"I think she knows better than to bring a married man with her to Aldrich!" She whispered "married man."

"But what if he's divorced by Christmas?"

"Shhh." She put her forefinger to her lip and then pointed to the dining room. I didn't realize that Daddy had come inside. I hoped he hadn't heard me say "divorce," the word that had given him so much pain.

"I wonder what my 'big surprise' will be from Daddy," I whispered.

"No matter what it is, I want you to act pleased. Sometimes things have to change, and often it's for the better so you just have to go along with it. Let me have the knife, Fiddle." I handed her the paring knife. "Those peelings are half the size of the potatoes." I wondered what GranRose meant by things having to change and having to go along with it. It sounded like fate—not letting it drag you. "You go on now," she said. "Find a good tree, but no bigger than nine feet."

"What did you mean about things changing? HOW are they changing?"

She looked at me. "Don't worry, Fiddle. It never does any good. It will all work out... Now you two take your time. I'm not going into the store until this afternoon so I won't need the car. Put on your leggings and galoshes, and tell your father the saw is in the smokehouse."

When Daddy and I got into the Pontiac, the heater was going full blast. That was the first time the car hadn't been cold that winter. The car was warmer than the house. Daddy was "handy," just as GranRose had said. We headed down the road in the opposite direction from town out into the country. The white covered the fields and the fences, and you wouldn't have known where the road was except for the speckled black weeds along the ditches beside it. The only boundaries were the thickets of fir and cedar and the crescent shaped stretches of willow that grew in the distance beside the branch. Until we got there, I didn't know we had reached Rocky Ford where Betty Sue and I had floated over the flats of slate in the summer. The water was frozen gray white. The car skidded on the ice close to the edge of the culvert bridge.

"I'm glad we didn't slide off into the creek," Daddy said, when we got to the other side.

"Me, too." We laughed to break the tension.

"We might have frozen our nether parts off." For Daddy that was funny.

"Do you know what a snowman asks God for?" I asked.

"What?"

"A good freeze."

"That's not bad, pal!" And then he said, "Old snowmen never die, they just melt away." I didn't fully catch on until years later, but I laughed as if it were one of Mom's ripsnorters.

"There's a place up here by the Kinders' farm where we can walk back into the field." Daddy knew Aldrich and the Kinders from his early days with Mom.

We drove up a hill and turned off onto a stretch of snow lined on either side by barely visible hedgerows. You couldn't see the road at all. After a few minutes, Daddy pulled over and stopped beside a wide metal gate. When he turned off the car and I opened my car door, I realized for the first time how quiet it was outside, how a silence had fallen all around us. Daddy pulled hard on the gate, scraping it open through the snow. As we entered the field, I heard dogs barking in the woods down the road.

164

"They're hunting down there," Daddy said. "We'll go this way over to those trees." He pointed with the saw to a stand of pointed evergreens.

It was hard to walk. My heavy galoshes crunched in the deep snow as we made our way from the gate toward the trees on the other side of the field. From a thicket of snow-covered bushes, came a sudden loud squawking of birds that swooshed up and flew off in a black whirl.

After a while I said, "Those birds scared me."

"Those were quail. We scared THEM."

At the edge of the woods, I saw three firs that looked right to me, but Daddy said they were way too big and I found a smaller, full one that grew straight. "Can I cut it down?"

Daddy handed me the saw, but I couldn't make it move so he got the cut started for me and then let me finish. "Timber," he said as it fell. Then he dragged the tree across the field to the car, put it in the trunk, and tied down the top.

As we drove home, it began to snow and the soft white of the fields changed color like the bluing GranRose swirled into a bucket of starch. By the time we got to Rocky Ford, Daddy was leaning over with both hands on the steering wheel looking for the road through the clacking windshield wipers. This time we made it over the frozen culvert on new fallen snow without sliding.

"If you'd gone any later, you would've been snowed in out there," GranRose said to me, when I came in the door.

We watched Daddy from the living-room window. He lifted the tree out of the trunk, shook the snow off, and hammered two boards on the bottom. The limbs scraped the door jamb as he pulled it into the house. It fit in the corner of the living room by the piano just touching the ceiling. GranRose had found two strings of lights with big pointed bulbs—red, yellow, blue, green. When we clipped them on and plugged them in and the tree lit up, I was pretty sure that this Christmas Eve had more promise than any other.

That night Daddy made a fire in the fireplace, and the three of us sat by the tree and ate angel food cake.

"I guess now is as good a time as any for my surprise," Daddy said. He pulled a little green booklet from his breast pocket and handed it to me.

"What is it?" I said. It looked like the alphabet book I had had in kindergarten.

"Read the front."

"Pass...port."

"Open it," he said.

"That's my school picture!"

"It's your passport photo now." It was like being given a new identity. My fifth grade image ensconced with a seal made me feel more substantial. "I was wondering if maybe you would like to go back with me to the Philippines," Daddy said.

In all of my puzzling over Daddy's "big surprise," I had not once considered the possibility that he would propose taking me to the Philippines. Instead of springing from my chair and embracing him, which is what he probably expected, I was stymied.

"The Philippines?"

"Yep."

I couldn't speak. Finally, GranRose spoke for me.

"When would she be going?"

"In February. With me. On the plane."

"That soon."

"Yes. I'll come up from Oklahoma on the bus, and we'll fly out from Springfield."

The two of them looked at me for a reaction.

"What do you think, pal?"

I didn't know what to say. If my parents were not going to get back together, I had made up my mind in the course of the afternoon that I would be going to Las Vegas where I might become a showgirl and from there, if I got a lucky break, a movie star.

166

"What about the Huks?" I finally asked.

Daddy laughed. "Oh, you don't have to be worried about them. We've got that under control."

"Could... Mom come, too? Just for a while?"

After a strained silence, GranRose said, "Your mother's got her place and her job in Las Vegas now."

I realized then that GranRose DID know about a "place" that Mom had gotten and that she also must have known that Mom was planning on taking me with her after Christmas.

What she said next to me, therefore, came as a shock. "It would be a great opportunity to see the world."

"What about Las Vegas?" I said.

"Well yes, but the Philippines... that's a horse of a different color."

I had never heard that expression but I could tell she wanted me to go with Daddy NOT Mom.

"Mom has always said she wanted to see the world. We planned to do it together..."

"Well now your mother... I don't think she'd be able..." GranRose was faltering.

"There is one thing I should tell you," Daddy said. "It's the really BIG surprise." He leaned forward, his elbows on his knees, and looked directly at me. "What I've been wanting to tell you is that I've met someone, a woman, a very nice woman. Her name is Conchita. I think, I KNOW you'll like her."

It took me a while to take in his big surprise, and I'm not proud of my reaction. On the other hand, wild horses couldn't have held me back.

"Who is this Conchita?" I snapped.

"Now that's no way to talk," GranRose said.

"Some Filipino floozy?" I blurted.

"Janet, that's not a bit like you. Your father has met a nice woman..." I could tell now that my father had confided in GranRose and that they were in league.

167

"How do YOU know?" I countered my grandmother in a hateful snap, of which I am ashamed to this day. "My MOTHER is a nice woman!" I exclaimed to them both. "She's not some floozy!" Then, my voice cracking, I turned to my father and feebly asked, "Are you going to marry her... Conchita?"

"Well, that's what I wanted to tell you, pal. Conchita and I got married... just before I left. She's looking forward to meeting you."

I put my head in my hands and began crying. "But what about Mom? What about Mom?"

I could feel my grandmother and my father together, angling on either side to boost me and keep me in tow.

"It'll be up to you, Fiddle," GranRose said. "You can go with your father or your mother."

"But my mother would be... heartbroken..." I had never used that word before. It sounded odd and frightening.

"Well there's time to think about it, isn't there, George?"

"Sure. There's plenty of time."

***

"Heartbroken." I repeated the word to myself that night, almost wanting it to be so. That I might be capable of breaking my mother's heart horrified me, but it also pleased me, because if it was true, it meant my mother loved me, deeply, maybe as much as she had loved any man. My father's marriage to Conchita and his overture to me to come live with them threatened my belief in my mother's love for me. If she WASN'T heartbroken by the prospect of my departure for Manila, I would be crushed. Without realizing it, Daddy had stirred my deepest fear about Mom.

On Christmas morning he gave me a tiny box from him "and Conchita." It was wrapped in the sheerest red paper and tied with a thin gold piece of twine. Conchita herself had probably wrapped the delicate package. Inside was a ring just my size. It was silver with a silver grape leaf and four tiny blue pearls.

168

"Do you like it?"

I loved it, but I only nodded my approval, "Uh huh." I had gone to bed and risen harboring my bad feelings and was on the brink of rejecting my father's kindness.

"It's beautiful!" GranRose looked at me intently. "Look at those beautiful little pearls."

Daddy produced another little box wrapped in green for GranRose. It was a silver ring with eight tiny pearls.

"Why, George!"

"Conchita picked them out. Grandmother and granddaughter rings she called them."

I didn't want to know what Conchita called them, but I kept quiet because GranRose was hovering. "It never pays to spout off at anybody," I could hear her saying. "If only your mother could have learned that lesson." Not that she ever actually said either one of those things to me. GranRose always chose indirection. But I could hear her just the same.

"Conchita certainly has good taste," GranRose said, prodding me with expectant raised eyebrows, meaning I had to say something nice to my father, who was innocent and guileless, and letting me know that such a moment, an offering on Christmas morning, mustn't be depredated.

"Does Conchita know how to make the flower necklaces?" I managed to utter.

"Oh, yes," he said.

"Thank you, George. I can't think of a nicer gift. Can you, Fiddle?"

I was still wavering, but when GranRose with her raised, trusting brows put me on the spot, I rose and went to my father with a ducked head and hugged him. Then GranRose went to the kitchen and packed a lunch for my father, and we drove him to Fair Play to catch the bus for Oklahoma.

"If you come with me, you'll have to get certain shots," Daddy said in parting.

"In the arm?"

169

"Yes. This is a big decision, pal. I want you to give it your serious consideration. Okay?"

"Okay."

"And you need to get the shots pretty soon."

"We'll attend to it," GranRose said, handing Daddy the lunch she'd packed.

"Maybe you had better get them, too, Rose. Just in case you decide to come along with us."

His overture tickled GranRose. When her laugh was followed by a whee, it was genuine and infectious. It showed how pleased she was by Daddy's invitation, and it made me and Daddy laugh as well. I do think that if circumstances had been different, GranRose and Daddy and I might have made that trip together and had one of those unforgettable times, but maybe I am dreaming. For one thing, there was Mom, who would have been bitter at the very least, and then, of course, there was GranRose's declining health. But I will always remember my father's show of regard.

As the bus pulled away from the Fair Play filling station, we waved at Daddy through the window, pointed to the rings on our fingers, and waved again.

"I'm proud of you, Fiddle," GranRose said as we left the bus stop and headed to Uncle Pat's to wait until Mom's bus arrived.

"What for?"

"You beat up on Satan this morning."

GranRose's praise was rare. She was suspicious of and embarrassed by adulation. Her few words, cloaked in metaphor, made me smile to myself all the way from the station, past the red brick downtown and the snow-covered lawns to Uncle Pat's native -stone house at the end of the main drag.

***

Aunt Pansy greeted us at the door. "Pat's up to something out in the shed. Come on in."

170

Pansy's old mother was sitting in the parlor in a wheelchair with a red-and-white quilt folded over her knees.

"This is Janet, Marge's daughter," GranRose said affectionately to the old woman.

"I remember when you stayed with us the first night you came to Missouri," she said in a ratchety voice. She was alert behind her withered skin, which drooped like thin fabric across her cheeks and then into folds of wrinkles. "I'm so glad you came to visit."

Aunt Pansy served us eggnog while her mother told me the story of what had happened one fateful Christmas Day when she was my age.

"You see those scars?" she held out her hands. Despite the brown, spotted skin and bulbous blue veins I could see the ancient pocked scars. "My little brother Gene was only two years old. He looked like a little angel. Back then the little ones all wore white nightgowns made of muslin. He followed along everywhere we went. If the hill was too steep, I'd put him on my back," she smiled, drifting into the past. "He'd left Mama's bed and started sleepin' with me. You know how a little one can feel like a part of you and when he's not there, somethin' is missing?" I didn't know, but I nodded thinking of Bear De Rowe. "That's how I was with Gene."

The old woman had become animated. I could see how her love for Gene was still alive, how all she had to do was think of those times and the love could rush back, and that was why she told the story. But as she continued, her eyes saddened, and I sensed the inevitability of an unhappy ending.

"On the mild winter mornings," she said, "my sisters and I went down to the creek to do the laundry in a big boiler over a fire, don't you know. Of course, Gene always wanted to go along. On the cold days, I'd put him on my back and throw a quilt over us, and we'd bounce along, Gene all warm with his towhead on my neck, laughing if I skipped and jostled him. When we got to the creek, I'd wrap the quilt around him and set him on the ground,

171

while we got the fire going and sorted the laundry. It was hard work, and sometimes he'd crawl out of the quilt and run around in his muslin gown. Whenever I felt my missing part, I'd look up and check on him.

"But one Christmas morning, maybe because I was excited about Christmas, I don't rightly know, but that day, when my back was turned, Gene ran over by the fire and his gown caught the flames and went up in a blaze." The old woman paused with a look of horror, her scarred hand on her chest. "When I saw it, I ran to him and grabbed him and rolled that little body over and over in the dirt." She leaned forward in the chair, lucid and acute. I could barely stand the pain of her awful Christmas memory. "But by the time I put him out," she said, "it was too late." She sat back in the chair as if to calm her fluttering heart.

"That was the Christmas of 1865," she said in a faraway voice. "It was a terrible time what with the war, but all I remember is Gene." And then, looking directly at me, she said, "You see I was at that age when things come to you clear and stark, like after a storm when it's so white and bright you can never see the same again." She held up her hands and looked at them as if she were startled. "So I remember Gene. Those scars don't go away." Now she folded her hands, putting them away for another time. "I was just about your age, don't you know." She looked at me with sad, loving eyes.

Aunt Pansy handed her mother a handkerchief that had a Christmas tree embroidered on the corner. Uncle Pat had come into the room quietly toward the end of the story. "Janet knows 'Away in a Manger,'" he said to his mother-in-law.

She pressed together the palms of her revived old hands. "Whee doggies!" she said. "Let's hear it!"

I sang all four verses, and together we took turns singing each person's favorite carol until we came to GranRose, whose favorite I did not know. Uncle Pat found the Cokesbury hymnal and taught me "I Heard the Bells on Christmas Day," and over the years the words come to me, "wild and sweet," as they do in the carol, alive with the spirit of that Christmas Day in Fair Play.

Chapter 21

Before we left Uncle Pat's to pick up Mom at the bus station, he gave me an antique that he had found in the shed and refurbished.

"It'll take you from the top of the hill all the way to the railroad crossing," he said, putting a small sled with a red stripe in the trunk of the Pontiac. "As good as new."

"When we get home, I'll go sledding!" I said to GranRose in the car on the way to the bus station.

"It'll be dark by then, Fiddle."

"I can go in the dark."

"You need more snow. Tomorrow it's supposed to snow."

"Can I just try it in the dark? You can drop me off by the hill. I'll walk home."

"You need warm clothes. Wait until tomorrow. The sun is going down."

"It's just behind all those clouds. I can't wait."

"Well, think about something else and see if you can stand it."

I weighed what she said as we waited in the car for the bus.

"GranRose?" I said after a minute.

"Yes, Fiddle."

"I don't think I can stand it."

About that time, the Greyhound came growling over the hill from Bolivar, which made me forget the sled.

Mom got off the bus all bright and cheery with a big suitcase and lots of packages. A man got off behind her with more packages.

"My heart sank to my heels when I saw that man," GranRose later told me.

"My heart leaped to the skies when he got back on the bus!" I replied.

Both of us thought Mom had brought a man with her, but he was just some "nice guy on his way to Humansville" she'd met on the bus who had "insisted on helping with the packages." Later, she noted in passing that he might come over for "a visit," but thankfully, that never materialized.

As we drove to Aldrich, the sky turned a dark blue, and the temperature dropped.

"The heater still works, thank goodness," Mom said from behind the wheel.

"Daddy fixed it!"

"I guess he's still good for something."

"He was good for a lot," GranRose said from the back seat. "He shoveled snow, brought in the coal, fixed the door on my range that's been broken for a year. I don't know what all."

"That's nice to know."

"Daddy and I went out to the Kinder farm to get the tree. I'm the one who sawed it down."

"Well guess what I've got to put under it? All of those packages!"

"Whee doggies!" I threw up my hands.

"You've turned into a regular Missourian. What's that you've got?" Mom pointed to my blue pearl ring.

"Daddy gave it to me! He gave one to GranRose, too. They're grandmother- granddaughter rings."

"Let's see, Mama." From the back seat GranRose put her hand out between us. The veins were as blue as the pearls, the hand beautiful and unscarred.

"Nice. But not as nice as what I got."

I was right about Mom's surprise. She had rented a small house in "a good neighborhood," mostly made up of Mormons who had "some crazy ideas about God and the afterlife," but who "set a good example," never drinking a drop of liquor or coffee or

175

smoking a cigarette. She said GranRose could come and stay as long as she pleased.

"So there. Daddy Shmaddy. Was that all he came up with? The rings? Was that his 'big' surprise?"

"He said maybe I could go to the Philippines."

"What? I can't believe he would come halfway around the world to take you away without so much as a word to ME about it."

"Just a visit," GranRose said.

"In the middle of a school year! What a dope. Your father..."

"I could finish the school year over there."

"Are you kidding me? Mama, I hope you told him how stupid that would be."

"Just a visit..."

"Who would take care of her over there? Did he think about that? George is off his rocker."

"Well, he has help..."

"Help. What? Some houseboy?"

"A girl," I said.

"Oh. Interesting. Some Filipino housegirl. I wonder what's going on there!"

"A woman that he met," GranRose said, "sounds like a perfectly nice... woman."

"They got married," I said.

"WHAT?" Mom almost ran off the road.

I didn't dare show her the passport. During the rest of the drive she sulled up, but after we unloaded the car and got settled in the house, she started in again.

"I worked a long time to get this place for us, and I've looked into the schools. I met your principal, for crap's sake!" She was apoplectic. "Your father might have had the decency to call me. Off on a toot with Miss Carmen Miranda. I'll bet she was all over Mr. Soldier in Uniform twice her own age, a ticket out of ... Manila or wherever she's from."

176

Mom couldn't quit. Even as we exchanged gifts, she kept lighting into Daddy.

"Well, I don't think he meant anything against you." GranRose tried to calm Mom. "He might not have thought about it…"

"He might not have thought about it!" Her mockery of GranRose made me wince. "Any dope could see what SHE's in it for. He's always been such a damn fool."

"Cursing never fixed anything," GranRose said, but Mom couldn't stop.

"Marrying some Filipino girl. There's no fool like an old fool."

At the time, I couldn't take into account the depth of my mother's feelings, but looking back it seems simple. The idea that I might go live with my father threatened her status as my mother, which she had always taken for granted. And in addition to that, she was jealous. She was in a fight with another woman over a man. That was my mother's baseline, and she succumbed to it remorselessly.

"Con-sheet-a, bull-sheet-a…" she said, prompting GranRose to leave the room.

"Your Grandmother is mad at me. Bad joke, I guess," she said. "I shouldn't have said that."

"No. You should've said Con-sheet-a is FULL of bull-sheet-a," which cracked up my mother and alleviated her misery. A joke went a long way with Mom. With her, you could always count on the fine line between gravity and humor.

"So what do you want to do?" Mom shifted to her serious interrogative mode. "Where do you want to go?" She was tense, waiting either to whoop or pounce depending on my response. "Will it be Vegas or Manila… bull shita." She couldn't resist adding the invective.

It took me a minute. I thought about my father, how I had promised him just that morning that I would give his proposal

177

my "serious consideration," and I thought about GranRose's tacit alignment with Daddy. And then I thought about Mom.

"You don't know? I can't believe you don't know..." Mom said. Looking back on Mom's reaction, I can't say if she was potentially heartbroken, but she was definitely flabbergasted. "Are you saying... What are you saying?"

"Vegas," I answered, "I want to go to Vegas, Mom." At the time it simply wasn't possible for me to refuse my mother.

My mother teared up. "That's about the best Christmas present I've ever gotten in my whole life. Come 'ere, kiddo." Then she called out, "Mama, Janet wants to go to Vegas!" She hugged me and said, "You know what that calls for? That calls for suet pudding with hard sauce."

I never told Mom that GranRose thought I should go with Daddy. It would have caused a terrible rift. I wanted to please both of them, which wasn't possible. It hurt me to think that GranRose preferred my father, that in her opinion "my own good" could mean separation from Mom. It seemed like such a mother-daughter betrayal. At the same time, I worried that GranRose was right, that I should take my chance to see the world and that she might think less of me for not doing so, but she never uttered a word of disapproval.

When she brought in the suet pudding, she simply replied, "She'd better not get mixed up with any Mormons." I'll never forget her remark. It was one of those blessed evasions of the truth. It took me off the hook with her. Had she not been distracted by a phone call, perhaps GranRose might have dared to say more. I wonder if she might not have aired a reservation about my decision, but she never sat down with us because of the three short rings of the telephone, which meant that Nola had a call on the line for her. I remember those rings because the three of us were eating the pudding in the living room by the fire with just the Christmas tree lights on when the ominous call from Kansas City came.

"I'll bet that's Ginny!" GranRose said, rising, eager to talk with her oldest child all the way from England.

178

While GranRose was on the phone in the other room, Mom told me about the junior high school and how she'd talked to the principal about getting me in. She said I would switch from class to class, and I wouldn't be stuck in one run-down room with a bunch of little kids any more. She explained to me how I would have a different teacher for every subject and after school I could be in Latin Club.

When GranRose came back from the phone, she was holding a piece of paper that shook in the shadows of the tree-lit room. "Lord, help us." She held out the shaking paper to Mom who was in the middle of telling me that when she got the "moola" I could take dance lessons again. Mom stopped cold.

"What is this?" she asked, taking the paper.

"I don't know what to think."

Mom read aloud my grandmother's frightened scrawl. "The Kansas City... what?" She pointed to the illegible word.

"I have to go to Kansas City as soon as I can, to that address."

"But the City what?"

"The City Morgue. The Kansas City Morgue."

"What for?"

GranRose looked blank. "They have a body."

"Is it Clay?" Mom asked.

"It could be. It may be...They found a body, but they don't know for sure."

"Where? Where did they find it?"

GranRose struggled. She placed one hand on her chest and took a breath. "Under a train." Mom put her fork on her dish and set the dish on the end table. "They want me to look at the items they found... to see if they're his," GranRose said. She walked to the large window in the living room and looked out. It had begun to snow.

"What items?"

"They didn't say."

"They want me up there. The sooner the better."

179

"We can leave first thing in the morning, Mama."

"Did my grandfather die?" I asked.

"We don't know. That's what we have to find out," Mom said. "You can go stay with Betty Sue."

"I want to go with you."

"You can take your sled. You and Betty Sue can go sledding. After this snow I'll bet there'll be a bunch of kids out there."

"Don't leave me here."

"Call her up now and ask to spend tomorrow night."

"How long are you going to be?"

"We'll probably be home tomorrow night, but it'll be real late. Call her up now, kiddo."

GranRose was standing, her back to the window, pale and nebulous in the light of the Christmas tree. I walked to her and put my arms around her.

"I could go with you," I suggested.

"You should stay here." GranRose looked at me just the way she had the night she had fired the shotgun.

"Do you want an aspirin?"

She didn't answer me. She just said, "And don't worry about us. Worrying never did anybody any good. And it never made anybody any better. Go sledding."

GranRose's exhortations didn't prevent me from worrying, back then or since. A worrier is a worrier. But they did teach me that worry is not in itself virtuous, that martyring oneself in the name of it is pointless if not vain, and that it is better, given the opportunity, to go sledding.

*   *   *

The next morning big dry flakes were falling, covering the crust of ice on the road. Mom attached my sled to the rear fender of the Pontiac with a rope she'd found in the trunk.

180

"That ought to hold it," she said, getting in the driver's seat beside GranRose. "Okay, kiddo, here we go."

I lay on my stomach holding the sides of the sled as it skimmed over the road, slowly, thrillingly, faster and faster. Flecks of fresh snow flicked up on my coat and on my face as I sped beside the white yards and fences like a low-flying bird. Hurtling toward the downtown crossroads, through the flurry, I began to see figures in snowsuits and beanies. All the kids in Aldrich were in motion, floating and alighting. I could see them at the top of the hill and gliding down the slope, one or two on a sled and sometimes three. I didn't want the car to stop but when it did and Mom came around and asked "Was it fun?"

I said "Yes," in a daze that made her laugh.

"Okay. Have a good time, kiddo. We'll call you tomorrow sometime." Mom untied the sled and got back in the car.

"Goodbye," I said after she closed the car door, but she was fiddling with the heater or something, and GranRose had her glasses on her head holding an open road map close up.

I watched them turn in the snow in the direction of the bridge. Until I saw the back of the Pontiac headed toward the river, I hadn't thought of the peril they might face going up the hill on the other side. What if they didn't make it to the top? What if the car slid backward down the hill? What if Mom lost control of the car and they went into the icy river?

"Wait," I yelled after them. "Wait!" But the car kept getting smaller until it was a dark speck.

"Janet, Janet, can I ride down the hill with you?" a voice from the opposite direction called as I watched the last speck of the Pontiac subsumed in white.

It was one of the first graders, a little girl I helped in reading at school. Beside her were two boys in red snowsuits smoothing and patting a snowman, and on the long sheet of white behind her the kids on their sleds laughing and shouting to each other as they glided downhill. In the direction of the bridge was all worry and fret; in the other, unalloyed play.

"Okay." I began walking toward the girl.

The kids at the foot of the hill were of all ages. When I got closer, I recognized everyone except the teenagers, who went to high school in Fair Play. Several younger ones called out to me and waved their mittened hands. The snow, which had let up, began again, big soft flakes that got in your eyes, flakes like the paper ones strung across the windows at school.

"Who were you hollering at?" the little girl said, looking up at me.

"My mother and my grandmother."

"How come?"

"I was worried."

"Don't worry," she said, so innocent and earnest.

"Okay," I said, and after the first sled ride, I spent the whole afternoon on the glorious, white hillside without a worry.

Betty Sue came, and we sledded down the crystalline hill, time after time, in the afternoon sun and later amid the blue snow flurries, sometimes letting the littler ones ride, jostling and breathless, along with us.

Chapter 22

GranRose never saw the mangled body of my grandfather at the Kansas City mortuary. She was presented with a pair of glasses, a jacket, and a comb. The missing arm on my grandfather's glasses had been replaced by a piece of string years ago. The glasses at the mortuary had a missing arm but no piece of string. His jacket was brown with a silk lining. The jacket that had been recovered was too torn to be recognizable. The tortoiseshell comb, which GranRose had given my grandfather when they were married, had his initials engraved in tiny letters on a piece of gold inlay. A comb had been found in the inside pocket of the lacerated jacket. It was unmistakably his.

"The minute they showed me the comb... that's when I knew it was your grandfather," GranRose told me. "Had it not been for the comb, we would never have known." Had it not been for the comb, my grandmother would have continued to live with the fear of the last twenty years—that her wayward husband could turn up in the night as he had the night of the gunshot and who knows how many times before that, as he perhaps had the night my mother was conceived.

But at the same time that the comb removed my grandmother's fear, it instilled failure and loss. She never broke down or came close to it that I could see, but of course, I was a kid. What I saw were her slowed gait and her hollowed eyes. She must have reflected upon what Clay had meant to her in the days when she gave him the comb, which he had carried the rest of his life. And their early years together when the town was booming and the store prospered and they were young parents, she had to have thought of those days—the high times before the store floundered, the Kansas City jobs dried up, and my mother, the menopause baby, came along. Despite the fact that there would be no more shameful bumming around, living in a lean-to on the Little Sac, nipping from a pint on the loafers' bench in front of the store, turning up at the house in the middle of the night, staggering and demanding, the death of my grandfather defined the failure of the marriage and the breakdown of the family as never before, and GranRose was overcome.

The body, what remained of my grandfather's mangled body, was shipped to the funeral home in Bolivar, and the graveside service, closed casket, was held at The Ridge. My uncle flew in from Germany, my aunt from England. Mom was elated. She idolized her brother, a war hero, and her accomplished sister, the wife of a colonel. And she hadn't seen either since I was four years old. In their company she flourished, garrulous and exhilarated, tirelessly flitting from one thing to the next, attending to undertaker, preacher, casket, and wake. There may have been those, the propriety sticklers, who were offended by her high spirits given the circumstances, but beneath her apparent heedlessness lay the fact that my mother had lost the parent she was most like, the father who had deserted her as a girl and whom she had unconsciously emulated throughout her life. For all her jokes and wisecracks, on the frigid morning of the funeral, I found her alone and miserable, sitting by the coal stove in the dining room in her navy blue gabardine dress with the pearl buttons. She was applying castor oil to her eyes to take down the swelling.

"Mom! Your eyes!" The lids were puffed up into gruesome narrow slits.

"It doesn't ever pay to cry all night. I can tell you that. This castor oil isn't worth a crap. What I really need is some ice…"

I found the ice pick on the back porch, stepped out the back door onto the cold concrete slab, leaned out under the eaves, and chipped pieces of ice from the top of the rain barrel.

"Thanks, kiddo. Your mother is eternally grateful." She rolled the ice into a towel and held it to her eyes. "I'll bet it was cold out there." She talked to me and to herself blindfolded. "It's a wonder they were able to dig the grave. That ground is harder than

184

a donnick. I hate to think how cold it's going to be out there. Poor Daddy, in the cold, cold grave." I could tell from her moving shoulders she was crying into the towel.

"I'm sorry, Mom."

"I wish I didn't have to go," she mumbled. "I wish I could stay with you right here by this warm stove. We could read the Bible… or maybe play some black jack."

"I'm going with you, Mom."

"Don't be silly." She lowered the towel and looked at me. "There won't be a single other kid out there."

"I don't care."

"It's not for kids. It could have a bad lasting effect. Plus you don't have anything decent to wear."

"I don't want to stay here by myself."

GranRose came into the room, carrying the fur-lined coat my uncle had given her. She had on a black crepe dress that made her face ghostly white except for the rosy veins on her cheeks.

"Let her come if she wants to," she said.

"The car will be jammed. Doc can't get his old clunker started. We have to pick them up."

"She can sit on my lap."

"Well, she can't go looking like that." Mom looked at me, so defeated by the nubby old sweater I wore to school almost every day, I thought she might start crying again.

"I'll have my coat on top, and my new beanie and muffler."

"That'll be fine," GranRose said.

"Well you're gonna have to do something about that rat's nest," Mom said, alluding to my hair.

I brushed my hair in front of the small mirror Mom had tacked to the wall of the back porch where the light poured in and you could see every freckle, bump, and pore. My hair had gotten darker and longer, almost down to my shoulders. Every tangle pulled and hurt and the porch was freezing, but I was determined not to be left behind. I knew that the minute they left, the house

185

would become a tomb, as lonely, moribund, and "lasting" an "effect" as any funeral. So I brushed and brushed until GranRose came out on the back porch and said my hair shone.

"Let me see," Mom said, checking the curls that remained from the Toni. "Okay. Get your coat and muffler."

My aunt, my uncle, Doc, Aunt Grace, Mom, GranRose and I, half on GranRose's lap crammed up against the car door, rode together to the funeral. The ground at The Ridge was brown, the dead short blades of grass poking up through a thin layer of ice. A dim sun came and went from behind the dark rolling clouds as the front moved in.

"It's getting colder by the minute," my aunt said, as the family gathered around the casket beside the freshly dug chunks of orange-brown soil.

"I'm perfectly warm," said GranRose in her black fur-lined coat with the hood up. She and I stood at one end of the casket looking down the silver metal cylinder at the preacher who stood, Bible in hand, fierce and sober, at the opposite end. He had on a black coat and hat and his black bushy eyebrows made a straight line across his forehead.

"I wonder where Pat is," GranRose said, looking nervously at the parking area as more people arrived.

"Late to his own brother's funeral," Mom replied in a jokey way, getting a big laugh simply because people, as I have since observed, will laugh at the corniest remark to ease the solemnity of a funeral. The more the sadness of the occasion set in, the friskier she became. "How do ya like that casket you paid for?" she asked my aunt and uncle in an irreverent, loud voice. "I saved you some moola." Mom was proud of the bargains she had gotten at the funeral home and at the monument company in Bolivar. "They threw in the ornamental handles with the rosettes. That style casket doesn't usually come with those." My aunt and uncle, probably mortified, said nothing. "You know why caskets are so expensive?" she kept on.

"Why?" I asked.

186

"Everybody is dying to get one." I burst out laughing.

"Don't encourage your mother," GranRose whispered, squeezing my hand.

A large circle of people had formed around the family and more people kept coming, many more than anyone had expected. With the exception of me, there were no kids, but everyone else in town, people from the countryside, and from Fair Play came despite the cold. They gathered as near as they could to the family, all bundled in coats and scarves waiting for the preacher to begin.

"We can't start until Unc gets here," Mom insisted. "Where in the devil is he?"

You could see beyond the crowded parked cars, and down the long road that crossed the top of the ridge for several miles. We waited for what seemed forever in the cold wind that had whipped up after the cars had stopped coming.

GranRose said, "We'd better go ahead and begin, Fletch" which was the preacher's name. "Pat must have been held up." She sounded defeated, demoralized.

Fletch held his Bible, the dangling red ribbon marking his place, ready to call us to prayer, but Mom couldn't quit her insistent jabber. It was the only way she knew to survive the moment.

"You know what the man who got fired for being late said?"

"What?" I said, automatically, forgetting myself.

"It was just a matter of time." When no one laughed but me, she briefly shifted to commentary. "It's so unlike Unc to be late."

"Even the Rock of Gibraltar can have a flat tire," I said, piping up in his defense, which made Mom hoot. GranRose elbowed me, grimaced, and put a finger to her lips.

"Look. I can see a car turning off the main road," my aunt, Aunt Ginny, said, stalling the minister. We all looked off beyond the cemetery across the dead stubbled fields to the faraway junction. A tiny car had turned and was moving toward us under the huge, gray-mottled sky. Everyone looked as the car grew larger. It was as if the life of the gathering depended upon the car and what it could deliver.

As the coned headlights and the hump of the Chevy hood took form, someone said, "That's Pat, by golly!"

"Is it?" I asked GranRose because the crowd had closed in, blocking my view.

"Yes, it is," she said.

"In the nick of time," Mom said as if Uncle Pat's arrival were a winning, last-minute draw.

I began clapping.

From behind me, I recognized Miss Sunbonnet's rasp: "It's Pat and two others!"

"He has Pansy," Aunt Ginny said, "and some man."

"Who could THAT be?" Mom asked, "...the man?"

"I can't make him out from here."

"He has on a uniform!" my mother said, getting a better look at the unidentified man. You could practically feel the swoon in her voice.

"Every woman in Aldrich will have her eye on HIM!" Miss Sunbonnet said with a nod of her black bonnet.

The crowd had parted, making an aisle for the three to get through. People were murmuring greetings to Uncle Pat, Aunt Pansy, and the other man and shaking hands with them as they made their way up to the casket.

Uncle Pat walked directly to GranRose. "Sorry I'm late, Rose. I had to wait on George's bus."

"Well, I declare," she said. "Look who you brought along."

From behind Uncle Pat, the man in the uniform came into view. It was Daddy. He was so striking, his appearance so sudden and timely, I could only gape. I still think of him at that moment: young and strong, in his brown uniform with the red and gold bars, his hat under one arm, my brave, modest father. He

188

walked over to me, leaned down, and whispered, "Hi, pal," and the preacher began.

Daddy put his arm around me and kept me warm throughout the preaching and praying. I was so happy he was there that I felt no remorse for my dead grandfather. Even as Uncle Pat broke down by the gravesite, the last to leave, I waited in the cold beside my father without a qualm. On the way back to the house, we sat together in the back seat of Uncle Pat's Chevrolet. He didn't ask me about the Philippines—what I had decided—and I didn't say a word. I was just glad he was there, not only for me but for Uncle Pat. They talked about the army, the weather, quail hunting. From time to time, Aunt Pansy looked over the seat and smiled at me, but we didn't speak. We let the men talk all the way back to the house.

I believe everyone at the funeral preceded us there. There were people crowded into every room. One of the men had lit a fire in the fireplace in the living room, another stoked the coal in the furnace in the dining room, and the oven in the kitchen had been turned on, but it was still chilly and people kept on their coats.

As many as could gathered in the dining room. Somehow, when Aunt Ginny asked me to help her set out the food, Daddy and I got separated, and I wound up second in line for food behind Miss Sunbonnet.

"If it weren't for that comb, who knows where your grandfather might've wound up," she said to me, "in the back corner of some graveyard out in Kansas, I spect…"

I was glad when the preacher interrupted to offer thanks. While the prayer labored on, I wondered when and where Mom and Daddy would actually face each other. Maybe they had greeted each other in the kitchen, which was where I expected she might be, or maybe they had gone out on the back porch where they could talk privately about my future, or maybe, just maybe they were in the bedroom kissing. I tried not to think of the latter, of something so impossible and dizzying but my hopes had reared

189

forward despite all logic by the time the preacher said "Amen" and the line began to move.

Mom and Aunt Ginny had put the leaves in the table, but the food barely fit on it. A ham covered in pineapple and cloves, two baked stuffed hens, a platter of fried quail, and a pot of chicken and dumplings lined one side of the table; pressure-cooked green beans, creamed corn, sweet potato souffle, scalloped potatoes, fried apples, tomato aspic, pickled beets, on the other. Squeezed together on either end were biscuits and rolls beside boats of gravy, jars of apricot preserves and red plum jam, and bowls of freshly churned butter. Those were just some of the dishes. I remember them because I helped Aunt Ginny organize them and because she took a photo of me with her Brownie camera standing beside the table and sent it to me, with "a gem and a jewel," written on the back. I remember them because they were standard Aldrich fare, because they represent the abiding sustenance of those days, culminating at my grandfather's wake. And I remember because the ritual seemed like some kind of winter feast, a coming together of the whole community that bore an unknown promise, some hidden flicker that could be counted on.

The dinner line wound out the dining room and into the living room. Miss Sunbonnet took a tiny serving of everything on the table, prattling the whole time, holding up the line. "I'm just glad Clay was buried in hallowed ground. That goes a long way toward entering the kingdom of God, don't think it doesn't," she said in a low wheeze. "Of course, Clay was a known tippler..."

I took a quail drumstick, a biscuit, and a dollop of jam. I carried my plate into the living room looking for Daddy or Uncle Pat, but neither was there so I sat on the carpet in front of the crackling fire and ate unnoticed by the adults all about. I made my way to the kitchen where I found Mom.

She had made coffee and put out the desserts on the kitchen table. You had to make your way through the people standing around the Coldspot to get to the pies and cakes. Someone had opened the door to the upstairs, and there were people sitting on the steps with plates on their laps. I kept wanting to talk to Daddy, but Mom put me to work. There didn't begin to be enough plates or cups or forks, so I wedged myself through the crowd to get the dirty ones in the other rooms to bring them back to Mom to wash.

"Can I take your plate?" I asked Miss Sunbonnet, who handed me her plate absently and kept right on nattering to Betty Miller.

"Some say 'What's a little nip or two?' But you know as well as I do a drunk can't pass through the gates of heaven any easier than a rich man."

"'Judge not, lest ye be judged,'" Betty Miller said. "That's what Christ says."

"Well, that's where me and Christ differ," said Miss Sunbonnet. "There's a time when you have to call a spade a spade."

"That time isn't at his funeral," Betty said.

I carried the plates in and around the people to the kitchen. Oneita had worked her way to a corner by the sink where she dried the dishes, handed them to me, and held forth for the benefit of all within earshot.

"Just once, I'm proud ta say, I beat Clay Dysart at marbles. He give me one o' the blue gray ones that was amongst his best. I still have it somewheres. If'n I can find it, I'll give it to you, Little Rose. Your Grandpa Clay was good at everthing where ya have ta take aim. He was the best quail shot I ever did see. Better'n my own father who was nuthin' ta snort at. Clay balanced them glasses up on his nose, looped the piece of string over one ear, and 'bam!' Got one ever time, by jacks. Daddy let me go along with him and Clay when I was jest a kid. They didn't let you go, Marge. You remember that? You was mad as a wet rooster."

"They didn't let me go because they were afraid you and I would get into a fight!"

"They was probly right."

191

Mom and Oneita laughed, lifting my sense of the past, as if they were repaired, akin in ways that rose above their childhood rivalries.

As the kitchen began to clear out and Oneita lost her audience, she shifted her interest to me. "Little Rose here is about ready for another Toni in my opinion. I thought them curls suited her to a tee."

"They were cute, but we're flying out to Vegas tomorrow."

Mom hadn't said a word to me about leaving the next day. When had she decided that? And what did she mean by "flying out"? I knew she was worried about work, but I didn't see how we could go off and leave GranRose so soon. To make things worse, Daddy came in the kitchen just as she made the remark. The cup in my hand fell into the sink and clinked against a plate. Everything was happening too fast. My parents were face to face for the first time since South Carolina, a moment I had stupidly longed for.

"Good Lord. I think it must be George Stephens," Oneita said when she saw Daddy.

"Is that Oneita Hicks?"

"It's what's left of 'er."

"How are you?"

"Good as you can be and be unemployed."

I was glad Oneita was there because I knew the conversation wouldn't flag. I was racing to think of how I was going to explain to Daddy that I wasn't leaving with him even though GranRose was on his side.

"Don't matter whether it's a wedding or a funeral," Oneita said, stacking the dried dishes, "it's just one hog after another." She talked on about the kitchen problems at the Nifty Café in Bolivar until she heard someone from the other room praising the chicken and dumplings, which she had brought and wanted to take credit for. When she left, the strain was palpable.

192

From the other room, we heard Oneita say, "I don't know if those dumplings are fittin' to be et," which was followed by the storm of praise she was looking for.

Finally, Mom broke the silence. "Hello, George," she said in a formal, clipped voice.

"Marge."

"I heard you tried to make off with my daughter behind my back," she said. It was a searing accusation. I could hardly breathe.

My father didn't respond. Instead he said, "Did I hear that you two are flying to Vegas?"

"I'm not sure," she said, though I think that may have been a lie which she mollified by adding, "There's a good bus route between here and there."

Daddy turned to me. "I guess that means you won't be coming with me then."

I could see he had been counting on me. He looked more than disappointed. He had the kind of forlorn look that coming from a man like Daddy could break your heart. But instead of letting the moment die, for my sake, my father, the soldier, rallied. "Well, maybe some time later…"

After a long, heart-hammering pause, during which I was speechless, Mom spoke up, changing the subject.

"Congratulations on your marriage," she said.

I couldn't tell if she meant it, if she was yielding, but I was so grateful when GranRose appeared that I wanted to hug her. And I would have except that I saw how pale and weak she was, how unsteady on her feet. In her black crepe dress, she moved toward the kitchen chair next to where Daddy was standing, steadied herself with one hand on the curved wooden back, and slowly sat down.

"I'm about played out if you want to know the truth." She leaned over and unlaced one high heel and then the other.

"Go rest, Mama. I'll see everybody out." Most of the people had begun leaving.

"Your brother and sister are taking care of that."

"Well, I can do the cleaning up. You go on and lie down."

"She'll want to soak her dogs first," I said, which provoked laughter though I was perfectly serious.

GranRose said, "I think your father is at peace, Marge."

"I do, too, Mama."

"He failed us. Wasn't like George here...always there when the chips are down." She reached up and patted the sleeve of my father's uniform. I could feel my mother's rising hackles.

"Clay came through some pretty hard times," Daddy said.

"I'm awful glad you were here for us today."

"I have fond memories of Clay."

"You didn't get any fishing in... no quail hunting..."

"Next time," he said, though I'm sure, given my decision to leave Aldrich, he did not believe that there would be a next time. "Goodbye, Rose." Daddy bent down and kissed my grandmother's florid cheek. It was something you didn't see back in those days, before intimate gestures became commonplace. Then he came and took my hand and we walked together out to the front porch and stood in the withering cold dusk while we waited on Uncle Pat and Aunt Pansy.

"Should I give you back the passport?" I asked.

"No. You can keep it, but keep it safe. Don't lose it."

"It's upstairs under my pillow."

"You can use it any time. You never know."

"I'll never lose it."

"That's good, pal."

Uncle Pat and Aunt Pansy came out the front door, and we all crunched across the thin layer of sidewalk snow to the car.

"Write to me," Daddy said. "Then I'll have your Las Vegas address."

"Okay." I was choked up.

"Goodbye, pal."

"Goodbye, Daddy."

"I'll see you after school tomorrow," Uncle Pat said, giving me a pat on the head.

I didn't try to explain to him that I would be gone tomorrow and would not be going to the store. I never thought once about what a hard day he had been through. I never gave him one word of thanks for picking up Daddy, bringing him to the funeral, and putting him back on the bus.

Instead I said, "Don't have a flat tire crossing Coffman Branch," which was just as well, because it made him smile.

Daddy hugged me and got into Uncle Pat's Chevrolet. I watched the tail lights disappear in the freezing gloom. It felt like the lowering of a casket. I must have stayed in the road several minutes after the car was out of sight, because I got so cold the tears froze on my cheeks.

As people were leaving, I could hear Oneita's horse laugh on her way to her car.

"I guess Marge will be around to help out Rose for a few more days," someone said to her.

"Nope. She's flyin' out tomorrow—on a bus." Oneita guffawed. "Ever heard o' that? I guess she flew in on a bus, too!"

I didn't understand why Mom had lied about flying, but I knew Oneita had seen through her fib and was mocking her.

When I went back in the house, GranRose had gone to bed, and my mother and her siblings, drained and beaten, sat in the disheveled chairs that had wound up at one end of the living-room. I sat on the floor in front of the fireplace at the other end of the room, my fingers aching from the cold.

Though my aunt and uncle adored their mother and were eager to have her visit, neither was willing to take her in on a full-time basis.

"I wish Mama could come back to Germany with me… When we get back to the States, maybe then…"

"I was thinking we could make room for her in our quarters for a couple of months in the spring… let me ask Peter."

195

"She could live with us in the house next to all of the Mormons," I said. My suggestion surprised the three, who hadn't noticed me huddled by the dying embers. "Without polygamy they're the very same as we are." I repeated what Betty Sue had told me. "And now that they don't HAVE polygamy…"

Mom interrupted me before I could go on about Mormonism.

"We don't have the room, kiddo. Besides, your grandmother wants to work at the store, part-time, for now. Uncle Pat needs her."

"But you said she shouldn't be alone here in the house."

"Life isn't perfect, kiddo. The most we can do is lighten her burden however we can. You'd better get on upstairs. You need to get everything you plan to take in the giant suitcase and get a good night's sleep. We have a long day ahead."

I went to the attic and put on the striped flannel pajamas Mom had given me for Christmas and her old plaid robe. Mom had hung up my clothes, the ones I hadn't outgrown, on a pole inside a closet enclosed on one side by the steep slant of the roof. The Samsonite was also in the closet, hidden in the deep recess farthest from the closet door. I hadn't seen it in seven months. As I pulled it out, I heard my mother and my aunt cleaning up in the kitchen, my mother's voice, raised and distraught, above the clatter of the dishes. I went down the staircase and listened to my mother breaking down in the aftermath of the day.

"If I don't get back to Vegas, I won't have a job to get back to. Do you know how long I've been stuck up here in Aldrich?" she said in a loud, bitter whisper. "Daddy couldn't even die right. All I can remember of Daddy is his back side on his way out of town," she said, her anger dissolving in self-pity. "He left so many times, one time after another, and now he has left for the last time."

"You've borne the brunt of these last weeks," Aunt Ginny said.

196

"I bore the brunt of the last twenty years! You were long gone, Ginny, when Mama started hiding the shotgun behind the door."

"That's true. I just meant I should have been here to help with the funeral arrange..."

"I just care about Mama!"

"Of course."

"It's not just the school thing. She's taking on the whole dang Army Corps of Engineers."

"You can't expect her to give up on..."

"Oh yes I can. It's a sinking ship. Throw in the chips is what I say."

"Well... maybe..."

"Maybe, my butt. It's a loser's bet, one that could cost her her life. Last month she traipsed all over the county with petitions for every lost cause known to the population of Aldrich, Missouri. No wonder she's exhausted."

"I know."

"Well, I'm not staying behind to watch it."

"No. Of course not."

"Hell, the town OUGHT to be flooded."

"Now, Marge."

"I mean it. There isn't anything here worth fighting for."

"What about the people? Their homes?"

"They'll be paid for them! They can move to Bolivar where they'll all be better off. As far as I'm concerned, they can sink the whole dang place. I'm not going to think about it. Janet and I are getting on that bus tomorrow and the devil take the hindermost."

"We all have to go on with our lives. All we can do is lighten her load. Mama knows that. When she starts slowing down, she'll give up the cause ... maybe in a year or so..."

"If she lasts that long. You heard Doc. The only thing all her kicking and screaming is gonna stop is her heart. Who'll be here when that happens? Who's going to take care of her?"

197

"I would take her if I could…"

"We all have our excuses, don't we, Ginny?"

"She wouldn't come if we begged her anyway."

"For which we are all too thankful, too thankful." There was a long silence before I heard my mother add, "The truth is nobody wants her."

After that there was no more talking. My mother's words gave me a heavy, sinking feeling, as if I were on the sinking ship of Aldrich with GranRose. I sat there slumped on the narrow step until a door downstairs closed and reminded me that my mother and Aunt Ginny, having given my uncle the downstairs bedroom, would soon be coming up to bed. Then, like a drudge, I climbed back up the steps, tripped on the hem of the oversize robe, and returned to Samsonite, open in the middle of the floor, the huge top ready to clamp down on all of my belongings. I was sitting cross-legged in front of the gorged suitcase when Aunt Ginny came up the steps.

"You certainly know how to pack a suitcase," she said, walking over to me. "I've never seen a neater job."

"My friend back in South Carolina showed me how." Thinking of Kay made me miss her. She would have helped me decide what I had to leave behind and told me stories about girls my age who were destitute and sinking but triumphed in the end.

"I talked to your teacher Lila Bauer today," said Aunt Ginny. "You know what she called you?" I thought immediately of Tutti Frutti, which I had chewed in class and for which I had been kept after school. "She called you a gem and a jewel."

"Oh." I had never heard the expression, but I was relieved.

"And Lila knows what she's talking about. A good teacher is a good judge of character." She turned her back to me, stepped out of her dress and underclothes, and pulled a nightgown over her head, all in a few swooping movements. Then she slipped one arm through the sleeve of a robe and then the next, and in a whirl tied the sash with the ease and rapidity that Mom made pie crust or mopped a floor. In ways, she and Mom were alike—both efficient, graceful, quick to laugh—but they were also very different. Aunt Ginny had a steadiness and leniency that made you unafraid.

"I want you to know how much we all appreciate what you did for your grandmother the last few months." What she said went straight to my secret core and made me begin to cry.

"What is it?" Aunt Ginny asked in her gentle, even voice.

Everyone had cried so much that day that tears seemed normal—it was a day for crying—but my answer to her question sprang from some unpredictable, subnormal place.

"I am a burden," I said, confessing my buried fear.

"Why, Janet, that isn't so."

"Until I came, GranRose was fine."

"You didn't cause her health problem. High blood pressure runs in the family. That was always coming. There was no stopping it."

I wiped the tears with the long flannel sleeve of the robe. "Was it inevitable?"

"Yes," she said, obviously pleased.

"Like fate," I said.

She smiled. "That's right."

"You can't change the fiddle but you can change the tune," I said, trying to apply Uncle Pat's metaphor. "Maybe if I'd changed my tune…"

"If anything, you made your grandmother better. You are one good helper. I saw the way you were coming and going with the dishes today." Some adults know how to solicit a child's feelings. Aunt Ginny was one of them.

"Did GranRose tell you about the night she got out the shotgun?" I asked her.

"Your mother told me."

"That's the only time I ever helped."

"You helped all the time, just by being here, by your presence alone. Your grandmother will miss you something awful.

She'll always remember this time you've been together, and you will, too. You'll have that all your life, Janet, what you did for her. You're not a burden. You're a gem and a jewel." I loved the soft "g" sounds of the phrase. "It's been a long day. We're all exhausted. You can finish packing tomorrow. Come on to bed." She turned down the covers of my bed.

I took off my mother's robe and got in bed. She asked me if I wanted a back tickle, which I did, and she reached under my pajama top and tickled my back until I fell asleep.

Chapter 23

When I woke up the next morning, a gray figure was making a bed in the corner of the attic. The movements were graceful as a swan, the white sheet flaring in the air and softly falling in place on the bed, the swift tucking in, spreading of quilts, and plumping of pillows. I thought it was Aunt Ginny, but when I was fully awake, I realized it was Mom.

"Where's Aunt Ginny?" I asked.

"The Kinders came at 6 AM and took her and your uncle to the airport."

Anyone would think I would've been cried out from the night before, but on waking I was faced with a flood of new reasons to bawl. It was Monday morning, and I was supposed to be going to school. I realized for the first time I hadn't even said goodbye to Betty Sue or Miss Bauer. But worse than that I was mixed up about Daddy. Buried beneath my shame of having hurt and disappointed him was the fear that I wouldn't see him again for a very long time. And then there was the matter of GranRose. Until that morning I had not reckoned with leaving her, aBANdoning her, as I had learned to call such an act. Of all the people in my life, I took her most for granted. In that way, I was just like my mother. And also, like Mom, of all the many reasons I had to weep, I recognized only the most immediate and apparent. So when Mom told me that Aunt Ginny had left, I sat on the bed and burst into tears, and when she asked me why I was crying, I gave her the most superficial of my many reasons.

"Aunt Ginny was so nice."

She walked over to me and raised my chin. "Are you sure that's all?" Her eyes were still swollen.

"It's sad about Grandpa Clay." I thought that was something my mother would want to hear, and I was right.

201

She sat on the bed beside me, her face sagging. "Oh, kiddo, you don't know the half of it." My mother loved her father more than she knew. "We just have to bear it and get on with our lives," she said, wiping each of her puffed eyes with the knuckle of her forefinger.

"Will you be okay, Mom?"

"Of course, I will."

"How will you get your mascara on?" I asked her, dead serious.

She rose and walked to the broken mirror hanging on the beadboard wall of the attic. "It's not going to be easy," she answered, equally serious.

After Mom went downstairs, I finished packing, but the Samsonite wouldn't close. I took out my tap shoes, which were now too small, my feedsack shorts and matching top, which I couldn't wear in the winter, the copy of *The Call of the Wild* that I had found in the attic what seemed like years ago, and Bear de Rowe. Before I closed the Samsonite, I talked to Bear de Rowe about why I had to leave him and explained that he was now in charge of the attic. This he accepted like the panda he was, leaning up against the pillow on my bed, looking lonely but proud. Then perched with both knees on top of the closed suitcase, I was able to clasp the fasteners in place. It was too heavy to pick up, so I slid it across the floor and bumped it down the stairs.

***

On the way to the Fair Play gas station, I sat in the back seat of the Pontiac with the Samsonite. The countryside was sheeted a treacherous blue-white, and the snow on the roads had turned to ice. Even on the level stretch of road out of town, the car would slide and Mom would have to correct it. We were all quietly worrying about the hilly part of the drive, especially the gully where we would have to cross Coffman Branch.

"This road is frozen hard as a donnick," Mom said, casually, trying to pass off the driving hazard we faced. "Where'd you get that hanky, Mama?" GranRose was breathing on her glasses and wiping the lenses.

"Pansy embroidered these for us," she said, putting her glasses on and looking nervously down the road. We were the only car on the road.

"They have a Christmas tree in the corner," I said.

"Cute," Mom replied.

Bill and Kelton Cole passed us on our way in their green truck. "It's Bill and Kelton!" I said, looking out the rear window and raising a forefinger at them.

When Mom skidded again on the ice, I couldn't hold back what we were all thinking: "We have to cross Coffman Branch and go up the hill!"

"We can do it," Mom said, but I wondered if GranRose could "do it" in the other direction on her way back by herself. "If the Cole boys aren't afraid, I'm not afraid," Mom said, resolutely.

"What if we can't do it?" I said.

"We can. You wanna know why?"

"Why?"

"Because I'm going to work tomorrow at 8AM in Las Vegas, Nevada, if it kills me. That's why."

"The roads will be better in a few days," GranRose volunteered.

"We could wait to go when the roads are better," I added.

"We're already running late," GranRose said.

"Will you two stop? The die is cast."

When we got to the top of the downhill slope of the branch, Mom said, "Do you see the Cole brothers stuck down there? We'll just proceed slowly. The hill on the other side isn't anything like as steep as the one at the bridge. No sweat."

As we began to descend, the car slid a little toward the middle of the road, but Mom got it back on track and accelerated so that we would be able to make it up the other side without

203

stalling. I could see all the way to the bottom of the hill. Ice had formed over the branch, and you couldn't tell where the branch began or ended. About halfway down the hill, we slid again, but Mom kept the car from slipping to the shoulder.

"You have to get the knack of this," she said, turning and smiling at me.

Seconds later we hit a sheet of ice and the car planed toward the trees on the side of the road. When Mom turned the wheel, we skidded sideways back to the center of the road and began descending, careening out of control toward the frozen water. As we hit the floor of ice, the car pitched forward, spun, whirring up and around, and then banging down hard and throwing us all forward, it gradually slid backward and stopped. We were turned around in the opposite direction at the bottom of the hill in the middle of the road in the iced-over branch.

"Are you all right, Mama?"

"Do you see my glasses?" GranRose had slammed against the dashboard.

"Are you okay, kiddo?" I had hit the front seat, and the Samsonite had smacked my side.

"I'm okay."

We sat there rattled and mute. Finally, Mom spoke. "Crap." And in another few minutes she sighed and said, "Kee rap," which was followed by more silence, another deep sigh, and the question at hand: "What the crap are we gonna do now?"

"We have to wait until someone comes along," I said, remembering Uncle Pat's words, "to pull us out."

"We could freeze between now and then," Mom said. She tried to start the car but it spluttered and died. "I'm sorry, you guys."

"Pat will be coming along on his way to the store," GranRose said. "It's just a matter of time."

"There goes my job," Mom said, looking at her watch. "The bus leaves in a half hour."

"Don't cry, Mom."

204

"See these eyes?" Her mascara had begun to run. "I cried so much yesterday a few more tears aren't gonna matter. I look like hell."

"Cussing won't bring down the swelling," GranRose said.

Mom was inspecting her eyes in the rearview mirror when she yelped, "Oh, Lord!"

"What is it?" GranRose said, flustered.

"Look there!" Mom turned from the mirror to look out the back window. "It's what's-his-name Cole." I looked out the back window.

"Bill!" It's Bill Cole!"

Bill and Kelton had waited in their truck at the top of the hill to see if we would make it, and Bill was walking toward the car. I heard a shrill, two finger whistle, which must've been Kelton who was still at the top of the hill. Mom rolled down her window.

"Are you guys okay?" Bill called out to Mom.

"We're okay. The car won't start."

"We can take you to Fair Play to the gas station and have them send somebody back here who can get the car out."

"How will we all fit in?"

"Well, we've got a load in back. Two of ya can ride up front, one on the lap of the other."

"We can still make it to catch the bus," Mom said looking at me as if the weight of the world had been removed. She called back to Bill. "Our bus leaves at 8:30."

"I'll stay here and wait. You two go on," GranRose said.

"Are you sure, Mama?"

I saw GranRose's glasses on the floorboard, practically under my feet, and with one foot I pushed them back under the seat. It was an involuntary movement. The tip of my shoe, automatically and irrevocably, moved the glasses out of sight.

"They'll pull you up the hill and get her started up," Bill Cole said.

205

"But how will you drive without glasses?" I asked GranRose.

"If you can't drive or if they can't get her started, they'll take you on home," Bill assured GranRose. "I sure was sorry to hear about your husband. He was quite a fisherman."

It dawned on me that Bill and Kelton had figured out my connection to the man fishing on the river and that it was no longer a secret I had to keep, which somehow made me feel better not only about them but about the Little Sac River itself, a place I no longer had to fear.

"We have two suitcases," Mom said. "Is there room for them?"

"We can probably tie 'em down on top of the load in back. Let's see what we've got."

"Mine is in the trunk."

"Mine is too big," I said, shielding the Samsonite.

"These boys will figure it out," Mom said. "The bus leaves in twenty minutes," she called out to Bill.

"I can't see a thing," GranRose muttered, looking for her glasses. I don't know how the whole glasses thing came to me. I had no strategy. All I can say is… the words came out of me, unthinking and unqualified.

"I'll stay here and look for GranRose's glasses."

"What do you mean?" Mom asked, aghast.

"I'll stay here, Mom. That's better."

"Better?"

"You go on. Don't worry about me." I said, aping GranRose. "I can come later when the weather clears up."

"But you'd have to come alone on the bus."

"I know. I can do it. I've done it."

The trunk slam jarred the car and Bill came walking by my window on the ice with Mom's suitcase.

"Where's the other one?" he asked Mom.

"It looks like only one is going," GranRose said, leaning down to look up at him through Mom's window.

Kelton had walked down the hill. I rolled down my window and leaned out.

"We're stuck," I said.

"It won't start?"

"Nope."

"We've got one rider to Fair Play," Bill said. "You ready?" He opened the door for Mom. "Watch it. Coffman Branch is pretty slippery today." She got out of the car, taking his hand. "We're gonna have to drive fast to get you there."

"Are you sure, kiddo?" Mom asked, looking at me.

"I'll see you next week or so."

"Okay. Take good care of your grandmother."

"She can take care of herself," GranRose said.

"I'll find her glasses."

"Okay, kiddo. If you're sure."

"Have a good trip!" GranRose said.

"Bye, Mom," I said.

"Goodbye, you two. I guess you know you two are the most important people in the world."

"Don't drag it out, Mom." That was what we always said when partings were too emotional.

"Okay," she said, fumbling in her purse. "Here is some moola." She handed me a twenty dollar bill. "For your trip. Don't spend it all on one bus."

I rolled up the window, got up on my knees, and watched out the back window as she and the Cole brothers climbed the hill and tied the suitcase to the top of the load in the back of the truck. Mom turned and waved at me before she got in the truck, and I waved back, though she couldn't have seen me.

After the truck disappeared, I slumped back down in the seat. I didn't know how to feel. The last thing that I had wanted had just happened. I was going to neither the Philippines nor Las Vegas. I was staying in Aldrich.

GranRose turned around and looked back at me and said, "Are you okay, Fiddle?"

207

"I think so."

"It wasn't easy, what you did just now," she said.

"It wasn't?"

"No," she said firmly, which made me feel so much better, as if she thought I had somehow in the last few minutes beat up on Satan.

"I found your glasses." I reached under the seat and handed them over to her.

"Thank the Lord! Not a scratch."

"I'm cold."

"Me, too." GranRose scooted over behind the wheel and rolled up the window. "I think I might try to start the car." She turned the keys in the ignition. The motor scraped and groaned. Then it sputtered, turned over, settled in a purr, and the drone of the heater came on.

"Hallelujah!" I said, clambering over the seat.

"My heavens. If that's not luck, I don't know what is!"

"That's a miracle!"

"At least we won't freeze to death."

"I don't know if we're stuck in ice or not." GranRose shifted, turned the steering wheel in a half circle, slowly let out the clutch as she stepped on the gas, and the car moved forward a few inches.

"We moved!" I said.

"It's not likely that we'll slide going up…"

"Bid'em high, GranRose…"

"We'll stay on this side away from where we slid before."

The sun had come out and the ice was glistening like foil. For a moment the wheels spun but then, miraculously, got traction and we slowly began to move up the hill.

When we made it to the top of the incline, GranRose said, "No longer stuck with Satan in the freezing pit of hell!" We laughed heartily, GranRose's whee turning white in the cold air. "We need to teach you to drive," GranRose said, driving about

208

twenty miles an hour, grateful to be moving along, both hands on the wheel.

By the time we got to the turn into town, Uncle Pat honked from behind and pulled up beside us.

"What's going on?" he called out.

"When you get to the store, call Fair Play to stop the tow truck," GranRose said.

"The tow truck, you say?"

"Call them as soon as you can."

"I'll stop it," he said, and then, looking at me, added, "I'm glad to see you'll be staying on."

I watched Uncle Pat drive ahead down the road and turn at the crossroads into town. "Staying on," he had said, as if it were the natural thing to do, as if he'd half expected it, as if I'd made an A on a Latin test that he'd prepared me for.

"I hope he gets them to stop that tow truck. They'll get to Coffman Branch and there won't be anybody to rescue."

We drove by Ray's boxcar house. I looked at it for the first time since his death. It seemed smaller. There was smoke coming out of the pipe at one end of it.

"I haven't seen Eudorrie since Christmas," I said. "She doesn't come to school anymore." As we neared town, life, where I had left off, began to kick in. "I could go to school."

"That would be the thing to do. Do you have what you need?"

"Today is Latin. Today we begin Caesar!" My copy of Caesar, which Solomon Sharp had lent me, was in the attic. GranRose turned down the road to the school. "I don't have my book."

"They'll understand."

"I can look on with Betty Sue."

"That's right," GranRose said, pulling up in front of the walkway. I got out of the car feeling like I had forgotten something. I stood there in front of the open car door trying to think.

209

"I'll see you at the store this afternoon," GranRose said, urging me on. I still couldn't think of what was missing. "Tell Lila Bauer I needed you this morning. She'll understand."

"Wait," I said.

I crawled back into the car on my knees, kissed GranRose's ruddy cheek, and backed back out. Then I closed the car door and hurried down the shoveled walk and up the steps into Aldrich School.

PART III

Chapter 24

As it turned out, I never did go to Las Vegas from Aldrich. By the time I went there, I was alone on a nearly empty plane out of San Francisco and hadn't seen Mom in years. It was a clear, sunny summer day, and the plane flew smooth as a ribbon, as Mom would say, not the least little bump of air to jostle the Coke the stewardess brought me. "That's a cute shirtwaist dress," she had said setting down the Coke. "I like the matching bow." The tailor who had made the dress cut a swath of the plaid fabric for a bow to tie up my ponytail. I sat forward in the seat looking out the window. I had been used to verdant landscapes, jungles of green, but below me now were brown mountains so bare I could see the pencil lines of roads crossing over and around them. I wondered who would drive on those roads, where they would be going.

It wasn't the first time I had looked down over a mountainous desert. I had flown in the opposite direction in the very same sky en route to the Philippines. That trip seemed like another lifetime, and yet the feelings I had had back then rose up like new, as poignant as ever. Things I hadn't thought of in ages, like Mom waving goodbye to me from the hilltop on the cold winter day of our accident in Coffman Branch, and my shameless lie. Like how I never did go to live with her and how I'd finished the year at Aldrich School, and like my unspoken duplicity with GranRose, who sent me to Doc Lawson for shots, which she said couldn't hurt and which I would need if I ever decided to visit my father. All of those buried memories were unearthed, uninterrupted, as steady as the drone of the engine in the cabin of the plane.

I recalled the phone call from Mom right at the end of the Aldrich school year. She had acquired a new boyfriend, a bartender who had come into the doctor's office with "a swollen lip almost as big as his ego," and who was "hog-wild" about her and had "tons of talent" and might get a gig singing at a bar in Caesar's. And I recalled my long flight with Daddy over these same mountains to the Philippines and how once there, I stayed on. And on.

As I continually defaulted in favor of living with Daddy and Conchita, I had told myself that Mom was not heartbroken. She had married the bartender at one of those chapels in Vegas and made "a go of it." She wrote to me of her "happy marriage" and said "as soon as I returned to the States," she wanted me to come to live with her and Bobby, the bartender, "to complete our family." So here I was, finally headed for Vegas. And for the most part, I was happy about it.

Parting with Daddy and Conchita at the airport in San Francisco had been shaky and tearful. They were traveling to Oklahoma and then to his new station in Kansas, and I was traveling alone for the first time since my bus trip from South Carolina. I was sad on top of being fretful. But once the plane began its approach through sunny, pastel blue skies, on the other side of the Sierras, I forgot my leave-taking and my past worries. In my excitement, I forgot everything but Mom—her easy laughter and irreverence, her optimism and daring, her resilience, her Dysartness. At heart I was a Dysart, too, and I couldn't wait to see her.

***

"Hey, kiddo!" Mom jumped up and down and waved as I descended the stairs at the Las Vegas airport. "Good Lord, look at Miss Ponytail!" She gave me a bear hug that lasted forever and then introduced me to Bobby. He had tan skin and jet black hair slicked back. "Look at her, Bobby. Didn't I tell you?" Bobby

212

shrugged. He was probably embarrassed. I know I was. "Look at that hair! Those shoulders! That waist! She could be a showgirl comin' into town for a job at Caesar's." She stood back and looked at me adoringly and started singing. "A pretty girl is like…"

"Mom, stop."

"Well, it's the truth. Give her two more years and it's the truth. Am I right, Bobby?" He didn't know what to say. "Well, am I?" She nudged him with an elbow.

"Yeah," he said.

"See!" she said to me, vindicated. "All she needs is a little STYLE." Mom started singing "A pretty girl" again, moved her shoulders backward and forward, and slinked in a circle showing off her new toreador pants. "Latest style. Do you like them?"

"They're cute."

"Thirteen bucks! We'll go tomorrow! Look!" she exclaimed, holding up a bucket of dimes. "I just hit a jackpot. You wanna play? Here. Try it." She handed me the bucket and pointed me in the direction of the dime machines. "You're supposed to be of age but nobody will notice."

"I don't know about that," Bobby said. Either his hair was still wet from the shower or he used something on it to make it shine.

"She's good luck, Bobby. We'll stand in front of her where they can't see."

Bobby was blasé and glum.

"Go ahead, kiddo. You put the dime in there." I put in a dime. "Now pull the handle on the side."

An old woman was playing the machine next to mine. I recognized her from the airplane. She had forced her way down the aisle and raced through the concourse to the slots.

"Hey. I was playin' that one, too," she said.

"Oh, too bad," Mom said with a moue. "Old bat," she whispered to me. "Go ahead, kiddo."

213

I pulled the handle and got three bells in a row. Mom let out a whoop. Bobby cracked a smile for the first time. Anyone would say he was a good-looking man.

The "old bat," who had been feeding my machine was outraged. I'd broken and entered her turf and stolen her hard-earned reward.

"She's underage," she barked.

"She pulled the handle for ME," Mom barked back. Then she said to Bobby, bragging on my suitedness to the slots, "She's lucky. It runs in the family!"

"Yeah. Yeah. Let's go, baby," Bobby said to Mom.

"You bet," she said. Mom was on a high. She was so glad to see me, we had won at the slots, and she loved being called baby. "Rake in those dimes, kiddo. We're goin' shopping in the morning."

We got my Samsonite from Baggage, and Bobby carried it to the car.

"You got rocks in this thing?" Bobby addressed me for the first time. Mom laughed wildly as though he had said something clever she hadn't heard a million times.

Outside, the sun was beating down on the parking lot, so hot the asphalt had softened. Beyond the lines of cars were hangars and storage units and after that nothing but treeless, flat desert that shimmered in the heat.

"Here we are," Mom said, arriving at a white Crosley she had gotten "a great deal" on.

Bobby clunked the Samsonite into the small trunk and without speaking took shotgun, rolled down the window, and lit a cigarette. I got into the sweltering back seat. He was so dour and taciturn, the ride was tense.

As we rode along, to make conversation Mom said, "See that house?" She pointed to a crude, unpainted farmhouse in the middle of the desert. It was a long, windowless rectangle that had been added onto, sitting amid rusted machine parts and a car propped on its rims. "That's a plyg house," she said. That was her name for polygamist.

"It's crooked."

"They add on a bedroom with each new wife."

"You'd think they'd get a window."

"Nope. Just a bedroom… to breed in."

When we turned down the street to the house, Mom wanted me to pick out "our house." All I had to do to guess right was to "pick out the prettiest one."

"That one?" I pointed to an odd pink-and-orange house with a yard of crushed rock instead of grass.

"Are you kidding?"

I laughed, and she realized I had been kidding.

"You see, Bobby? I told you ya have to watch this one. Oh Lord, it's so good to have someone around with personality," Mom said, and then she added, "No offense, honey," which Bobby ignored with a grunt.

"THAT one," I said from the back seat, and Mom let up a whoop of approval and pulled into the driveway of a pretty ranch style house flanked with blooming cacti.

"I planted all those cacti myself," Mom said as she made lunch. "Anybody who believes that, stand on your head." She flipped the tortilla in the skillet.

Mom had mastered all the popular Mexican dishes that were Bobby's favorites. The spread included enchiladas, taco salad, quesadilla, and her special salsa. I had never had any of these.

"Dig in," she said.

"Anybody want to join me in a cold beer?" Bobby spoke!

"No thanks, you ole drunk," Mom said.

"So what do you call a drunk, Miss Know-it-all?" he asked.

"Somebody who falls off the stage on the floor in the middle of a song. That's who."

He held up his beer and said dead serious, "I didn't spill my beer, did I?

"Nope," Mom conceded.

"Not a drunk," he said, conclusively. "You girls sure you don't want to join me?"

"It's too early for me," Mom said.

"Too early for me, too, age-wise," I said.

Mom laughed. "Isn't she funny?" She raved on about my long, thick, blond hair and how we might restyle it with a big roll in front. Or I could get a pixie cut, which was the rage.

During the afternoon after a few more beers, Bobby brought out his guitar and began picking and strumming, a desultory this and that.

"Bobby can sing," Mom said, urging him to play something.

"Nah," he said.

"Oh, come on. Please. Say 'please,' Janet. Bobby likes to be implored, don't you, honey." Then she started singing and snapping her fingers. "A goodbye Joe, you gotta go…"

"Do YOU wanna do the singin'?" Bobby barked and put down the guitar.

"Sorry," Mom said, tiptoeing with raised hands and curled fingers in mock fear. She had thought of ways to pass off his brutalities, pretending they didn't humiliate and embarrass her. I half expected him to leave the room, but thankfully he picked up the guitar, strummed a couple of chords, and began singing.

A goodbye Joe, you gotta go, me oh my oh
He gotta go-pole the pirogue down the bayou…

That night after Bobby left half-lit for work, Mom and I were able to be ourselves, but I was too tired to stay up and talk for long and went to bed in the second bedroom, which she called my room and which we were going to fix up to suit me just as soon as she had time to move all the stuff out of the closet. I got a few

216

things out of my suitcase to put in the chest of drawers, but it was full, too. In the top drawer, I found all the letters I had written Mom from the Philippines and a blue velvet purse with a drawstring that was full of old jewelry. I emptied the purse on the bed—a locket, a woman's pocket watch, a brooch, earrings, and in among the jewelry Grandpa Clay's engraved comb. The pieces all came tumbling out onto the bed, the frivolous and fateful mementoes alike, all in a snarl. In among them, caught up in a string of glass beads, I discovered with a bittersweet gasp the blue pearl ring that Daddy had given GranRose.

While I was in the Philippines, I had thought less about what my life had been before. I had made new friends, though none so close as Betty Sue. I had very much liked the school on the base, though no teacher was so stirring as Lila Bauer. And though the news of GranRose's fatal stroke hurt for days, the Philippines, so removed and reference free, softened the blow of death. But now, as I held the blue pearl ring, her demise and also Uncle Pat's, which soon followed, seemed more real and recent, fresh sorrows to be reckoned with. I had saved the photograph Mom sent me of Aunt Ginny standing beside the flower-laden grave at The Ridge. I had nothing of Uncle Pat's funeral in Fair Play, which Mom had not attended. "I couldn't stand the pain of going back to Aldrich after Mama died," she had said in her letter, and I believed her. Does a loving daughter ever fully recover from her mother's death?

* * *

The next morning. while Bobby was sleeping and it was still cool, Mom and I sat on the patio outside the kitchen, drank California orange juice, and looked at the desert. From the back of the house there was nothing to mar the view, not one building or telephone pole.

"If you go that way, you'll wind up in Utah," Mom said. "I thought we might take a road trip. It takes a long time to get to

217

them thar hills." She pointed to a dim line of distant mountains beyond a stretch of iridescent sand. "That's the only drawback. That and the Crosley is so dang cramped and hot."

Mom had taken off a week from work to take me around. "First I wanna go by work, just stop in to show you off and make sure the place hasn't fallen apart without me, and then we'll go by your school to check you in. It's a brand new building, the latest adobe style. After that, we're home free. We can do anything we dang well please."

"What about Bobby?"

"Bobby can take care of himself. He has a friend who picks him up for work and another guy who brings him home."

We went back into the house and crept around not to wake Bobby while we got dressed to leave for the day. I was hoping he would have left for work by the time we got back that afternoon, and he had. I think Mom probably had planned our excursion with that in mind.

It was a full day. We went by the office where I met the doctor who'd been taken to the cleaners and who now had a young nurse girlfriend, and then we drove to my new school, a sprawling, muddled pink building on the desert fringe of the city.

"It's closed," I said as we drove through the empty school parking lot.

"Dang it. Oh well, we'll come back next week and get you registered. Right now we ought to attend to what really counts. Like having a little bit of FUN."

"Let's have fun!" I said.

"You know what? We could go pool-hopping if we had our bathing suits. Oh, my gosh, that would be fun. We'll do it tomorrow. You just go to a casino pool looking like you're a guest. Take a swim. We could check out several of them. Improve our tans."

"I don't have a tan. And I don't have a bathing suit."

"Well, we can fix that, Sis. Let the fun begin!"

We went shopping for toreador pants and a bathing suit for me at a glitzy mall, we took in a matinee—a long chorus line of fans and sequins and near-nudity—using the free tickets Mom had somehow acquired, and we bought groceries at a neon-lit store with rows of glossy red and green produce. The opulence and newness of everything entertained and distracted me as it might any first-time visitor to Las Vegas, but it also unsettled me. It was more spectacle, more fun than I could tolerate. Having just come from overseas, from such natural, modest surroundings, I was slightly sickened by the abundance and vulgarity of the place. When we got home, Mom heated up the leftovers from the day before, and we ate outside on the patio and looked at the desert and the stars, which made me feel much better.

The next morning, when I got up I couldn't decide what to take out of my cram-packed Samsonite. It sat open against the wall across two chairs with nothing "stylish" to offer. My cotton dresses and shorts all seemed out of place, from another world. My new bathing suit was still in the sleek plastic department store bag, wrapped in a piece of white tissue paper. "Catalina" the tag read. I put it on and looked at myself in the full-length mirror Mom had bought especially for my room. I was skinny and flat chested, but I liked the suit and wore it into the living room. Mom was sitting on the couch drinking coffee and reading the newspaper in her robe.

"Hey, look at you," she said. "You make me feel fat as a hog."

"I'm straight up and down."

"Who says?"

"A boy in the Philippines. At the club pool."

"Skinny is good, kiddo. Look at Grace Kelly. Catalina doesn't go on sale this time of year. We got lucky on that suit. A good buy is hard to find. So is a good guy. Remember that. Get yourself some cereal."

While I was in the kitchen, I could hear the shower, which meant that Bobby was up. I poured the milk over the last of the bran flakes, carried the bowl to the coffee table, and sat down by Mom. The phone on the wall in the kitchen began to ring.

"Want me to get it?"

"Nope. Just let it ring."

"This cereal doesn't go snack, popple, and crap," I said.

Mom laughed. The phone kept ringing. "Oh crap." She folded and slapped down the paper and went to answer it just as Bobby, his wet black hair slicked back, entered in a silk bathrobe and sandals.

"Hi," I said. *Good morning* seemed too cordial, too demanding of a response. He made a noncommittal grunt, better than nothing, and walked by me toward Mom, who was holding the phone with the long coil of cord blocking the kitchen doorway. She kissed his cheek and leaned toward the door jamb to let him by.

"Yeah. Okay," Mom said, plonking the receiver back on the hook. "Guess what, you guys," she said, exasperated, talking to both of us from the doorway, "That dumbbell whose temping for me has messed up the appointments, the bank deposits, and the books. I've gotta go in. I won't be that long, I hope. A few hours. Maybe." She paused on her way to the bedroom to get dressed. "We can still go pool-hopping. We'll go in the heat of the day, when it's hottest, okay, kiddo?"

She left the room. I was alone with Bobby. I would be alone with him the whole day. When he came from the kitchen with a mug of coffee, he stopped and looked at me and I realized I had his end of the couch, where he always sat. I stood up.

"Sorry. I've got your seat."

He shrugged and took a drink from the mug. I picked up my bowl, scooted by him to the kitchen, washed and dried the bowl and Mom's dirty cup. On the counter beside the coffee pot were a pint bottle in a brown paper bag and behind it some car keys. I could hear Bobby in the living room shuffling the cards and clacking the deck on the table. When I came out of the kitchen, he was sitting in his seat, flipping the cards up and over with a little snap so that they fell softly face up on the coffee table.

"Know how to play solitaire?" he said.

"No," I said, "Is it fun?"

"It's somethin' to do by yourself." He took a swig of the spiked coffee.

"I guess I'll read my book."

I started to my room, but he kept talking.

"Book, eh."

"Uh huh. I have a summer reading list."

"What're ya readin'?" He talked while he studied the cards, looking for a move.

"Different books." My English teacher had given me several paperbacks as a going-away present.

"Like what?"

"*The Odyssey.*"

"Yep," he said.

I thought he was responding to the poem, but he'd seen a play.

After he had moved part of a card stack from one place to another, he said, "Is it any good?"

I didn't know what to say. "It's a poem, a long one."

Mom came into the room dressed and ready to leave, holding her purse, which looked like a lunch pail.

"I never was much of a reader. I liked cards," Bobby said, ignoring her. "I was a dealer for a while before I got into music. Dealer of CARDS, that is." He glanced up to see if I had caught on. I smiled and his lips curled, bordering on a smirk.

Mom said, "If I may interrupt you two, I can't find the car keys."

"Don't ask ME," Bobby said, returning to solitaire.

"They're not in my purse," she said, holding out the open lunch box purse.

"So?"

"So you must've used the car last night."

"I think they're in the kitchen," I said. I walked past her and Bobby to the kitchen and picked up the keys behind the pint bottle. They were on a ring with a pair of dice that dangled from a chain.

"Here they are," I said, coming out of the kitchen and taking them across the living room to Mom.

"Thank you," Mom said curtly, snatching the keys from me and walking toward the back door.

"See you later," I said weakly, pulled up short.

And then she turned around and said to me, "Are you going to parade around the house in front of my husband in that swimsuit all day?"

She didn't wait for an answer, not that I had one, not that I could have fathomed a response. She walked through the kitchen and out the back door, bristling, without another word.

We never did go pool-hopping. I went to my room, closed the door, and sat on the bed, panicky and trapped. When my heart stopped pounding, I couldn't find any Kleenex, and rather than leave the room, I used the sleeve of my doffed pajama top to wipe my tears and blow my nose. Once I had collected myself, I changed into a worn sundress made of soft Filipino cotton, and put the bathing suit back in the store bag and under the bed.

I sat on the bed and thought about my previous life. In the Philippines I had learned "please" and "thank you" in Tagalog and how to dance between clacking bamboo poles. Daddy took me on rides in a jeep through the jungle that surrounded the base. Conchita and I sat under the trees outside our quarters and made leis of the ginger flowers that fell from the branches above. It seemed impossibly far away.

I got in bed with *Jane Eyre,* which was in the side pocket of Samsonite, half-read, knowing that *The Odyssey,* which had to be studied, could not take my mind off my mother's reprimand. I read the same pages over and again until Jane's trials finally consumed my own and I fell asleep. I spent the whole afternoon in a dead slumber as only a teenager could, up until Mom came

222

banging into the house and lit into Bobby for not having gone to work. I listened to them squabble over the fact that Bobby's ride hadn't shown up and Mom would have to drive him, late, to work.

After they banged out the kitchen door, I ventured out of my room, reassured myself that I was alone, and rushed to the bathroom to pee. From the toilet, I noticed Mom's loose powder and puff on the side of the sink where she'd left them because she had gotten ready for work in a hurry. For some reason they made me cry. It wasn't just Mom. Now I missed my father. I sat on the toilet and had myself a good cry. Next to the powder puff was a box of Kleenex, for which I was thankful. I dabbed my cheeks, went to the kitchen, and poured myself a Coke. It tasted as good as any Coke I'd ever had, even a fountain Coke at the Aldrich café.

I made a sandwich with some bologna I found in the refrigerator. By that time, it was cooling off outside, so I sat on the patio and ate the sandwich and drank the Coke, looking at the desert sun go down behind the blue line of mountains.

If my stay in Las Vegas had ended twenty-four hours earlier, with me and Mom eating Mexican leftovers in the back yard, things might have been very different. Had that been the case, the two of us might have been able to look back on the time as a happy reunion, a sign that we would always, deep down, be at one. But that chance had dimmed as I retreated to my room that day, and sat alone eating my bologna sandwich that night. And then it was eclipsed, at about three or four AM, when Bobby came rip-roaring home and ended any possibility of Mom's salvaging her self-respect, which was key to her sense of permanence with me.

Bobby's debauched argument that morning was threefold: Mom, he said, was "throwing her money to the wind," she had "the morals of an alley cat," and she was "plain as a mud fence." I don't know if Mom's anger over his use of the Crosley had triggered his barrage or if my presence had caused it—maybe I was the wind she was throwing her money at—but it was worse, I'm sure, than Mom was used to. The alley cat she might have been able to laugh off, but the mud fence was especially cruel. And then there was the fact that all of these charges were couched in some other, larger wrongdoing. For all his drunken slur, I am fairly certain Bobby accused my mother of "throwing away" his "baby."

As I lay in bed, I tried to block out the meaning of his words. I drifted in and out for a few more hours, but it wasn't possible to sleep. Finally, after it was light, Mom cracked my door and whispered to me.

"Kiddo? Are you awake?"

"Yes."

"Get up. Get something on and bring your suitcase."

"Are we going some place?"

"Shh. Yes. We have to be quiet about it."

I put on my new toreador pants and blouse, stuffed my slept-in Filipino dress into Samsonite, thought about the bathing suit and decided to leave it under the bed as if by mistake. I remembered the blue pearl ring and took it from the velvet purse, stashed it in the satin suitcase lining, closed the silver clasps, and carried Samsonite from the room, cringing as it bumped up against the hallway wall. Bobby was splayed out face down on the living room couch. I would have to tiptoe by the snoring, passed-out troll. Mom waved me through to the kitchen, and we left by the creaking back door. Samsonite barely fit in the trunk of the Crosley. I closed the top with a gentle thud, Mom turned the ignition, I slowly pulled the car door to with a click, and we escaped down the road into the breaking dawn in the direction of the distant mountains.

"Thank the Lord we're out of there," Mom said.

Like a gang moll, she pulled a roll of bills out of her top and tossed it on the seat between us. I could see the tears trickling down below her sunglasses. "Men are no damn good. Remember that." I handed her a tissue from a packet she had in the glove compartment.

"I'm sorry, Mom."

"Yeah. Me, too."

224

"Are you all right?"

"I am now. Now that you and I are off into the blue." I held the steering wheel while she blew her nose.

"Where are we going?"

"I don't know. Where do you want to go?"

"You mean here in Las Vegas?"

"No. I mean here in these United States." Mom pulled up to a gas station with an adjoining diner that had a big, steaming cup of coffee at the top of a tall sign post. "You and I are about to hit the road, Sis." She reached in front of me, opened the tiny glove compartment, which smacked my knees, and pulled out a map of the United States. "Take your pick," she said, handing me the folded map. She took a few bills from the roll and got out of the car. I studied the map without looking up until the gas attendant had filled the car and Mom had returned from the diner balancing two coffees and clenching some bills between her teeth. She handed me a coffee through the open window and threw the bills on the seat. "So what do you think? Where do you want to go?"

"I'm not sure," I said.

"Well, make up your mind, kiddo. We're free as the breeze."

"Well, I'd kind of like to go…" I hesitated.

"Quit waffling," she said. "I've never seen anybody hem and haw so."

"All right." I knew where I wanted to go but had been afraid to ask. "Missouri," I said. "I want to go to Aldrich."

"You DO realize that most of greater Aldrich has probably been moved by now."

"That's what you said…"

"So it's not gonna be like you remember it."

"I'd like to see it, what's left of it."

"Your wish is my command." Mom turned on the ignition, shifted into gear, and raised her coffee cup to mine. "Missouri it is!" she said, and down the road we went a whizzin' in full free-as-the-breeze mode. Mom had recovered from Bobby, at least for the time being.

She was at her best as we moved through Nevada and into Arizona. She was breaking loose. We were doing as we dang well pleased, devil take the hindermost. But the spree died down as the caffeine wore off and the car heated up.

"It's a long drive," she said, as we sped down the white-hot highway in the blistering sun with the windows open. "We ought to shoot for Tucumcari. If you can hold out until then, they've got a good Mexican restaurant that's cheap right across from the best motel."

"Let's go there, then."

I found two rubber bands in the glove compartment so that we could tie back our hair. The wind blew in our faces all the way to Tucumcari.

"That's it," Mom said, pointing to a bright neon sign in the shape of a sombrero.

"My kingdom for a margarita. That's Shakespeare."

"My kingdom for the horse. I could eat one."

Mom laughed riotously. "What a relief to be with someone who's heard of Shakespeare and actually has a personality."

***

The next morning we slept until check-out time. Mom used the roll of bills to pay for everything—gas, food, tip, the room. Just before she paid for anything she'd sing, "If I've got the money, honey, you've got the time." Then she'd peel off a bill and hand it over to the waitress, the gas station attendant, the motel clerk. She was as carefree as a teenager. If she was worried about the future—about Bobby, or me—she didn't show it. "We'll go honky-tonkin', and we'll have a time."

I don't know if she had won the money that had allowed us our lark, or if she had had the money socked away, hidden from

226

Bobby, or if she had taken it off Bobby after he passed out and felt entitled to a trip on him. However she had come by the money , she was out to spend it. It was free money. We were on a roll. On the way out of Tucumcari, she screeched off the highway and into the parking area of a Western dry-goods store. She bought me a leather jacket with fringe on the sleeves.

"I'm glad I happened to notice this place," she said to the man behind the register. "You need a bigger sign out there. I dang near missed it. There you go," she plunked down three twenties on the counter. "How far is it to Amarillo?" she asked. "I hope they've finished the road through town."

Mom knew all the conditions and stops along the way. The road was her turf, and she was unafraid. For all her misadventures with men, she believed she was innately lucky. No matter if the map didn't show the way. She'd get there "by guess and by gosh." No matter the means of travel—the food, gas, accommodations, or the possible perils along the way—she was confident, in charge. The freedom of the road, however fleeting, arrested all worry, and her aplomb put my worry to rest. I've never known anyone who was any more fun to travel with.

"Nevada may be hot now, but when we get back you'll be able to use that leather jacket," Mom said as we sailed through the desert.

I didn't ask her when that would be, when we would "get back." It was the first reference she had made to the future, but her assumption was clear. She expected me to return with her to Vegas. You might think that we would have been making plans, that we would have been wondering about what was going to happen in six days when Mom's week off from work was up, but you have to understand how drained Mom was, how incapacitated Bobby had left her. In the immediate aftermath, time had been suspended. Figuring out what was next wasn't something she could talk about, not to me anyway. For now, we were on the road. The two of us were bound in an immediate goal which saved us from consideration of the parlous future. Aldrich was our stop-gap. As

227

we drove along, it became more than our destination. It became an act of faith. We were on a pilgrimage that would somehow enable us to endure.

Going back to Aldrich was not something that Mom would have considered had I not been there. Once GranRose died, she thought of herself as having left Aldrich forever. But now with her latest relationship in shambles, a return was something she was capable of undergoing. Life was so bad that looking back was tolerable. And I was there. It was a thing I needed to do and that we could do together, and that she could do for me. So we headed to Aldrich as if the place could deliver us. But a few hours the other side of Amarillo, we began to falter.

"This road goes on forever. We got up too late. We can't make it before dark. What are we doing this for?"

"It was my idea. It was too far to go."

"There's no turning back now."

As we entered Texas, I began to wonder what Missouri would bring, and by the time we reached the border of Oklahoma, the dread of the reality we faced, of Aldrich without GranRose or Uncle Pat, began to weigh on both of us. On the map I found the little Oklahoma town where Daddy and Conchita were visiting my paternal grandparents before they went to Kansas. I was wishing I could be with them.

"That's where Daddy and Conchita are," I said to Mom, putting my finger on the town in the tiniest print. It was the first time I had mentioned them.

"It's a hole. Out in the middle of nowhere Oklahoma. Everybody poor as dirt... So, your father is going to be stationed in Kansas, the flattest place in these United States... I guess they're happy... Your father and she... get along...?"

"Yes."

Conchita was pregnant and Daddy was the happiest I had ever seen him. I was supposed to have phoned them to tell them how "things" were going, but "things" had been too tumultuous to explain. My life with them now seemed remote, and it was obviously not something my mother wanted to know about. After her one question, she never referred to them again, and I understood that neither should I.

By the time we reached Missouri, we had been driving through flat, arid country in oppressive heat for hours.

"This road is wearing me out," Mom said, breaking a long silence.

I was beginning to wonder why I had launched us on a trip that could only lead to emptiness and sorrow. I could tell Mom was depressed, too. When we stopped at a scorching border town to fill up, I almost asked her if she thought we should turn around, but in less than an hour after the desolate gas station, the road began to dip and turn. I began to come out of my funk. There were outcroppings of rock on both sides of us as we cut through the rolling hills to a ridge, and then there were open fields and long descents, and bridges over creeks amid woods of oak and poplar. In a matter of minutes, we were transformed.

"Missouri is so beautiful I can barely stand it," Mom said.

"It's so beautiful I'm gonna cry," I said.

"It's so beautiful, I'm gonna laugh."

We started laughing.

"Oh, we have to stop here!" Mom said.

Mom pulled off the highway at the bottom of a hill and turned down a drive that led to a small park.

"I know we're running late, but you absolutely have to see this." We parked the car beside a wood of maples. In two years I had not seen the dense shade of those trees, the flickering mass of pointed edges. From the parking lot you could hear rushing water. We followed a path into the trees. It led to a wooden footbridge that crossed a swift, brimming stream flowing downhill through thick woods. We stood on the narrow bridge in the din of the gushing water and cooled off in the damp air.

"I thought I was gonna die of the heat," Mom said loudly above the torrent.

229

"We've died and gone to heaven," I shouted back.

A breeze blew a spray up from the river.

"Oh boy. My hair is gonna be limp as a rag."

"Who cares?"

On the other side of the bridge was a stone building that had a huge wooden door, the bygone entryway to the workings of a dam. The building was locked. We were after hours. But a map behind glass showed where we were in the Show-Me state. We followed the path behind the building away from the noisy water to a quiet, placid lake by the dam. We sat on a bench and looked at the ducks and swans.

Though I was afraid of killing the moment, I took advantage of the tranquility to confess.

"I found GranRose's blue pearl ring."

"Oh, yeah?"

"Yeah."

"Does it fit you?"

"Yes… I took it. I brought it with me…"

"Good," she said, absently.

I wanted to put my arm around her, but I was afraid such a gesture would reveal the depths of my gratitude and affection for the ring, which she might resent. I tried to think of a way to change the subject, to pass off the moment casually when I realized that I was over-reading the past, worrying needlessly. Mom was staring at the water, oblivious to the ring.

"There are so many pretty places in Missouri. I don't know why I ever left," she said, The meek last rays of light wavered over the silver lake and turned the reeds along the shore a faint gold. "Remember that. If you're ever down and out, head for good ole' Missouri, sacred ground. The trip was worth it for the sight of that stream. You know what, kiddo? I think I've come to terms with what I'm going to have to do. I'm replenished!"

Mom didn't elaborate on what she was "going to have to do" and I didn't ask, but I was hopeful, secretly praying, that she

230

was leaving Bobby, and I'm ninety percent certain that's what she meant. She was on a high that allowed her to imagine a new life.

As the sun began to set, we drove in the failing light past the white farmhouses, the cows grazing in the fields, and through the little towns of houses with porch railings and swings half hidden in the long shadows of the trees. After the glare and desiccation of Vegas, Mom and I were revived and united by the cool lush lawns, the deep green foliage.

We drove until nightfall before we gave up looking for a place Mom had remembered where we could eat and spend the night.

"I guess it was on the road that went through Arkansas," she said, disappointed in her memory. "What I wouldn't give for a swig of Wild Turkey right now."

"What I wouldn't give for a hamburger and a Grapette." I had longed for a Grapette for three years.

As we entered the outskirts of the next town, Mom said, "We'll be lucky to find anything open after dark in a one-horse town in the Ozarks."

"I could eat the one horse."

We slowed down on the main street looking for a restaurant. "Cafés close down early here in these parts," Mom said as we came to the end of the business district. "Shoot."

"That's the last town for a long time," I said, looking at the map.

"Crap."

The road out of town wound uphill into the dark. When we came around a bend at the top of the hill, we almost passed a native-stone motel with a matching gas station and diner.

"Ha haaa!" Mom said, slamming the brakes and swerving at the last possible moment into the parking lot. "Whew. I knew this place was out here somewhere!"

231

Chapter 25

The lights were on in the café, but the woman inside was closing down.

"I have some soup left and a blackberry pie," she said, without looking up as she wiped the counter. She was young and soft-spoken.

"Great. We'll take some," Mom said, sitting on a stool. The woman sat two frosted glasses of water in front of us. Mom took a big gulp and followed it with a long *aah.* "Good ole Missouri branch water," she said, putting one elbow on the counter and clunking down the water like an empty shot glass. "Better than Wild Turkey."

The woman smiled, too shy to look directly at us. She placed the silverware on the counter.

"After dinner, I'll be ready to plop down."

"We've been driving all day," I said to the woman.

"We'll need a room for the night," Mom said.

The woman walked to the end of the counter and reached up on the wall to a board of hooks with keys. She was wearing a dotted swiss blouse with a drawstring that pulled up and showed a pale pink roll of midriff.

"You can have Number 6," she said. "It has two beds."

"That's a cute peasant blouse you have on," Mom said.

"Thank you," she said modestly as she left for the kitchen.

When she was out of earshot Mom said, "Of course, she'd look about ten times better in it if she didn't have those arms. Did you see?"

"Mom…"

"They were like a couple of loaves of bread."

Nailed on the wall behind the counter was an old Coke sign with a picture of a dark-haired girl holding up a bottle of

Coke. Her arms were thin, her soft, blurred face was smiling and rosy-cheeked.

"You know who that looks like?" Mom asked, holding her glass of water up in the direction of the sign as if she were toasting the image.

"Nobody. She's too perfect."

"Okay. Well, give her a freckle or two and a slightly larger nose."

"You? You used to wear your hair like that, the top tied up and the bottom turned under."

"Bull."

"You did. I remember it from when I was little."

"Well, it's not me. I can't believe you don't see the resemblance."

"GranRose, then. When she was young."

"You're getting warmer."

"I give up."

"Oh, come on. It's YOU, kiddo."

"I have blond hair, Mom, something you've never seemed to notice."

The waitress returned with two bowls of soup, which she placed on the counter.

"Would you like some bread? It's homemade."

"Thank you. I'd love some. Would you, Mom?"

"It's not part of my diet plan, but yeah, bring me some, too, with a big slather of butter, if you don't mind." After she left, Mom carried on with her emphatic observations. "A girl can go a long way with looks like yours."

Mom flattered me as she wished to be flattered. Her adulation had to do almost solely with appearance, her physical summations of me, herself, and the women she encountered based on a savage male perspective. As we headed to the motel room, she lit into the waitress again.

"She has pretty good skin and her features aren't bad, but if she doesn't do something about that weight, she's gonna get stuck in a café waiting on people for the rest of her life."

"She was friendly," I said.

"Anybody with arms as plump as hers shouldn't be allowed to wear a peasant blouse. Thank your lucky stars you got those beautiful thin arms. Do you have a peasant blouse?"

"No."

"Well, they're the rage here in the States. I'll get you one at Delarues. You need to wear them with a tiered skirt, with flounces, not a straight skirt like she had on. That skirt showed every roll of fat."

"She had a good complexion."

"She desperately needed lipstick and some mascara. Nobody that plain can go around without makeup."

"You have to admit she was pleasant," I said.

"Yeah. A-."

Mom did not intend to be mean. She thought she bore a new, wider understanding, a higher grasp of the female plight, something a limited country girl, somebody who had never gotten away, couldn't perceive. Her dictums were delivered out of a mix of pity and disgust. How come that poor, ignorant waitress didn't DO something for herself? At the same time, however, they were a means of achieving superiority, which she assumed ruthlessly.

The next morning Mom and I went back to the café for breakfast and ate in silence. Each of us was privately absorbed by the realities of the new day—the emotional reckoning of what we might face in Aldrich in a few short hours and of the disarray left behind in Vegas. The homemade biscuits and gravy improved us.

Mom left the "pleasant peasant" a big tip to reward her for the "good country cooking." That's what she said afterwards, but the tip was also to impress the others at the counter, especially the "nice-looking older fella" wearing cowboy boots.

"Those were the best biscuits I've had since I left Missouri," she said, dropping a twenty on the counter with affected nonchalance. "Keep the change."

I have to say Mom had an innate sense of a man she might attract and how to go about it. She gave the man a perfect opening.

"We might better try the biscuits," the man said to the older woman he was with. "Hear tell they're pretty good." He looked over at Mom and smiled.

"Were they made with lard?" the old woman said loud enough to be heard in the kitchen.

"Well, I don't know," the man said. He had a deep resonant voice.

"I think they used Crisco," Mom said confidentially to him.

"Where're you gals from?" the man asked, pivoting on the stool, one boot on the floor, the other on the rail.

"We're just a couple of hillbillies from southwest Missouri," Mom said, which made the man grin. "But we've been away for a long time... in Nevada."

"I'm up from Amarillo," he said, "visiting my mother." He indicated the elderly birdlike woman sitting next to him.

"I love the view out there," the old woman said loudly. "It increases your perspective. Always a surprise." She was deaf, but astute.

"Will you be here in town?" the man asked Mom, which had to have given her a rush.

"No. My daughter and I are paying a visit to my mother in Aldrich."

The man's mother leaned forward with her good ear tilted toward us. "Where's that again?"

"Aldrich. It's up above Springfield," Mom shouted.

"Oh yes. We used to have people in the country up that way, not far from Bolivar."

"Oh, really?"

"They're all gone now, of course. Scattered like dust and leaves..."

"Isn't that where the dam is going in?" the man asked. He needed a shave and stroked his chin.

"Yes. At some point..." Mom began, but the deaf woman didn't hear.

"Lake Stockton is what'll be there. It'll take over," she said. "It'll be a big fishing area once they finish moving everything and flood the place."

"Have they already started moving the town?" Mom asked abruptly.

"What's that?" the deaf woman said.

"I didn't know they had already started moving the town," Mom yelled back.

"Oh, my lands, yes. It's an awful hard thing for those people to have to pick up and leave what they've known all their lives. It's taken a terrible toll."

There was a lull and then the man said in his velvet voice, "I hope your mother won't be affected."

After a distracted moment, Mom smiled and said, "Oh, no. She won't be affected..."

***

Before we got on the road, Mom went to the motel office to make a phone call. I packed up our things and loaded the car. I could hear the whirr of a lawnmower behind the motel and smell the cut grass. From the parking area, I noticed for the first time the trellis of roses on one side of the motel, and across the road a stand of slender, peeling poplars. I dawdled by the car, waiting on Mom, and then wandered across the road. On the other side of the poplars, I discovered the view the deaf woman had mentioned—a sweep of fields and woods sloping downhill toward a distant line of hills. The road, white in the morning sun, surfaced in the clearings as it curved down through the valley. I stood

236

looking until the car door slammed. By the time I crossed the road, Mom was backing up, champing to go.

In the car, as we left, she was invigorated. I wondered if the man's attention at the café had given her a boost.

"Nice fella in there attending to his old mother," she said as we sped down the road that curved through the valley.

"Yeah. He was cute for an old guy."

"I couldn't bring myself to say that Mama was gone. You know?"

"I know."

Something had made her decide we were in a hurry, some impulse born perhaps of the phone call or something she'd remembered while we were eating breakfast. Or maybe she just wanted to get it over with—going back to Aldrich. Whatever it was made her speed downhill, taking the bends so fast she had to enter the oncoming lane on every curve. I was glad when we came out onto a straight double-lane highway. Between towns she drove twenty miles over the speed limit, but at least the road was safer.

"Let's go through Walnut Grove," she said on the bypass around Springfield.

"Not through Bolivar?"

"We can go straight to The Ridge."

"It's actually a little faster," I said, studying the map.

"The roads are better, too."

We turned onto smaller and smaller roads until we came to the narrow, winding one that went through Aldrich. Finally, she slowed down, here where we knew our way by heart.

The line of maples along the level stretch beside the old railroad bed and then the contour of the rolling countryside brought a flood of sentiment. The scenery was nothing I had thought about or could have called up, but every dip and turn was a homecoming, a sudden poignant recognition. We passed the little clapboard houses of Walnut Grove with their lilacs and spireas in full bloom, the tall brick edifice and steep steps of the Baptist Church, so close to the road the steeple was invisible from the car. At the sharp turn

237

on the outskirts of town, we passed the big white farmhouse, the barn, the silo, the fields of alfalfa until we came to the red brick gas station and grocery at Eudora, then the country church set back behind pecan trees, and the steep decline down to the farmhouse on one side of a creek, the barn on the other. Each forgotten sight was at once familiar. I knew the hills and hollows, the houses, barns, the creeks, the fencerows of wild roses, the long ditches of daisies and dusty weeds.

As we approached the turn to The Ridge, the air became cooler, and across the meadow the sky darkened above the trees that bordered the cemetery. We turned onto the orange-brown gravel, crunching past cows grazing by a pond and past the doorless, one-room schoolhouse where Uncle Pat had once taught Latin, and which was now filled with hay. There, by the corner of the old school we turned onto the dirt lane, a grass strip down the middle, that led to The Ridge. I could see beside the white church, a field of pink and fuschia, a profusion of blooms so thick that only the tall pointed stones on their high plinths rose above the blanket of flowers.

"Mom, it's pink. Look. The whole cemetery."

"The peonies are in bloom. Thank God for the peonies!" Mom said, as if the huge blooms with their plethora of diaphanous petals could soften the awful loss she was about to relive.

We got out of the car and walked through the pink to GranRose's gravesite where she lay next to Clay. A peony had taken root beside their rose-colored stone and the gorgeous blooms covered part of the inscription. We stood in dumb grief for several minutes.

"It's criminal that she died so young," Mom said. "Sixty-six years old."

She walked a few feet away and sat down on a stone bench under a flagpole. Behind the flag was a line of clouds streaked with blue and black. I had never thought of my mother as old, but as she sat there, under the darkening sky, missing my

238

grandmother, she seemed ancient. I realized it was not possible to comfort her in her single-minded suffering.

I walked to the back corner of the cemetery to the grave that had beguiled and haunted me and Betty Sue. "Unknown man who fell under train, 1934." The lonely words had once expressed the very essence of the mystery of life. Now the fact of the unidentified body lying in the ground before me was unnerving. He was no longer a romantic figure. He was just a young man whose life was taken under the rails and perhaps under the influence of a pint of liquor. The injustice of his early death should've made me feel better about GranRose's, but it didn't. It made me feel worse, because I knew that his fate was eventually mine and hers and everybody else's—that it was a mere matter of time before dear GranRose's grave would not be visited or known by any living person, and that at the heart of all separations lay that truth—that eventually we are all unidentifiable.

The sun went behind the clouds and a jangling wind came up. I heard the clang of the flagpole chain and looked up across the cemetery. Mom was no longer sitting on the bench. I thought she might have gotten back in the car to get out of the wind, but then I saw her over in the old section where my great -grandparents were buried.

"Mom," I called out. "It's going to rain." She waved and started walking back to the car, holding her hair back from the wind. I hurried back between the stones to GranRose's grave, picked one of the peony blooms, and got to the car just as the first big drops splashed on the dusty windshield. Mom was in a trance behind the wheel, looking straight ahead as if she were studying the rain, trying to figure out the pattern of the splotches.

"Mom?" She was too preoccupied to answer me. Finally, she turned her head and looked at me with a helpless, intransigent expression. She was decided about something.

"What is it, Mom?"

"I was going to tell you... I talked to Bobby this morning, on the phone at the motel," she said. The rain started pouring down. The pattern on the windshield disappeared in a myriad of pounding drops. "He's really feeling bad about what happened."

"Oh, Mom, Mom," I said, hoping I could arrest what I knew was to come. "What about...?"

She interrupted me before I could go on. "I promised I'd give him another chance."

I wondered if that was exactly true—if Bobby begged her, as she implied, or if he merely capitulated. At another time I might have protested her obvious decision to go back to him, but I decided to do as GranRose would have done and say nothing, because it would do no good. The wild horses that couldn't stop my mother from doing what she set out to do was my mother herself. Her wild, untamable will was beyond my power to restrain. What I had to figure out was not how to extricate Mom but how to extricate myself. As we sat in the car, the dark folds of the clouds drifted toward Fair Play, the rain began to let up, and Mom, dogged and hopeful, turned the ignition.

We drove from the cemetery across the meadows of the ridge toward town. Before we got to the bridge, we saw bulldozers and trucks where men were working in the first stages of cutting a new road through rock.

"Look at that," Mom said, marveling as we drove past the construction and down the hill toward the iron bridge, but I couldn't think of anything except the nightmare of Bobby and Vegas. "That's amazing," she said, slowing the car to look up the river as we approached the old bridge. "I guess that's where the new bridge will be." She stopped the car between the latticed trusses of the old bridge to get a better look. "Amazing. Cutting through all that rock." Now that she had told me that we were headed back to Bobby, she was talkative and unsentimental. "It'll change the whole dang lay of the land."

You could see a huge gap in the cliff which followed the curve of the river and which had been always been covered in trees. The Little Sac River was rippling and silver in the wind, and the odor of the water and the rain came through the car window.

"What will happen to this bridge?" I asked.

"Oh, they'll have to take this down. All this will be underwater."

"The whole river will disappear," I said, mournfully. "The swimming hole and the fishing spots, Grandpa Clay's lean-to."

"Yep. Including Clay's lean-to. Everything will be underwater, the whole road, right up to town."

"Including town?"

"Including town, eventually. That'll take quite a while. That's what the man and his mother were saying at the café this morning. It could take years. First it'll be a big swamp."

The road into town looked as it always had, but the houses along it, including Ray's boxcar, had already been removed in preparation for the flooding. Along the way you could see the daffodils growing in wet glistening clusters where they had always been, outlining the missing walkways and porches.

We crossed the defunct railroad tracks and the vacant sites of the mill and the Christian Church, but when we turned into town I could see the bell tower of the United Methodist Church with the cross on top and the rows of red brick buildings. There were no people, no cars, no signs of life, just the buildings, empty and forsaken, but still standing. We drove to Dysart Brothers, which was boarded up and locked.

"Let's get out and look around," I said, to get Mom to pull over.

"The devil is beating his wife," she said, because despite the sunshine, it was still sprinkling.

"I don't care. I want to get out."

"I don't know why. There won't be a thing in there, but okay."

She let me out under the canopy at the front of the store. Between the crude wide boards nailed across the openings where the display windows had been, I could see the desolate interior. It

241

had been emptied of every counter and shelf. Only the tin ceiling remained. I stood there listening to the patter of rain on the metal canopy and looking at the silver ceiling inside the barren store trying to think of how I could endure the ride across Oklahoma, Texas, New Mexico, Arizona, and Nevada back to Bobby.

"I wish I could have a square of the ceiling," I said when I got back in the car.

"Oh brother," Mom said.

"Let's drive by the church."

"I hope we're not going to have to drag this out," Mom said, driving around the square toward the church.

The weeds were grown up behind and around the stores, but the lawn of the church was mowed and sparkling green, and the marquee was current.

"Look. There's a service on Sunday!" I said, as if I had made a life-saving discovery.

"The Methodists are indestructible," Mom said, heading toward GranRose's house—where it had been.

Of the houses along the way, Doc Lawson's and three others, which sat on slightly higher ground, had been spared, but once we got to where the sidewalk ended, every house had been removed, and I braced myself for what lay ahead. At the crucial turn, the front yard maples appeared lush and glorious. For a moment, I imagined the porch, the two-story frame, the roofline with the pointed gable, the whole of the house immutable behind the rustling trees, but of course it was missing, and so were the garage, the smokehouse, the chicken coop, the outhouse, the shed with the corrugated tin roof.

Since the rain had stopped, Mom got out of the car with me. The leaves of the trees were glistening, still dropping water.

"Crap," Mom said when a droplet hit her head.

We walked around the ravaged grounds in the pale, yellow light looking at the red and purple hollyhocks that had sprung up, locating the trumpet vine by the missing porch, the grape arbor in the backyard, and the pear tree behind the missing

242

chicken house. The back field was a solid expanse of goldenrod, wet and sparkling, all the way to the railroad track.

"Look," I said to Mom, gasping, pointing across the field, "The school is gone!"

"We've gotta go, kiddo. I've gotta get out of here and get back to Vegas. You know?" Mom had lost patience with retracing the past. She began walking back toward the car.

"Mom, I... I'm not ready to go...," I said, but she kept on walking as if her stubborn stride could pull me away with her.

"We have to make it home in time to get a rest before I have to go to work..."

"I know. But I don't think I can go... at this time."

Now she stopped and turned around in an open space.

"What? What's that supposed to mean? You just wanna wallow in this wreck of a place?" She swung her arms around in the deserted space, a big square of damp earth where the house had been. "I've never seen anybody so hung up on the past."

"I want to see Betty Sue and her mother, and Uncle Pat's grave in Fair Play..."

"Oh, my Lord. If you drag this out all day, we'll never make it to Tucum..."

"Mom, I want to stay on here in Aldrich for a while."

It took everything in me to say those words. We were standing in what I imagined to be GranRose's living room, about where the fireplace was, about where I sat the night after Grandpa Clay's funeral and listened to Mom and her siblings try to decide what to do with their mother.

"I can stay with Betty Sue. I'm always welcome in her home."

Mom was puzzled. I had surprised her. I had thought she might explode, but instead she eyed me, trying to figure out my motive. Before she could deny me, I said, "Let's go up to their house, anyway. I can't leave without seeing them."

I had taken my mother on, point blank, and she knew it. I thought she might be relenting by the way she stalled and toed the

243

dirt. I imagined that she was thinking of Bobby and how the making up might be easier without me when she got back to Vegas.

"All right. I guess we can go by there," she said. But then she looked me in the eye and added, "A short visit, and then the TWO of US hit the road."

***

On the drive up the hill to Betty Sue's, the pillaged landscape with its missing parts ended, and the past was gloriously restored. The yellow and purple iris and the snapdragons along the incline, the sturdy red brick home halfway up the hill, the gray stone bungalow with its steep front steps, and beneath the shimmering catalpa trees at the top of the hill, Betty Sue's shining, white farmhouse, all were mercifully, beautifully intact. When we pulled up in front of the house and got out of the car, Betty Sue came running out of the house barefoot. She was as pretty as ever, prettier.

"Janet!" she said, her eyes twinkling into slits. "I had no idea WHO you were until you got out of the car!"

Betty Sue was no longer a child. She was a stunning teenager with a lip-sticked smile, a lithe, enviable figure, and a pixie haircut.

Her mother came out of the house swiping flour from the sides of her dress.

"Watch this," she said to us. She untied her apron, threw it over the railing, lifted her skirt, and kicked up one leg to the porch rafter. "See that, Marge Stephens? I can still kick my leg over my head!"

It was the funny, genuine welcome of an old-time countrywoman, one who had known you all of your life, who was of your people, salt of the earth. My mother, bent over, head in hands, laughed in a way she never laughed with Bobby. I thought then as I do now that for all her protestations, Mom needed Aldrich, what it had been and become, just as much as I did.

244

"Oh, Betty. It's so good to see you," she said. "I wish I could kick that high."

"My heavens, Janet." She hugged and inspected me. "Look how you've grown. You know you look a lot like your grandmother despite that blond hair."

"I've always said that!" Mom said. "Same eyes, same forehead."

"Same flat nose," I said, scrunching up my nose and looking cross-eyed at it. That was GranRose's only bad feature, and I had definitely gotten it.

"Stop that. Don't make fun of the Dysart nose!" Mom said.

"I miss Rose somethin' awful," Betty said to Mom.

"We were just down there... at Mama's. It's a sad sight...without the house..."

"What they've done... we couldn't stop it, Marge," Betty erupted, visibly shaken. "You've never seen anything like it. You could hear the bulldozers down the hill day after day, slamming into the stores and then the houses leaving these ugly giant scars on the ground where people had lived and raised their families..."

Mom hesitated. "I know it was a... cross to bear," she said, her uncharacteristic words chosen for Betty's sake.

"It was RAPE," Betty said, countermanding her.

The word slashed out at us like a crude expletive. But for the depth of her feeling, her use of it was unthinkable. But, coming from Betty, it was a testament—no sweeping away the truth under the guise of "God's will." She stood in her loose, flour-dusted dress like an Old Testament matriarch.

"We all have to pray for Aldrich," Betty Sue said, putting an arm around her mother.

"How long are you going to be here?" Betty asked Mom.

"Well, I'm sad to say we're on our way out of town. I have to be at work on Monday morning..."

245

"But I... I could stay a few days, if I could stay with you," I said. My words erupted as unexpected as Betty's jolting cry of "rape."

Betty Sue looked at me wide-eyed. Then she squealed, clapped her hands, and began jumping up and down.

"Are you sure?" Mom asked me, looking so sad I wondered if I could carry out staying in Aldrich and whatever was to follow.

But then bolstered by Betty Sue's "Yes! Yes!" I said to my mother, with brazen innocence, "I can take the bus from Fair Play," knowing in my heart that I was lying, that when I boarded the bus in Fair Play a week later, I would be headed for Kansas, not Nevada. "It's a good route on Greyhound," I said, remembering and reiterating my mother's own words, "better than the plane out of Springfield..."

"P-l-e-a-s-e," Betty Sue said.

"We'll see that she gets on the bus," Betty said.

"Well, I know she couldn't be in better hands..."

"That ought to settle it," Betty said, patting my shoulder.

I got Samsonite out of the little trunk of the Crosley and together Betty Sue and I dragged and pulled it across the pebbly concrete walk to the big concrete block that served as the front step to the porch.

"C'mere, kiddo." Mom opened her arms. "You know how I hate to part with you." She gave me her special bear hug.

"Don't drag it out, Mom," I said, affirming my lie by couching our parting in intimate banter, as if it were unexceptional.

"Okay, kiddo," she said.

With that, Betty Sue raised her arms and turned a cartwheel in the middle of the soft, wet grass. It was slow, graceful, perfectly balanced, with her legs practically in a split, and she came up smiling with her hands over her head in a V.

***

My lie wasn't something I had mulled over—it had taken root at The Ridge, grown in the sunny rain on the drive through town, and flowered when Mom and I were standing in the dirt that had been GranRose's living room— but once I committed it, once I told Mom I would take the bus to Vegas knowing I would not, I began to think of my future differently and more clearly. During that week in Aldrich, the last time I ever spent any length of time there, I went to the Liberator's Parade in Bolivar, got a pixie haircut like Betty Sue's, visited Uncle Pat and Aunt Pansy's grave in Fair Play, and learned to do a slow, steady cartwheel.

At the end of the week, I phoned Mom and told her the truth, which hurt as much as anything I've ever done. Then I got on the bus in Fair Play for Wichita.

Chapter 26

After I spent a year at Wichita High School, Daddy was transferred to a base in Virginia, and I was chosen for early admission to the University of Kansas. During high school and my early college years, I never returned to Aldrich. But one fall during graduate school, after I broke up with a boyfriend, I tore out of Lawrence, Kansas, and drove to Aldrich looking for escape and solace. I had thought many times of making the trip—Aldrich was just three hours from Lawrence, but I had never had a car before. It was a foolish thing to strike out wildly in the early evening, but I was distraught and slightly drunk.

By the time I got to Fair Play in the pitch gloom, I was sober enough to realize I should check into a motel. The closest one was in Bolivar, according to the clerk at the new convenience store where I pumped my gas in the near freezing cold. I drove slowly by the abandoned red-and-white gas station and on down the dark road to Bolivar. On the outskirts of town, I came to a low, long brick motel from the thirties, a place that had intrigued me as a child. The identical doors in a row, which were fun to number and count, now looked smaller, closer together, and hapless.

The clerk gave me Number 5 which had a "working heater," a tall rectangle in the wall that came on periodically with a clang. After a tearful, restless night, I was glad to have the distraction of driving to the square the next morning, though winter had exposed every mean feature of the drag into town—the denuded trees and exposed telephone poles, the brown leafless tangle of vines on peeling houses and fences. And apart from the defoliation, there was a general decrepitude. It gave me a boost to see Lady Justice with her sword atop the Bolivar courthouse, but the stores below that surrounded the square were dilapidated, many of them vacant. I parked in front of the building that had been

248

Delarues, the department store that had drawn women from all over the county. The dejected secondhand shop that had replaced it sold plastic flowers, three bunches of which I purchased and carried with me past the beauty shop that had replaced the Spit Curl to the still extant Nifty Café. There I bought a cup of coffee to go and was advised of the best way to get to Aldrich.

The new road, paved and level, curved through naked woods and fields until, just outside Aldrich, it joined an old corrugated road. When I first came to the junction of old and new, I had no idea where I was. The whole lay of the land had changed, just as Mom had predicted. After I turned on the washboard road, however, I realized that I was driving on the remnant of the main drag that led out to the iron bridge. There were no longer signs of houses along the road or yards or paths or old flower beds, just overgrown brush. The desolate road narrowed as the ugly scrub thickened on either side. Then it turned to mud and dead-ended where the lake that had formed began. I got out of the car and walked in a cold, raw wind to the edge of the water. For twenty feet out, dullish gray water lapped the knees of roots. Beyond that was nothing—no iron bridge, no Little Sac River, no tree-covered banks, just a vast, bland lake from which stuck up, here and there, rotting jagged trunks, the sunken ruins of the woods of Aldrich.

When I went back to the car, I got my peacoat out of the back seat and put it on. Then I turned the car around and drove on the new highway to where I thought GranRose's house once sat, but the area was now an unrecognizable marsh of willow and sumac. I pulled off the side of the highway where I could have sworn the old road turned and went by her house, though there were no silver maples to identify the front yard, no barren branches jutting up against the autumn sky as I had imagined. Instead, there was a swamp of reeds and bullrushes and a thicket of bushes with large soft blooms, each with a million tiny, feathery buds, a pale tenuous white.

I could feel the car pull in the wind as I drove over the wide, new concrete bridge and uphill to The Ridge. Amid the

249

ravages of late November, the sight of the gaunt church house, the gray rows of headstones, the brown stubble of the yard made my heart fall. What had I expected? When I got out of the car, the wind whipping across the ridge slammed the half-open car door shut. Whether I liked it or not, I was alone in the empty cemetery as I had wished. "You brought it on yourself," some naysaying voice said to me. "Ah, the hazards of nostalgia," it said. But I was hopelessly caught up in a bludgeon of emotion. I buttoned my peacoat and walked to the gate.

The clang of the flagpole chain led me right to GranRose's grave. I stuck the bound stems of the plastic daffodils into the ground beside the pedestal. Next to her and Grandpa Clay, Mom had put up her own stone. She had told me that the price of monuments was going up and that buying now was a "good investment in the future." It was pretty, as monuments go, a large rose-colored hunk of granite with her name and birth date. I walked out to the Unknown Man, laid the plastic roses on him and thought of Betty Sue, who had married and moved to Montana. On the way back to the car, I walked through the old section where my great-grandparents lay. It was too cold to further indulge the past, but as I was exiting the cemetery, I noticed Ray Parson's small primitive stone. It had begun to sink and was lopsided. I put down my last bouquet there, the one intended for Uncle Pat. Then I drove, with the car heater full blast, to the Fair Play Cemetery, visited with Uncle Pat and Aunt Pansy for a few minutes, and headed back to Lawrence.

***

After that, I went back to Aldrich only once during the course of thirty years. I would have gone often, despite the near disappearance of the place, for it had given me solace or perhaps I should say perspective, but I moved away from the Midwest, and Aldrich was too far away for a car trip and too out of the way of my cross-country travels. Recently, though, when my mother-in-law died in Arizona and my husband and I were driving her Buick back east across the desert, I persuaded him somewhere in New Mexico, probably as we drove through Tucumcari, to take a detour to Aldrich.

Of course, he had heard all about the year I had spent there. He knew all of the main characters, their stories and sayings. My idolization of the place amused him. He liked to tease me about "Alllldrich," dragging out the syllables and looking heavenward wistfully. But he was perfectly amenable to changing course and half-way through Oklahoma, bore north toward Missouri.

As we left the flat, tedious country and entered the foothills of the Ozarks, I looked for familiar sights along the road —the riverside park, the native-stone motel, the small-town diner. But when Mom and I had taken our trip that once, she had cut over to the top of Arkansas, whereas we were on a newer, more direct route.

"The old roads that go through the little towns are prettier," I said, looking at the map on my phone.

"We can get off the highway if you want to."

"No. I want to get to The Ridge before dark."

"The Ridge?"

"The cemetery. Where everybody is."

***

By the time we pulled into the grassy parking area outside the cemetery gate, the sun had begun to go down. There were no other cars. We had the cool, May evening, the setting sun, the humming and clicking of insects, all to ourselves.

"The cemetery has doubled in size," I said, breaking the quiet.

"It's no little country churchyard."

"The peonies are in bloom."

"Everywhere."

251

"GranRose is over near the flagpole," I said, leading the way.

The light had turned the grass a deep, gorgeous green, and the sky was orange and a bright pink, the color of the peonies.

"It's so beautiful I can't stand it," I said.

"It's pretty beautiful."

"It's the most beautiful cemetery in the world, and I want to be buried as close to GranRose as I can get."

We found her stone and stood for a few minutes looking at the swirling gray marble in the last rosy rays of light and listening to the fireflies.

"Mom's stone is down here," I said, walking in the green grass down to the "hunk of granite" Mom had put up for herself many years before. "She called it her 'long-term investment,' the best 'hunk' she ever invested in."

My husband laughed and followed me down the row.

"Oh no," I said, looking at the stone.

"What's wrong?"

"Look! There's no death date," I said, bewildered. "Why?"

"Well, what's-his-name, Bobby, Herman, Jack, I can't keep them straight… He never had the death date added to it."

"Jack. That jerk. All these years."

"Just two years."

"But two years, and he still hasn't done it. He said he would do it."

"YOU could have it done. I guess you might need the death certificate."

"I can't believe he didn't do that one simple thing." I felt like sitting down in the grass and bawling. "She should have been buried here."

"Well, he buried her there in Vegas."

"But she should have been buried here, close to GranRose."

"It's water under the bridge."

"I hate that saying."

"What's done can't be undone."

"That's almost as bad," I said. "He could have given me some of her ashes. I could have brought them here."

"That ship has sailed." He was trying to lighten the mood. It was a kind of joking he did when I got stuck in the past.

"One old cliché after another. Can't you think of anything different?"

"Time marches inexorably forward" he said, which was pretty good, good enough to bring me round.

"Uncle Pat could have said it in Latin," I said.

"Uncle Pat was an all-around guy."

"He was so great and so was GranRose. They both knew their Latin."

"*Requiescant in pace*," said my husband.

"I'll go to the monument company in Bolivar tomorrow before we leave, to see about adding the death date."

"Good idea, my love."

We walked through the newer part of the cemetery looking for Betty Sue, straining to read the stones in the waning light. We found her on a row near the edge of the cemetery next to her parents.

"I can't believe Betty Sue, who was the soul of goodness and beauty, married a womanizer and died a painful death. There's no justice."

"No. There isn't."

"She never complained or got angry about her illness. You know why?"

"Why?"

"She said she wanted to glorify her Lord. That's what she told me over the phone from her deathbed. 'I want to glorify my Lord.'"

We lingered there, in the beautiful twilight, beside Betty Sue, amid the humming and chirping in the tall grasses and trees outside the cemetery.

Then we drove over the huge lake on the new bridge and turned on the extant portion of the old road into town. It was rutted and potholed, but I wanted to see Dysart Brothers one last time. We passed what had been the Aldrich Methodist Church. There was a rusted mowing rig and some other old farm equipment in the weeds that had grown up where the smooth, mown lawn had been. Someone had moved in and hung sheets in the lower half of the arched windows.

"The store is just down the road," I said. But as we bumped down the rutted road, I saw through the dusk that the lone red brick building, the last vestige of town, the proof of what had been and marker of my childhood, like all of the other buildings, was now gone. I got out of the car and stared at the empty lot of flowering weeds that had grown up where Dysart Brothers had stood. In the fading light, I could see in the field where my grandfather had played croquet a pile of red brick that had been left behind. I stumbled and almost fell as I made my way through the brambles over to the pile to retrieve a brick.

***

That night in bed at the Days Inn, Bolivar, I couldn't sleep.

"Do you think my mother was a redneck?"

"No," my husband said, half asleep.

"Why not?"

"Her high voice."

"Rednecks can have high voices," I said.

"Not like hers. Hers was mellifluous." My husband and Mom had gotten along.

"She got raked over the coals by all those men."

"Yeah."

"All that clobbering. It coarsened her. You know?"

"I'm dog tired."

254

I ignored him. I needed to talk. "She was so afraid of being perceived as some ignoramus from Missouri."

"Well, I never thought that."

"I once heard someone call her a tough old broad."

"Well, that person was mistaken. For all that raking and clobbering, your mother was never hard-bitten. She had a lilt about her, right up to the end."

"I love you."

"I love you, too. May I go to sleep now?"

"Okay."

"We'll talk about it tomorrow."

"I loved her voice…"

My husband fell right off, but I stayed awake processing. I thought about Mom's hillbilly penchant for showing off. Usually, it was good natured, for the laugh, but sometimes it was mean. In her later years the meanness became more pronounced. She set herself apart by telling people off. She boasted of her clever berating of strangers— the "hateful old bat" who took her slot machine when she went to the restroom. She told HER a thing or two. The "horse's ass" who pulled into the gas pump in front of her. She stopped him in HIS tracks. The bridge partner who "went to bed with an ace." That was the last time she was playing with "a rank amateur." During the last years of her life, she unleashed her unhappiness onto her closest friends.

Her girlfriends, on their nights out, tried to divert her when her stories turned into sour, self-interested spiels.

"Excuse me," she once said to one of them who had interrupted her when she was midway through a long diatribe about a car mechanic who had tried to rook her. "Are you aware of how you interrupt people?"

The woman was flummoxed. "Sorry," she said after an . awful, silent interval.

Mom had taken me along on Girls' Night Out to show me off, even though I was well into my forties. First the girls played the slots and drank for free and then they would break for dinner. When the waitress came to the table, Mom was loaded.

"Don't mind if I do have one more little snort," she said.

It was unlike her to drink too much, but she was drowning her sorrows having lost on the machines. It was after the last little snort that she "took" the interrupter "down a peg or two" and "called her number."

After dinner I overheard from the restaurant bathroom stall, two of "the girls."

"I'm not doing this one more time. She's ruined our Girls' Night Out."

"We'll have to disband and then start up again without telling her."

"She expects us to listen to her go on and on. You can't get a word in edgewise."

"She drank too much tonight."

"She does it stone sober."

"Her daughter is so different."

"If she tells me one more time about how 'educated' that daughter is…"

"You know she deserted her when she was a little kid."

"No. Really?"

"Yes. She didn't even raise her."

"I knew something was funny. She seemed hamstrung with her mother blathering on like that."

"It gets worse."

"Tell me."

"She never wanted her, tried to abort her…"

"Really."

"She broke down and told me all about it one night, back when we travelled together."

"That tough old broad broke down?"

"Oh yeah."

"When was that?"

"Years ago. A bunch of us girls went out to Yosemite, and she and I shared a room in that big lodge. We talked all night. She was only eighteen when it happened. She was married but he never knew a thing about it. She was back in Missouri visiting her mother. She'd gotten a redneck friend to drive her to some little town out in the sticks where she could get rid of it, but on the way they had a flat tire and she wound up not going through with it. She said a flat tire decided the course of her whole life. A flat tire and a redneck."

"Talk about the pot calling the kettle black."

"She wasn't always so bad."

"She always had that mean streak."

"It got worse over time."

"I'll bet she's put that girl through the wringer. She's nothing but a mean redneck from Missouri."

There was a pause and then another, different voice, someone who had entered the restroom.

"I wondered where you girls went off to." It was Mom. "We're in there tryin' to figure out the bill. You two 're gonna have to shell out to cover the tip."

"We're well aware of that, Marge," the angrier woman said, the one who had been interrupted.

When I heard the women leave, I came out of the stall. Mom was holding a tube of lipstick and studying her face in the mirror.

"Good Lord, I look awful. I ate off all my lipstick. Did you have a good time?"

"Yes. Thanks." I washed my hands.

During the conversation that followed, we never looked directly at each other. We glanced instead at each other's mirror images. Which was a good thing. Anything more potent—the actual, extended sight of Mom—might have made me weep, WOULD have made me weep.

"I drank too much tonight, kiddo."

"We drank a lot."

257

"Ya know how drunk I am?"

"How drunk?"

"I tried to put on some lipstick, but I couldn't hit my lips." Mom dropped the lipstick in her handbag and began powdering her nose. "Did you get a load of those two biddies?" I glanced at her narrowed eyes in the mirror. "Either one of them could buy or sell me. If you think I was about to let them run off to the restroom and stick ME with the tip, better think again. They would take me to the cleaners if I let them." She kept talking to me but looking at her own mirror image. "Why do you think that is?"

"I don't know," I said, putting on my lipstick, holding the tube close so that my hand wouldn't shake.

She paused on the cusp of insight, but then as if unable to achieve it, broke her gaze and looked at my image, puzzling over my face. "You know what?" she said, wagging her forefinger decisively.

"What?" I asked, looking away, replacing the lipstick, trying to sound neutral, wishing I could run out of the room, wishing I could collapse in tears, alone.

"I think we need to go shopping..." I could feel her pondering my mirror image and when I looked back up she met my mirrored eyes and said, definitively, "Yep. You, kiddo, need a good moisturizer."

On the way out of the restaurant, Mom struck up a conversation with the waiter, "a good-looking kid."

"Did you enjoy your meal?" he asked us.

"I didn't enjoy paying for it," Mom said, looking for a laugh. But the waiter was too young to recognize her dated, silly humor and didn't know what to say.

"You know for a schmancy restaurant like this with a schmancy tab you could stand to make some improvements."

"Oh...?"

"Do you know what an unflattering light you have installed over the mirror in the Ladies Room?"

***

Though I had ten years since recovered from the Ladies Room incident—the hate-filled gossiping voices, the fury of the one woman, the shocking disclosure of the other—I fretted through the night at the Bolivar motel. The next morning, I left my husband in the motel restaurant, went to the monument company, which required only money to add the death date to my mother's stone, and to the Walmart where I purchased a pair of clippers and some moisturizer for my dry, travel-worn skin. Then, to spare my husband, who was content to read all day, I drove alone in his mother's Buick to The Ridge via Fair Play.

If I had known of the devastation of Fair Play, of the terrible collapsed roofs, the fallen brick walls, up and down the main drag, the surrounding scrub grown up through porches and out windows, I might have gone directly to The Ridge. I might have spared myself the sight of the rotten frame of Uncle Pat's house, hunks of the broken native stone lying in the brush. But perhaps going there served a purpose.

After Fair Play, the placid gray lake which had displaced Aldrich seemed like mere monotony and The Ridge? The Ridge was heaven. With the clippers, I trimmed back the peonies until I could read the name, Rose Dysart, 1888-1954, and placed the freshly cut blooms in front of the stone of my mother, Marge Stephens, 1924. I thought that maybe when the monument company sent me a photo of the stone, the inscribed death date would help me lay Mom to rest. Maybe, I thought, I could quit asking myself if I had done right by Mom.

It isn't that I didn't see Mom over the years. I did. I went to Vegas after she divorced Bobby and stayed for several weeks, and many times after that I visited her during the summer. Once we went to Yosemite, which she still called YOSE MITE. I remember laughing and singing as we rode along. But the truth is we grew apart. It was a slow, fated pulling apart, something we couldn't stop.

259

"Men are no damn good, except for that one you snagged," Mom said to me in one of our last phone calls. "Now you married well. Your grandmother should never have let me marry so young. I should have gone to college instead. If I'd had the chances you had... Of course, those were hard times. Oh well, it's all water under the bridge."

***

"Only in Missouri would they let you keep the room five hours after checkout and not charge you," I said to my husband as we departed the Bolivar motel.

By the time we got on the road, the sun was already setting.

"Oh, Mom..." I sighed, a few minutes after we were out of town.

"What about her?" My husband indulged me as I reflected upon my mother, even though it was his mother who had just passed away.

"She died without ever finding the marital and familial love she longed for." My answer came out unexpectedly corny and stilted.

"She had a lot of fun," he said.

I left it there. I had been consumed by my own past for long enough. After a while I said, "I dragged you all the way to Aldrich."

"I was a willing victim."

"I don't know why I cling to it."

"It's your family—all of them—GranRose, Uncle Pat, Betty Sue... the Unknown Man. Everyone should have such a place."

"It's a place which brings one's sense of injustice into perspective," I said, trying to justify my attachment.

"Exactly. It's a perfect burial site—the cemetery, the missing town, none of the ugly squalor of Fair Play."

260

"I've talked about it so much. I thought you should see it."

"You were right."

"It's just a little town that went underwater. Nothing to go back to…"

"It gave you the family that sustained you." My husband knew just what to say.

"It gave me all those memories…"

"Right."

"And what is family if not memory?"

We rode along in his deceased mother's Buick with the windows half-open. For about an hour we drove on narrow, winding roads through the fragrant rural darkness, the same roads that had taken me to Fair Play fifty years before. It was unaccountably beautiful. And then, at a critical junction, we raised the windows and turned on a wider, well-lit road that skirted the larger towns and led to a major highway.

"It's a beautiful place, southwest Missouri," my husband reflected as we crossed the state line.

"Isn't it, though," I said.

We turned onto a ramp that looped up and around onto the interstate.

After we had settled into the flow of traffic, he said, "Aldrich is special. I see that now." He turned and gave me a comforting little smile.

"It's sacred ground," I said, leaning across the console to kiss his cheek, knowing, as he did, that we would never come back.

END

Book Club Questions for *Aldrich, MO Pop.199*

1.The novel is divided into three parts: before Aldrich, the year in Aldrich, and visits back to Aldrich. What is the time span of each part? How old is Janet in the beginning? In the end? Janet, the adult, narrates the story, intervening throughout the action. In which part is she least present? most present?

2. Who is the antagonist of the novel? Are you at all sympathetic to that character? Janet is called "irresolute." Why might that be? Do you think people who try hard to be different from a parent succeed?

3. Describe the main characters of the book and the degree to which they affect Janet. How is Betty Sue both a double and a foil of Janet?

4. What is the basis of the contention between Marge and Oneita? Does one or both have a "hillbilly" complex? In an angry retort to Janet at the cemetery, Oneita hints at a buried truth about the past that involves Marge. What does she imply? How is this confirmed in the Ladies Room scene in the third part of the book?

5. As a coming-of-age story, the novel deals with the loss of childhood illusion. With what adult reality must Janet struggle? Do you believe she makes the right decision at the end of Part Two? How might her life have differed had she decided otherwise?

6. A sequence of dreams is used in the story to express Janet's fears. (See pp. 7, 22, 37, 152) What are her main fears? Noah and

the ark is the subject of the Sunday School lesson. Where else in the novel does a flood occur? Does Janet fear drowning?

6. Janet's fears are countered by fantasies. Into what unreal worlds does she escape? Explain her identification with birds. Do all children enjoy such fantasies?

7. Do you agree with the sentiments regarding memory which are expressed in the two epigraphs of the novel? What do you make of Janet's husband's remark, "What is memory, if not family?" Is Janet too sentimental, too attached to the past? Do you consider yourself to be nostalgic? How common is the idealization of the past?

8. The book deals with the concept of inevitability. Do you believe that fate is predetermined, self-determined, or completely random? Marge quotes Seneca on the subject of fate. How is Seneca's viewpoint different from Uncle Matt's?

9. The novel expresses both the fear of being trapped in a "one-horse town" and the yearning to return to a more untrammeled place—that is, both the desire to escape and the longing to return. How do you explain this contradiction?

10. The end of Janet's childhood coincides with the decline of the town of Aldrich. Does this geographical backdrop, the virtual disappearance of a place, suggest a larger loss of innocence in terms of our country — the America of yesteryear? What do you make of the allusions to Longfellow's *Evangeline* and the displacement of the people of Acadia?